LORD
OF THE
DARKNESS

WILLIAM ALTIMARI

"Lord of The Darkness," by William Altimari.

ISBN 978-0-9728726-8-3 (softcover), 978-0-9728726-9-0 (hardcover).

Published 2017 by Virtualbookworm.com Publishing Inc., P.O. Box 9949, College Station, TX 77842, US. ©2017, William Altimari.

ACKNOWLEDGEMENTS

I thank my niece Veronica Altimari for employing her exceptional editorial talents in the preparation of the manuscript.

DEDICATION

To the memory of Monty Simmons, caring and gentle and wise,
who brought me into the world of the great cats,
from whose grasp I have never been able to escape.

(1917-1996)

And to the memory of MIDNIGHT, noble, mysterious, and
incomparable, whose hair-trigger temperament never let the hammer fall,
and who granted me his most carefully guarded gift—trust—and shared with
me the secrets of the leopard's soul.

(1970-1987)

SECRETIVE, SILENT, SMOOTH AND SUPPLE
AS A PIECE OF SILK,
HE IS AN ANIMAL OF DARKNESS,
AND EVEN IN THE DARK, HE TRAVELS
ALONE.
--*Maitland Edey*

FOREWORD

This is a work of fiction. However, "fictional" should not be confused with "fanciful." This tale derives from the author's long and close interaction with leopards, from the work of other naturalists who have conducted field studies of leopards or who have reared leopard cubs, and from hunters' forays into the bush to deal with leopards who, through some mischance, usually human ineptitude or folly, have been forced to resort to killing and eating human beings. Over a half-century ago, hunter Alexander Lake, often credited with more than a few tall tales of his own, wrote a book in which he remarked, only half-jokingly, on the dangers of "animals lying in wait and hunters lying in print." There is no need for that forewarning here. Nothing concerning the behavior of leopards or about humans' encounters with them has been invented, altered, inflated, or contrived. In fact, some of the more startling details about these mysterious felines have been left out in order not to strain the reader's trust. As someone once observed, a novelist forever works under the maddening constraint that fiction must stick to possibilities, whereas reality surely does not.

William Altimari
Tucson Mountains
waltimari@comcast.net

1905

PART ONE

YINGWE

1

UNTIL LIONS HAVE THEIR HISTORIANS, TALES OF THE HUNT SHALL ALWAYS GLORIFY THE HUNTER.
--AFRICAN PROVERB

BIG GAME HUNTERS forever roam outside the frontiers of normality. By hunters I mean, of course, not the people who occasionally dust off a deer rifle to secure a slab of venison for the table. I refer to those who travel thousands of miles to swelter by a waterhole in the off-chance of bringing down a Cape Buffalo. Those are hunters. They are not normal men. And, like all outliers, they seek the company of their strange kind.

As one of them, so do I. That is why a cold winter evening at the New York Safari Club conferred such pleasure. Sleet whipped against the windows, but in the sitting room, adorned with tusks and hides and horns, we savored the comfort and warmth of the rich brocades and Persian rugs and wassail and buttered rum.

Until two years earlier, the Christmas season meeting had been problematic. A lecture highlights each month's gathering, but rare was the speaker who could find the time in December. Consequently, the Speakers' Committee — in fact, a single harried officer — annually endured what one member wryly called "Advent anxiety."

Then in '03, I was asked at the last moment if I could fill the bill and give a brief talk. I sat on the edge of a desk and chatted — it was that casual. I spoke of the Garhwal Man-Eater. The talk was a sensation. In the years since, I have brought lantern slides, and now this heretofore unknown tale of the Indian bush has become as eagerly anticipated a Christmas delight as a turkey dinner. Even an occasional reporter has stopped by for a quick story to fill some space. The hunt, the stalk, the quarry, the kill — all the colors of the palette. I always attempt to minimize my own role and speak mostly of the cat, but that is difficult at the Safari Club, where a puffed up chest is no vice.

"Well, done, as always," said a friendly voice off to the side of our crowded sitting room.

I turned to the right to bring my good eye into play.

My old friend Paul Bentley approached with two whiskey glasses. Nowadays, he always uses very tall ones. Otherwise his limp would cause the contents to spill onto the rug.

He held out the glasses. "Bourbon or cognac?"

I laughed because he knew the answer. I took the whiskey.

"I can't understand ingesting something that was laid down around the time Napoleon took Vienna." I settled into a wing chair near the fire. "Tastes like a mouthful of timber."

Bentley draped himself across the maroon cushions of the chesterfield. "You're looking well, Hil."

"More than fair."

Which was more than I could offer about Bentley. He seemed thin and tired after recovering from being half-trampled by an elephant. He savored some brandy and rested the glass on the arm of the sofa. Then he just stared at me.

"Ah, the pensive look," I said.

"Just thinking. . . . Why don't you speak of one of your more recent hunts? Why always the Garhwal tiger?"

"It's expected. And I like the fact that the details can be verified."

That seemed to puzzle him. When I went no further, he said, "I don't understand."

"Long ago I wearied of hunters' stories that were written on the wind."

He grinned and took some more cognac.

"I don't want to be remembered that way."

"Remembered?" he said with a laugh as hard as a monkey's bark. "Are you dying?"

"We're all of us dying."

That numbed the conversation.

Finally, after a long pause, he said, "You have a talent, Hil. You tell a story like no other."

I nursed my bourbon and gazed away into the fire.

"No matter how often you spin a tale, it's as fresh and spontaneous as if you thought up the words two seconds before you spoke them. You inspire the young and reassure the old and thrill everyone between."

"I take no credit for God's gifts."

"You should. He could just as well have given them to someone else. But He chose you. He must have had a reason."

I knew that, and I was still searching for the reason.

"In any case, why not talk of Africa next time? That's where your heart is. You pulse with the beat of the lowveld."

I turned and smiled at him.

"Give me that as a Christmas gift next year," he said. "I don't need another hundred dollar bottle of cognac. Tell us a fresh tale of a lion hunt in the African bush."

I held up my glass in salute to him. "My friend, I'll consider it."

It was the only marginally dishonest statement I had ever spoken to Bentley. I would not consider it. I could not, because I had not shot a cat in eleven years.

"By the way," Bentley said, "our old friend is here tonight. Did you see him?"

Sarcasm was Bentley's favored currency, so I eyed him as skeptically as a tiger spying a staked out buffalo.

"Who charms us tonight?" I asked.

"The Baron."

"Ah . . . tidings of comfort and joy."

9

"The word is that he's returned with one and a half metric tons of trophies."

"Don't they have taxidermists in Germany?"

"He lives here now."

"Well, *that'll* strengthen the Republic."

"He sees you as his rival, you know."

"Rival at what? I haven't bagged half the game he has."

"Rival in reputation."

"You're joking."

"I'm not."

"Then he's a fool. It isn't mine. No honest man can lay claim to his own reputation. He holds it in trust."

"You see, that's why you're so fine a speaker—these little poetic flourishes of yours."

I turned back toward the fire.

"Good evening, captain."

He had come up on my blind side, the customary tactic with Prussians.

I stood up. "How do you do, Baron?" I held out my hand, but he kept his distance. He brought his heels together and bowed slightly at the waist.

Erich Von Roon looked as if he had been carved from silver. The short hair, the crisp moustache, the gray suit. I again felt a bit disappointed that he did not wear a monocle.

"An excellent presentation as always, captain."

"*Danke.*"

"*Bitte.*"

Petty though it might have been, I was always rankled that he wore British tweeds. My late father was British, and the fact that Von Roon donned clothes bought in Bond Street appalled me. As did the fact that his Germanic English was spoken with a British intonation—a two-headed monster if ever there was one.

"Quite a cargo this time, as you might have heard."

"Yes," I said.

"Three fine Grevy's stallions among them."

Bentley cleared his throat. "Won't you sit down, Baron?"

Von Roon had told me about the zebra trophies for a specific reason. One evening a few years earlier, I had drunk too much bourbon and had remarked within his hearing that anyone who shot a horse should be thrown off a cliff. Von Roon had snapped off a brittle laugh, but he knew I was not joking. What he did not know was that I would later ask a *Sangoma*, a witch doctor of sorts, among my Shangaan friends to use his powers to ensure it would one day come to pass.

Now Von Roon was tossing the dead steeds onto the ground in front of me. Prussian subtlety is like British cuisine. One searches for it in vain.

"I expect that to your home you'll be soon returning," Von Roon said.

"On Central Park?"

"No, no," he said, tut-tutting me ever so gently. "To Africa. You have a home on the Sabi River, do you not?"

"Yes."

"To hunt the man-eater."

"I hadn't heard of it."

"Two days ago a cable I received. There is even a reward, though the honor is enough. You are expected. Who has shot more man-eaters than you?"

I drained my glass and set it aside. "I never enter an area where a reward is being offered. Too many fools on the ground. Besides, Africa is overflowing with lion hunters. One of them can handle it."

"Ach, no," Von Roon said, pausing for effect. He, too, had a taste for the theatrical. "No man-eating lion prowls the Transvaal."

Even the languid Bentley straightened now from his slump.

"I speak of a man-eating leopard. Terror stalks the land."

I stood with the heavy drapery pulled aside and gazed down onto the street. The lamplight glowed softly off the snow, and a lonely hansom made its way back to the barn. I knew I would be walking home tonight.

Despite the rumble of conversation in the sitting room, I heard Bentley's loping steps as he approached behind me. I turned and through the bluish cigar haze I saw he had with him a slender and sandy-haired young man whom I vaguely recalled from the lecture.

"Captain Hilton Rixton, allow me to introduce Mr. Jonathan Stratton."

I shook his hand. "How do you do?"

"Very well, thank you, sir."

He had the optimistic eyes all young men should have.

"Mr. Stratton is a journalist. He would like to write a piece about you."

Bentley sported the bemused expression he always did when he had succeeded annoying me.

"Mr. Stratton, I believe Baron Von Roon would make a far better subject."

"No, not at all, captain. Please . . . ."

He gestured toward the chairs near the fireplace.

"Briefly then," I said.

He sat and pulled out a notebook and a pencil. "I work for the *Herald*, but I also write for other publications. I thought I might compose a portrait of you for *Collier's*."

"Why?"

That seemed to hit him between the eyes like a .400 express. Evidently no one had ever said that before. I guess everyone on earth felt he was worthy of a portrait in *Collier's*.

"I was fascinated by your talk. I spoke with some of the other members, and they all hold you in high regard. Many said you're the finest sportsman on the planet."

"They're very kind."

He held up the notebook. "May we?"

I gestured with two fingers to Winwood, our steward.

"Very well," I said. "Proceed."

Stratton dabbed the pencil point onto the tip of his tongue. "May I ask when you were born?"

"A couple of decades before you."

"And where?"

"Montana."

He smiled as if I were telling him a joke. He stopped smiling when he saw I was not.

"Truly?"

"You thought I was British."

"I wasn't sure."

"I'm half."

"Your accent. It seems as if — ."

"As if I were born somewhere near the middle of the Atlantic."

"That's it." he said, laughing.

"My father was British. A retired army officer. I've picked up some of his inflection and tone. I was born in Montana, but I spent most of my childhood in England."

"And your mother?"

"A wild Montana filly. My father was hunting pronghorn and got caught in a thunderstorm. He found shelter at a cattle ranch. There he met my mother. He was smitten at once."

"I see. An unusual match."

"Oh, yes. A tight-lipped High Church Anglican of the old school and a flame-haired Irish Catholic. Madness. My mother ran away from him as fast as she could — until she caught him."

Stratton burst out laughing. "I love stories like that!"

"I spent a great deal of my youth in England. My father was an educated man. Latin and Greek."

Stratton failed to realize he was insulting me with his skeptical look.

"And he loved the opera. Took me to see *Rigoletto* when I was eight. My mother and I moved back to America after he died."

Winwood appeared with a tray and a pair of bourbons.

"Winwood, you're worth your weight in ivory."

"Thank you, sir."

And away he went.

"Mr. Bentley introduced you as captain. I was wondering — I mean . . . so many sportsman supposedly have military rankings that — ."

"You were curious if it's an honorary appellation?"

"Yes."

"It's genuine."

"The American army?"

"Of course."

"Infantry?"

"Cavalry. I served in Arizona under Colonel McGregor and Colonel Hargrave. And my best years were later as an officer in the Tenth."

"Did you —."

"That book is closed. Let's move on."

"Very well. May we talk about big game?"

"Briefly."

Stratton took a sip of his bourbon and seemed to be gathering his thoughts.

"You've stalked man-eaters?"

"Didn't you attend the lecture?"

"I mean other than the Garhwal Tiger."

"I have."

"Baron Von Roon is returning to Africa to hunt a man-eater. He told me it's marauding near your home there."

"So I'm led to believe."

"He asked me to accompany him if I'd write up the adventure. All expenses paid."

"And you turned him down?" I said in surprise.

"I'm a city boy. I'd be lost out there." He hesitated as if he knew he were being dishonest. Or at least not telling the entire truth. "And he makes me uneasy."

I was impressed. "Very insightful."

"Will you go?"

"After the rainy season. I'll celebrate Christmas here."

"I understand. Would it be possible for me to wish the compliments of the season to your family? And perhaps speak with them a bit?"

"I've never married."

"I see. Let's return to the hunt. Can you tell me your exact feelings at the critical moment?"

I had known that was coming.

"What moment is that?"

"The squeeze of the trigger. Can you elucidate that for the non-sportsmen among my readers?"

"That's like trying to explain lovemaking to a virgin. It's—my God, man, don't write that down!"

He dropped the pencil into his lap.

"And I have no time for old maids of either sex who try to tsk-tsk sportsmen to death. So if you're writing for them, we'll end this now."

"I'm not writing for them, captain."

I took a sip of bourbon and savored it. "At the climactic instant, there's a profound communion between the stalker and his quarry that defies simple explanation."

"Can you try?"

"Well, I'm not talking about a butcher with a firearm. There are too many of those. I mean a true sportsman. A transcendent fusion between the man and the animal burns white-hot and exists beyond ordinary human comprehension."

Stratton folded his notebook and set it aside.

"And," I went on, "as with lovemaking, there's often a terrible letdown afterward. And even, sometimes, as with the carnal, a hint of shame."

He looked baffled. "I don't know how to understand feelings like that."

"Perhaps someday you will."

"Captain, might I see some of your trophies?"

"I have no trophies."

"I don't understand."

"I gave them away."

"All?" he said, obviously astonished.

"All." It was only a partial lie.

"Why, captain?"

"A trophy is just dried skin stretched over a form. With eyes of glass. It's nothing. Less than nothing."

He seemed troubled now. Groping. "Might I ask you something personal?"

"Everything is personal."

"Yes, I suppose it is. Your eye . . . ."

"Snatched by a tiger's claw."

I wished he had not broached that topic because late in the evening the black leather patch always began to make my skin itch, and when I started thinking about it, my skin itched even more.

"A man-eater?"

"The Garhwal Tiger."

"But you never mentioned that in the lecture!"

"The talk was about the tiger, not me."

He leaned over and pulled aside the fire screen and threw his notebook into the flames. "Can you tell me?"

"It was my own fault. After the lucky shot in the dark, I approached him and saw he was still breathing. There's a protocol hunters use when advancing on a downed animal—put one more into him to be sure. I didn't follow it."

"But why didn't—?"

"I don't know why, so don't ask me. There he was—the demon of Garhwal. Merciless slaughterer of the innocent. But he was not. He was just an old tiger. With a broken left upper canine and a half-crippled left rear leg from some stupid and gutless hunter. So the failing old gentleman of the forest began taking the only prey he could catch. And for that I had brought him down. And saved countless lives."

"Can you tell me what happened?"

"Well, I should've finished him off right then as he gasped his last. But I paused because I noticed something I'd never seen before."

I turned away with my bourbon. I had no desire to go on.

"Captain . . . please."

I still stared into the fire. "I saw the light dying in his eyes. It was as if I'd dropped a pair of lit candles onto the ground and was watching them flicker out. And with his last measure of strength he leaped up at me and exploded with a savage roar and slashed my eye from my head. Then his candles sputtered and died. And stalking him taught me more about tigers—and more about life—than any books could hope to tell. And it was worth the eye."

Stratton gazed at me for a month. At last he said, "That was long ago."

"Very long—eleven years."

And it was yesterday.

2

. . . A FLEETING GLIMPSE, ONE PRESS OF THE TRIGGER AND – IF THE AIM HAS BEEN TRUE – THE ACQUISITION OF A TROPHY THAT SOON LOSES ITS BEAUTY AND ITS INTEREST.
--SPORTSMAN AND NATURALIST JIM CORBETT

TO ME, the silence of a snowfall is one of nature's most soothing tonics. And when one is surrounded by New Yorkers, silence becomes a blessed thing. I walked home in peace.

Letty, my housekeeper, was asleep now, but she always had a fire ready for me in my study on these cold December nights. I removed my overcoat and slouch hat and set them aside and warmed my hands before the blaze. A kettle of hot tea gleamed at the edge of the hearth. She was a treasure.

After pouring some tea, I went to my wing chair. I took my revolver from my coat pocket and laid it on the side table. An Iver Johnson .32 hammerless, the pistol had been given to me by a retired Pinkerton agent for whom I had done a small favor. The three-inch barrel and the hammerless design make it ideal for its home in my pocket. Defiantly unnecessary are the gracefully carved mother-of-pearl grips the detective had commissioned for his secret sidearm. Of course, the lockwork of the weapon lacks the careful hand fitting of its famous competitor from Hartford. The canny Norwegian had certainly known he could never provide that nicety for the price at which he was offering his pistol to the man who calloused his hands for a living and who could not afford a Colt. Yet Johnson had produced a tough and reliable revolver nonetheless, and so I took it to my gunsmith in Johannesburg for him to perform his own subtle magic. He refined the tolerances by stoning and polishing the internals, and he changed the mainspring to lighten the trigger pull and then returned to me my personal Excalibur. Unlike the uncertain heart of man, my silent guardian never wavers, never dozes, never betrays. Always alert, it waits without weariness for my summons. Several years ago, four times it roared its single fearless word and saved the lives of three innocent girls in the heart of the African jungle. With its discreet reassurance and unassuming valor, it is beyond price. I would not barter it even for the Star of Africa.

I pulled off my eye patch and dropped it onto the table and sat back and savored the tea.

Stratton and I had talked for over an hour. He could not get enough. I cherish the enthusiasm of youth. Many of the middle-aged fear it, for they fail to remember their own time boiling in its stew. Woe betide the dreary graybeard who forgets that.

After a time, Stratton had excused himself, and I had assumed he had departed. A half-hour later, as I was buttoning my coat, he appeared and handed me a sheet of paper.

"Just a quick draft of the opening," he said and thanked me for my time, shook my hand, and was gone.

I now set down my tea, lit a panatella, and pulled the folded paper from my vest pocket.

RIXTON OF AFRICA

Many are the men widely celebrated who, if truth be told, have done very little. Conversely, there is a smaller number of individuals who have performed startling deeds but remain unknown. I will not say they "languish" in anonymity, for their obscurity is carefully guarded. At the New York Safari Club, I recently had the bracing experience of conversing with one such man.

Captain Hilton Rixton, late of the United States Army, is half-British by blood, a Montanan by birth, and an African by adoption.

18

More importantly, he is a man of adventure to his fingertips. Yet I suspect he would dismiss such a description out of hand.

I met him on the evening he gave a thrilling lecture about his hunt for the Garhwal man-eating tiger in India over a decade ago. He spoke of those events with an unusual detachment, as if they had happened to another. I have encouraged him to write them down for all to sample, but he has demurred.

The captain is in his middle forties, and large for a horse soldier, approaching six feet. His short black hair is combed back smooth with Brilliantine. His straight black moustache is neatly trimmed. These features are, however, the ones noticed last. Most prominent is the tragic loss of his left eye, relic of the tiger hunt. A black patch of African buffalo hide adorns that side of his face. Somewhere beneath it begins a scar from the tiger slash that gouges deeply down his cheek. Oddly, his strong features, dark from tropical suns, are somehow enhanced by this savage badge, but he shrugs it off as nothing more than the mark of folly.

When the captain speaks informally, his tones are low but always alive with irony. He converses in an almost offhand way with a casual eloquence that most men could not attain with pen and paper and hours of contemplative thought. Also, and unique in my experience, is the fact that, when he speaks, he enunciates every soft sentence with a clarity and cadence that says this will indeed be the most important sentence he will ever speak in his life – and he has reserved it for you. This curious circumstance has the effect of drawing one in as with the pull of a powerful tide. One feels helpless to move away. This gift, and that is precisely what it is, I am certain is a talent of which he is completely unaware.

Well, not anymore, I thought, smiling.

The ring of the doorbell at this hour could have meant only Bentley. He was a wretched insomniac, though he suffered greatly from the cold and it surprised me that he would be out and about now. I slipped my patch back on and went to the door.

My shock was total when I saw Stratton standing in the lamplight. He looked as frozen and stiff as a dead caribou.

"Come in, come in."

I took his hat and coat. As we went toward the study, I saw on the hall table an envelope I had not noticed before. It looked like a cablegram. However, my clearly disturbed young friend took priority. I slid the envelope into a vest pocket.

Stratton warmed himself in front of the fire while I poured him some tea.

"What's wrong?" I said as we sat across from one another.

He glanced at the revolver on the table. "Was that with you tonight at the club, captain?"

"It's always with me."

"Truly?"

"It never leaves my side. The right-hand pockets of all my coats are lined with leather. There it waits. I might sleep, but it never does."

"And you've found it necessary?"

"Yes."

"Life is a mystery, isn't it?"

"Indeed."

"I've been walking around for an hour and wondering if I just made the worst decision of my life." He paused.

"Go on."

"I told Von Roon I'd accompany him to Africa."

"I'm sure he was delighted."

"Ecstatic."

"So why the anguish?"

"I'm unsure."

"About what?"

"Von Roon."

"I see." I offered him a panatella, but he declined. "Your instincts are good."

"How do you mean?"

"Von Roon is a dangerous man."

Stratton stared at me over his teacup. "Please tell me how."

"He has a relentless drive to prove himself. Like all Prussians. So safety and good sense are sacrificed to that. There's no more dangerous man to be with in the bush."

"Then what should I do?"

"Why ask me?"

"Captain, whom else can I ask?"

"You can ask yourself. Rely on your own judgment."

He sighed and set down his tea. "I'm afraid I don't have enough knowledge about hunters, good or bad, to make a judgment."

"Well there are many kinds of hunters. Some are brilliant, some are fools. Some are butchers, some are sportsmen. It depends."

"On what?"

"Mostly age."

"Can you give me some particulars?"

"When hunters are very young, their biggest desire is to get plenty of shooting done. They don't even care much about hitting anything. The thrill comes from banging away, smelling the powder. Testing the weapon. That's why young shooters can be very dangerous fieldmates unless they're carefully supervised."

"But Von Roon would be beyond that, wouldn't he?"

"Yes. But there are also other kinds to consider, and that's where he comes in. After hunters develop their shooting skills, they often become obsessed with a new god—the bag limit. They want to bring home the maximum number of every animal they can find."

"Is that Von Roon?"

"Yes, but with a risky twist. Most hunters mature. They go beyond the sophomoric stage I just described, and they become trophy hunters."

"And what exactly does that mean?"

"They don't want to bring down five lions. They want one lion—the biggest, the heaviest, the one with the most beautiful mane. And they'll spend years searching until they find it. They won't litter the veld with corpses. These are honorable men."

I paused to let him absorb that.

"Please go on."

"Von Roon reached that stage, more or less, but then partly slipped back to the previous one. He's a charming combination of the two. He wants trophies—only the best—but he wants tons of them. He's like a maharajah I know who's bagged over a thousand tigers. Can you imagine it?"

"No, this city boy can't imagine that."

"These grotesques use hunting not to be one with the pulse of nature. Not to walk as a predator and participate in the flow of life and death. They kill to flaunt dominance. Mastery of beasts they see as inferior to themselves."

Stratton hesitated. "So you think there's no hope for them?"

"Do you? I've known some of them to kill nursing females and leave their young to starve. Von Roon has done this. One time he even shot a leopard dozing on a branch. And he's not the only hunter who has."

"I had no idea of that sort of thing."

"Pompous fools desperate for trophies. Why not just start a rock slide and crush the sleeping animal under some boulders? Then drag out the corpse and skin it and make a rug to impress your drinking cronies? There's a special circle of Dante's Hell waiting for those barbarians. And for Von Roon."

Stratton looked toward the sideboard. "May I have something stronger than tea?"

I got up and poured him some bourbon.

"There's something I left out," I said. "A final level of maturity beyond that of even the trophy hunter. This is the true sportsman."

"Tell me."

Stratton took a delicate sip of the whiskey and settled back more comfortably.

"The real sportsman savors the entire experience. And that means more to him than a dozen heads on the wall. Living in the bush, sharing evenings under the stars with friends, smelling the campfire, telling stories, swapping lies, and bagging the occasional trophy. And not weeping if he fails to do so."

Stratton smiled. "And is that you?"

"Only a fool presumes to judge himself. But there are a few. Selous is one."

"I don't know that name."

"Frederick Courtney Selous. Learn it and don't forget. He's the greatest sportsman alive. Or dead."

"And he embodies that sort of maturation?"

"He's alone at the lofty summit. But it's been a long journey. When he was young, he was quite the slaughterer. He was an ivory hunter and took the titans down like wheat. In those days, with the weapons he had to hand, it was the most dangerous occupation on earth."

"He's told you about it himself?"

"He doesn't speak much about it now. But he has a weakness for champagne. Pop a cork with him and after a while you'll see sadness, like a cloud drifting across an African moon. He'll tell you he dropped far too many tuskers just so English snobs could have their billiard balls."

"You know him then?"

"Only slightly. Through friends. But we've shared a bottle or two. Selous is a giant. He's well into his fifties now, but still a man of iron."

"He should write his memoirs."

"The common wisdom is that Rider Haggard used him as his model for Quatermain. But no novelist could encapsulate that man. It's a nice *homage*, but it's just Plato's shadows on the wall of the cave. Selous is uncontainable. May he live to be a hundred."

"You're all such a strange breed," Jon said, shaking his head.

"Stranger than you think."

"Do people ever criticize you outright? Say that killing an animal for pleasure is immoral?"

My laugh must have sounded as brittle as cracking glass. "Times beyond counting. And usually behind my back. But a good hunter hears all the chattering in the jungle."

"And how do you answer them?"

"I don't."

"If I were to ask you, would you answer?"

"Are you asking?"

"I am."

"I'd say killing an animal for pleasure is *not* moral."

His stunned expression was priceless.

"And," I went on, "I'd further say hunting prey for sport is also *not immoral*. It's neither."

"What? I'm lost."

"Hunting for pleasure and satisfaction is a basic human drive. Because it's an instinct, it prowls its own solitary way *outside* the strictures of morality."

"How on earth can you say it's an instinct? Millions of people don't hunt and never will. You don't make sense."

Young people are, in the main, happier than older ones. I suspect it is because they are so naïve. No middle-aged man enjoys subverting such sacred ignorance. Aiming at that target always gives me buck fever.

"I have you, don't I?" he said with satisfaction.

"You have nothing."

"Refute me."

I admired his audacity. "Why?"

"Because I'm challenging you."

"Who will be the better for that?"

"Truth will be better."

I had to laugh. "Truth? That's the great lash that whips us all."

Now his expression of superiority became insufferable even to a man as patient as I. He was as cocky as a monkey who failed to see the leopard on the branch above him.

"Well, Mr. Stratton, the—."

"You may call me Jonny."

"That's a child's name. Let's make it Jon."

"Go on—hunting instinct."

"The drive to procreate is one of the most powerful human instincts. Do you agree?"

"I do."

"Yet countless people choose not to do so. Many voluntarily foreswear conjugal love and suppress that drive for one or more of a whole catalogue of reasons."

"All right. So?"

"Are you going to tell me that because not everyone employs it, the sexual drive is not an instinct? Or will you say these people are not human? By your reasoning, it must be one or the other."

"Well, no . . . I . . . that's not fair."

"An argument one loses is never fair."

He downed the rest of his bourbon, but it was too much for him and he coughed like a consumptive.

"And consider one thing more," I said. "When people sit in stadiums at sporting events and smile as one team hunts down and destroys the other team, or when they see one prizefighter demolish another, what do you think the audience is doing?"

"I never really —."

"They're hunting — in the deepest dungeons of their soul."

"But how can you — ?"

"They've simply hired others to sweat and bleed for them. Even the carnage of the chessboard brings death to the other side. Big game hunters are more honest — they stalk, kill, collect their trophies, and move on."

"You make it sound too simple."

"The most important things in life are *extremely* simple."

"But you're saying an ordinary game is —."

"Don't for a minute think that sporting contests are about scores and wagers. They're not."

"Then what — ?"

"They're tales of the hunt. All the thrills and fears of a jungle stalk — codified and stylized for the genteel. Only a child would think otherwise."

"And I'm being childish?"

I smiled. "There's always room for growth."

"But even something as optional as —."

"Optional? Hunting is universal and ineradicable. A fundamental fire in the human spirit. If you must, blame God."

Jon stood up and went to the fireplace. He set the heels of his hands against the edge of the mantle and stared into the flames.

"I came here for reassurance tonight. I'm not getting any."

"For that you need a priest. I know a few. In fact, one is a very fine duck hunter."

He turned back to me and could not help smiling.

"You know, captain, you're relentless."

"I have to be. I'm a man of the veld."

"And Von Roon?"

"Go with him. Just be careful."

He had a pleasant smile, even if a bit weary now.

"Did you enjoy what I wrote?"

"Very flattering."

"That's just a raw draft. I'll let you see everything before I commit it to print."

"That's not necessary. You don't need my approval."

"Perhaps not, but I want it to be correct. Shall I continue it?"

"If you wish. Be aware, though, that it'll cause me problems."

He laughed. "You're not serious."

"The last time someone wrote a piece about me, I received four discreet marriage proposals."

He laughed even harder. "In person?"

"By mail."

"And not one was worthy?" he asked in a bantering tone.

"Hardly the point. I'll never marry."

"Why not?"

"My standards are as lofty as Kilimanjaro."

"In what way?"

"She'd have to be a wild and untamed woman. Nothing less."

"As your mother was when your father met her?"

"You begin to understand. And there aren't any of those anymore."

"You shouldn't give up."

"A man knows the world he lives in. And accepts it. I'll die alone. A feeble graybeard wheezing his last. Or, preferably long before that with an animal's fangs deep in my throat."

He just stared at me, and then turned away and went for his coat and hat. While he did so, I opened the envelope I had slipped into my vest.

"Stop." I said.

Startled, he froze.

"First thing tomorrow, wire Von Roon and tell him you've changed your mind and you're not going to Africa with him. Will you do that without question?"

He hesitated only a moment. "I will."

"Good. You're going to Africa with *me*."

I handed him the cablegram.

YINGWE STOP TWO DEAD END

"What does it mean?"

"*Yingwe* is the Tsonga word for leopard. This is from Joseph Mpunga, my headman and tracker. It's the man-eater. My people are going to need me. They're in danger."

"Your people?"

"The Shangaan. Those are my people."

Jon put back his coat and hat and sat down again.

I thought for a while until he became impatient.

"Do you think it was any of the men who work for you who were killed?"

"No. Joseph would've told me."

"Will we go soon?"

"Not while it's raining. There's no point to that."

"There's no hunting during the rains?"

"There can be, but it's problematic. Sitting out at night in the rain waiting for a cat—who probably won't show up—ruins your health and your spirits. It isn't very good for your firearm, either."

"I can imagine."

"And it's much harder to get a clean shot when the foliage is lush. On the other hand, there *is* an advantage to it. If you're going to bait your quarry, wet weather is better than dry. So you have to weigh all—."

"Why is wet weather better?"

"During the dry season, the hoofed animals congregate at waterholes. They become easy pickings for a cat, so he's not nearly as likely to come on to a bait—which he knows he didn't kill and which he sees as something he's stealing from another predator."

A slow smile softened Jon's features. "This *is* a science, isn't it?"

"Of a sort. In the rainy season, the ungulates are scattered and more difficult to come by, so he's more likely to look favorably on a free meal — your bait."

"And your people — are they safe for now?"

"Oh, yes. As protected as if I were there myself. Joseph is the guardian of my hearth when I'm away. He's a master of bushcraft, so he'll know if the leopard is in the area. With a Holland and Holland he could shoot a poppy seed off an ant's head."

"So everyone is safe then?"

"The most important thing is for my people to stay in at night. It's almost unknown for a man-eating leopard to stalk a man in daylight. Joseph knows this. They'll be fine."

"I got the impression that Von Roon is leaving immediately."

"Sounds like him. He wants to be first on the ground. Before I or any other hunters take to the field. But it's a waste now. By the way, you never mentioned if you're married."

"I'm engaged to be married."

"When is your wedding?"

The question clearly startled him. "Early June."

"Then this could complicate matters. We might not be back in time."

"When would we leave here?"

"We should sail in early fall."

"Nine months? We'd wait that long? And how would that disrupt my wedding in June?"

His tone annoyed me. I could see that Jon was one of those people who quickly took liberties of familiarity with those who had opened their door for him. Not surprising, of course, in a journalist. More than irritating, it was dangerous at the beginning of a perilous venture. I decided to keep my gate open but also to notch his ear with a .22 for stepping through too quickly.

"Have you attended college?"

He looked defensive. "Columbia University."

"Well, I guess that'll have to do. Haven't they stumbled on the equator there yet?"

He stared at me for a few moments and then said, "I don't understand."

"It's summer below the equator now. Fall begins in March."

His face reddened. "Well, if you're talking about South African time . . ."

"I *think* in South African time. From today onward, so will you."

He remained silent. The bloody ear was working.

"Do you still have borrowing privileges at Columbia's libraries?"

"Yes."

"Good. I'm going to give you a list of titles to read before we go. I want them all finished by the time we leave. They're hunters' accounts."

He nodded. "I can do that."

"I'll never ask you to do something I think you can't do."

He seemed uncertain. "Thank you."

"And when you read these books, take them with several dozen grains of salt. Especially the danger. Hunters always ratchet that up a few notches. And don't pay too much attention to hunters' verdicts on animals' intelligence. Hunters are like everyone else—they think the smartest animals are the ones that act most like people. Never make that mistake."

"I'll remember that."

"One thing more. Avail yourself of Columbia's gymnasium. Get into the best physical condition you can in the next few months. A pasty-faced writer softened by Manhattan's fleshpots will shrivel and die under Africa's glare. Your fiancée will thank you for that."

"My fiancée? Why?"

"Because if you follow my advice, you'll be coming home in a stateroom instead of in a box."

Before I slipped into bed that night, I stood before my dresser and gazed at the statue I had bought many years before in Assisi. It was a rendering of St. Francis stroking the Wolf of Gubbio, the fierce man-eater he had tamed so long ago. I lowered my head to my patron and prayed for guidance. Then I opened the cedar box next to it. I slid my hand across the tiger pelt within.

"Old friend, I need your wisdom now," I whispered as I caressed the orange fur. Then I picked up the tiger claw threaded on the leather thong and looped it around my neck. "We will go together."

3

LEOPARDS ARE CERTAINLY THE MOST DIFFICULT TO UNDERSTAND, MORE INTELLIGENT THAN LIONS OR CHEETAHS AND LESS RELIABLE.
--NATURALIST JOY ADAMSON

JONATHAN STRATTON STUMBLED over a treasure where he least expected it. The *Herald* offered to finance his African trip in return for a serialized account of it. I warned him we might revel in nothing but failure, but his optimism was irrepressible — for the moment. And my more or less generalized loathing of the Fourth Estate encouraged me to allow him to squander as much of their corroded silver as possible.

We visited Owens Outfitting. Robert Owens was a translocated Welshman who had been a military tailor in London. Now he provided ermine and silks for the American sportsman.

Jon purchased the best garments available. At my instigation, he bought a tan bush coat similar to the one I wear and several shirts and trousers. I had the coat and trousers customized with patches of heavy leather over the shoulders and even thicker coverings on the thighs.

"That doesn't look very comfortable," he said when he heard me give instructions to Mr. Owens about the leather.

"You'll live with it," I said, looking over some new shirts for myself. "And that's the point. To protect your lily white skin."

"The man who speaks in riddles," Jon said, laughing.

I set aside two shirts and looked at him. "Most of the people who've been killed by leopards didn't die in the drooling demon's crushing jaws. They died a day or two later of blood poisoning."

"From cats?"

"They're the cleanest animals on earth, but there are two exceptions to their sterling hygiene. Any guesses?"

"I'd assume their mouth, since sometimes they eat rotten meat."

"Very good. But there's one other deadly area—their claws. The undersides are slightly concave. That lightens them without decreasing their strength. Like a fuller in a knife blade. But tiny particles of decaying food contaminate those grooves."

"So when they slice you, they're inadvertently injecting you at the same time?"

"Now you're learning. We use carbolic acid, but it's always pointless. Every big cat slash turns septic. No exceptions."

I pointed out a variety of serviceable hats, including a tan coober pedy like the one I have worn since Noah made landfall, but Jon would have none of that. He insisted on a linen covered pith helmet—"To look the part," he said.

Ah, yes, that would seduce the carnivores.

Medium-weight boots gilded this Manhattan lily, and then we were off to meet Bentley for supper.

The ancient Pompeian columns of Delmonico's welcomed us. Bentley was already there. The three of us ensconced ourselves at my favorite table at the shadowy and distant edge of the dining room.

I always came to "The Citadel" when I was in New York. That Delmonico's served the best steak in America was arguable, but it did offer the finest slab east of Billings and west of Mars. That night we ate like decadent tribal chieftains.

"Ready for your adventure?" Bentley asked Jon when we were well into our dessert, a superb port.

"I doubt it," he answered with refreshing honesty.

"Wisely spoken," Bentley said. "No one can ever be ready for Africa. Are you familiar with firearms?"

"Familiar?"

"Can you hit anything other than your feet?"

"I've hunted squirrels."

"I see." Bentley gazed at me with that bemused expression. "*Ngala* beware."

"He'll be all right," I said.

"I'm sure he will." Bentley looked back at him. "You'll be with the best shot south of the Limpopo."

"How many man-eaters have you hunted, captain?"

I could not recall, so I concealed the lapse with a leisurely sip of my wine as I searched my memory. "Eight—well, nine I suppose. Four tigers, three lions, one leopard. And another leopard who outsmarted me. I understand he still stalks the Panar River Valley in Almora."

"Not like you to give up, Hil," Bentley said.

"I didn't. He vanished into mist—as only a leopard can. He reappeared after I was gone."

"And he's still there?" Jon asked.

"So I've been told. The last I heard, at least eight sportsmen have taken to the field to slay him. He's eaten them all." I poured myself some more port. "A nicely definitive way of rebuking one's foes."

"It certainly is," Jon said.

"Have some wine." Bentley poured him a bit. "It'll soothe your soul."

"I assume you know what we can expect," Jon said.

"Of course," I answered. "And everything we expect to happen won't. And whatever we don't expect will."

"You've never mentioned if you're married," Bentley said.

"I told the captain I'm engaged."

"Insurance?"

He hesitated. "Some."

"Good."

"Stop it, Paul," I said.

"I'm just teasing," Bentley answered, smiling. "No reporter for the *Herald* has been devoured in Africa for at least three or four months."

"Oh, for God's sake!" I said.

"All right, all right," Bentley said and patted me on a forearm. "Just testing his mettle."

"Why should I be afraid?" Jon said to Bentley. "I'll be with the greatest *shikari* I know."

"How many do you know?" Bentley asked.

"One."

All three of us laughed.

"But do tell me about the Carnivora," Jon said to me seriously.

"Hunting them is every sportsman's dream. Sometimes it's as easy as aim, squeeze, boom, trophy. Other days, it's a mad folly."

"I assume that in Africa the lion is the most prized."

"He has the mystique of a god."

"And there are many ways to do it," Bentley said.

"How many?" Jon asked, looking at me.

"Four will cover it," I said. "You can hunt The King by stalking him on foot, galloping him down on horseback, sitting up over a kill or live bait, or running him to ground with dogs."

"Which way do you prefer?"

"The finest sportsman always chooses stalking on foot," Bentley said before I could answer. "Nothing is more taxing. Or more satisfying."

"And one of the worst is sitting over live bait," I said. "It's effective but it's corrosive. Listening to a goat bleating in loneliness and fear for hours is maddening to anyone with even a shred of feeling."

"I can't imagine what that must be like."

"Of course, eventually the goat stops and lies down to go to sleep. But the hunter has a string tied around one of its ears, and he yanks it to get the goat to keep bleating. After a night of that, your nerves are raw — or else you've become an insensate brute."

"And what about dogs?" he asked.

"Some use them, but no true sportsmen should use dogs to hunt lions or leopards. They do, though. I've never heard of it in India, but it's fairly common in the Transvaal, especially for leopards. It disgusts me."

"But what if—?"

"If you're a Montana rancher and a cougar is snatching your stock, by all means bring out the dogs and finish it. You don't have a choice."

"I don't understand. Why not?"

"You can't bait a cougar like a leopard, because a cougar won't eat another animal's kill. In fact, I've never known a cougar to come back even to its own kill after it feeds on it once. And the terrain out there isn't sandy or dusty enough to track a cat. You have to use dogs."

"But not with leopards?"

"With *Yingwe* you have other options—sporting options. Never let anyone tell you that hunting leopards with hounds is sport."

"Do most other hunters agree?"

"Most other hunters *don't* agree. But their agreement, or the lack of it, doesn't concern me." I had to laugh. "It's funny because my dissent does annoy *them*. But I'm indifferent to their fury. Let them think I'm attacking their character."

"Are you?"

"Shamelessly."

"Hil is an army of one," Bentley said. "Not that there aren't at least some hunters who agree with him. If a bit more gracefully."

"The honest ones. They know that when you hunt with hounds, you don't hunt at all. The dogs do. But that doesn't matter to some greedy hunter who's leading a safari for paying clients."

"But it's his job to produce results, isn't it?"

"Of course, and a leopard is one of the toughest results to come by. But with hounds it's all an illusion. The client doesn't get to hunt the cat. The hunter doesn't even hunt it. They don't come close. Can you guess why?"

He shook his head no.

"Because they can't keep pace with the hounds. Half the time the *houndsman* can't even do that."

"I never thought of that."

"So they arrive out of breath at some tree where there's a terrified and snarling leopard at bay over a pack of yelping trail hounds that have the collective intelligence of a handful of sea shells."

"It seems like a bit of a cheat."

"Then the client assassinates the cat—if he's any good at shooting a fish in a barrel. He then swaggers home and happily shows his drinking companions the results of the murder."

I saw Bentley smiling to himself, so I knew what was coming.

"What am I missing?" Jon said as he noticed Paul's smile.

"Well, our friend Captain Rixton has been known to wax philosophical and even poetical when soothed by a fine whiskey." Bentley glanced at me. "Would you care to expound?"

"And deprive you of the pleasure? Perish the thought."

"As it happens, friend Jon, one evening a new member of the club was regaling everyone with the tale of his leopard trophy gotten with hounds in Mpumalanga. He prattled on at length about the glories of hunting with a fine houndsman. What he failed to realize was the dangers of doing so when the old *shikari* was deep into his third bourbon. . . ."

Jon smiled. "Go on."

"Naturally, I couldn't resist the pleasure of goading the good captain. I said, 'Well, Hil, what do you think of that feat?' But he didn't answer. . . ."

"And?" Jon asked.

"Then the unfortunate fellow turned toward Rixton of Africa and said, 'Yes, please, tell me what you—' But Hil stopped him short with a wave of his hand and said, 'I think, young man, that color and contour are the only differences between a houndsman's heart and half a pound of dead rats.'"

Jon choked on his wine in mid-swallow. "Hil," he said, coughing and laughing simultaneously, "couldn't you be more specific?"

I spread my arms but said nothing.

"Can I put that line into my article?"

"Carve it into your soul," Bentley said and then looked at me. "Remember Ruslav, Hil?"

I laughed with a brutal pleasure that should have embarrassed me to myself but did not. "Who could forget him?"

"What happened?" Jon asked.

"Some Russian count." I said. "His manners were worse than Von Roon's."

"Can you tell me about it?"

"He wanted to hunt leopards in the Transvaal and do it with dogs. Sometimes a hunter will follow up a wounded leopard with dogs and survive the encounter because the cat is weakened, but hunting a healthy leopard with hounds is always extremely dangerous. . . ."

"Some hunters will tell you that a wounded leopard is the most dangerous of all the game animals," Bentley said. "They're wrong. An *angry* leopard is the most dangerous game animal. He doesn't have to be wounded to be furious. And nothing incites a leopard's wrath more than being chased by hounds."

"When a leopard is above you on a limb over a pack of yammering dogs," I said, "he's in a rage. Now he's no longer your prey — he's your enemy. . . ."

"Go on," Jon said.

"Ruslav had three or four trail hounds. They did their job. They tracked *Yingwe* and treed him. Ruslav thought it was over. Squeeze the trigger and go home. But this was no timid puma. When Ruslav got to the tree, the leopard just sneered at the yapping dogs and leaped onto the Russian and shredded him. The elegant count lived for less than an hour. His dogs died of old age."

"Do leopards always go into trees if they're being chased?"

"Only if they're being chased by dogs. If it's a man, usually the cat does the opposite and goes low. Heavy bush along riverbanks. Or down into a dry riverbed and up into the dense shrub on the other side. And there he waits for the hunter. And if the hunter's an amateur, he'll follow."

"And then?"

"It depends. If the cat's been wounded and thinks he can't get away fast enough, he might just wait there in the brush and hope he's not seen. But if the hunter makes eye contact with him—or even if the leopard believes he *might* have made eye contact—he'll charge. And then the hunter is a dead man."

I stared down at my drink in silence. After a while, Jon started to say something, but out of the corner of my eye I noticed Bentley wave him off.

"And there's one thing more," I said, finally looking up. "If you learn nothing but this from your association with me, it'll be enough. When you're sitting with your eye on a kill the leopard has cached in a tree, you're going to witness something that few are privileged to see. The cat will fly up the trunk of the tree without effort. He'll walk gracefully along the branch toward the carcass and then gently settle down to dine. He's now the king of his world and doing exactly what he was created to do. Stunning, supreme, and sublime. If you're a true sportsman, you take him at that moment. One shot."

"Just one?"

"If you're a true sportsman. And he never feels it. In fact, he never even hears it, because the bullet travels faster than sound. There will be no more ugly aging for him, no scrounging for scraps, no arthritic crippling, no final starvation. He's at the pinnacle of his life, relaxed and serene, and then the next moment he steps into eternity."

"We should all be so fortunate," Bentley said in his melancholy way.

"Or," I said to Jon, "you can drink from the dregs of the foulest dishonor and bring him to bay with howling dim-witted dogs. Now the last things he sees will be blank-eyed hounds. The last sounds he hears nothing but brainless yelps shattering the serenity of his gallant soul. There's no escape and this wise cat knows it. The majestic leopard's final moments will be terror and hopelessness, panic and despair."

Jon glanced at Bentley and then back at me but remained quiet.

I stared down into my wine, and we sat in silence for a long time until I looked up again. "Anyone who just for the sake of a trophy sits out all night jerking the ear of a crying goat is in danger of losing his soul. Anyone who uses hounds to hunt leopards has already lost it."

I paused and looked away, and Jon seemed afraid to speak.

"And horses?" he said after a while. "Can't that be just as unfair?"

"Yes, it can be," Bentley said. "But not necessarily. Tell him, Hil."

I knew what he was getting at—Somaliland.

"He should hear it," Bentley said.

"Hunting lions from horseback is like tickling scorpions. A delicate business."

"You'll have to explain that to me," Jon said.

"High speed, maybe a bad horse, inaccurate shooting. Hitting a running lion from a galloping horse takes staggering skill."

"Then how is it done?"

"First you have to understand most lions prefer to move off and avoid man. They see no point in fighting. The lion is a peaceful king."

"But . . . ?"

"But, if you ride close enough to him, he'll pivot and charge because he knows he can't escape. Now you have a choice—shoot from a moving horse, bring your horse to a halt and fire from the saddle, or dismount and shoot from the ground. And that last is the most dangerous sport on earth."

"But a lion is a big target, isn't he?"

"Not nearly as large as you think. Much of that head is really mane. His skull is less than a foot wide. At a hundred yards, it looks the size of a penny."

"Well, then, how can—?"

"And because of the backward curvature of the skull, if you go for a brain shot it'll probably glance upward and over. Especially if you're using hard bullets. The last shot you want to take with a lion or leopard or tiger is a head shot."

"Then what do you do?

"You can try for a lung shot, but that's not always effective unless you get both. And the heart is a fair size, but even if you hit it, that's no guarantee. I've seen a lion run fifty yards after taking a bullet through his heart."

"But doesn't your rifle have a greater range than that?"

"In the right hands. Most of the time I've used a Jeffery .450/.400 Nitro Express for tigers and lions. It's a double. I've brought down large game at over a hundred yards with a double rifle, but I don't recommend it."

"Why not?"

"It's really a short range weapon. I don't like to push it past fifty. And a lion is too small anyway for you to waste a shot at over fifty yards."

"That sounds so strange because a lion seems big to me."

"Trying to shoot a lion at a hundred yards is like trying to shoot a mouse at ten yards — not something you want to bet your life on."

"Then what do you do?"

"You can wait until he closes to twenty-five yards, but that's awfully close."

"My God . . . ."

"No, at that range, you won't have time to pray. An enraged charging lion is closing at about sixty feet per second. Think about that."

"I *am* thinking about it."

Bentley poured him some more wine.

"So if the lion is a hundred yards away," I said, "in two and a half seconds he's already closed half the distance. But you might not want to fire yet unless you're an expert, because fifty yards is too far for most hunters to ensure a lethal hit on a charging lion."

"Then what can you do?"

"You wait another second. Now he's about thirty yards away. Here's the moment of truth."

"And?"

"And if you miss with the first shot, there's a good chance you won't have time for a second one, even with a double rifle. But if you do, you'd better drop him with it because there's absolutely no time for a third. And at thirty yards, there's definitely no time for a second if you're using a bolt action. Even a straight pull like my Mannlicher, which is faster than a turnbolt."

"Then what do you do?"

"Get him with one shot or with two from the double, or you've bought a ticket to Heaven. Or Hell."

"Still with the Mannlicher, Hil?" Bentley said in a bantering tone.

I smiled but said nothing.

"What's wrong with it?" Jon asked Bentley.

"Shoots high."

"True," I said.

"I don't understand," Jon said. "Why?"

"The '95 is a military rifle," Bentley answered.

Jon looked confused.

"It's designed to hit enemy soldiers at long range," I said. "At less than a hundred yards it shoots about ten to twelve inches high."

"Then why use it?"

"Because it suits me."

"But *how* do you use it then?"

"I compensate."

"Instantly? In a crisis? How?"

I had to laugh. "I have no idea."

"Because he's intuitive," Bentley said. "And I hate him for it."

"Now do you want to hear the best part about charging cats?" I asked Jon.

"As long as you can hit him with the Mannlicher!"

"A leopard—especially a wounded charging leopard—is far more dangerous than a lion."

Jon seemed skeptical.

"You don't believe me?"

"I didn't say that."

When I said no more, he went on, "Can you tell me why?"

"First, he's faster. He can charge you at about seventy-five feet per second. So if he's a hundred yards away, you've got three seconds." I paused.

"All right."

"Two, when he charges you, he usually doesn't run straight like the lion does but in a jerky sort of zigzag that makes hitting him difficult at any range. Three, he's so much smaller than the bigger cats that a headshot—which is a shot of desperation with a tiger or lion—is nothing but a lunatic's fantasy with a leopard."

I paused and let that marinate.

"Hil," Bentley said, "you left out the worst thing of all."

Jon looked at him and then back at me. "What is that?"

"A leopard never charges from a hundred yards away. He waits until you're much closer. So those three seconds are really only two—or less."

"Then what can you do?"

"You can be quick and accurate. And you should do what a dismounted cavalryman would do—drop down to one knee and fire from there. But that's obvious."

"It's not obvious to me!"

"Think about it."

He did, but then he just spread his arms in confusion.

"A head shot is out. And you're not going to try for a spine shot if you can help it. It's wiggling all over the place and it's constantly moving out of your sights as the animal gets closer. Does that make sense?"

"Yes."

"The only constant target is his chest, which is getting larger as he's coming at you. But even then it's still tiny."

"So what are your chances then?"

"A friend of mine said that scoring a hit on a charging leopard was like trying to shoot a baseball hurled at your chest by a professional ballplayer from ten yards away."

"Did he do it?"

"What? Hit the leopard?"

"Yes."

"No. He was mauled to within an inch of his life."

"Then you're doomed?"

"Possibly. The best way to hit the cat's chest is to be as close to level with it as possible. Always try for the flattest trajectory you can get."

"That's why you drop down," he said, obviously proud of his insight.

"The problem is that many hunters don't want to go down on one knee. It makes them feel too vulnerable."

"They are, though, aren't they?"

"No, because you can't outrun a cat no matter how you're standing. So drop down, brace one elbow on your knee, take a breath, exhale halfway, hold it, fire."

Bentley cleared his throat.

I glanced at him and then looked back at Jon.

"Paul insists I tell you about an incident in Somaliland." I sipped my wine.

"He should hear it," Paul said.

"I was with a very well-known sportsman and a young English lord out for his first lion. I'll leave out their names, but you can probably track them down in your newspaper's archives. His Lordship wanted to hunt on horseback. He was a fine rider, polo and all that. It took us half a day before we found a pride. There was a big black-maned fellow lording over it. And then the chase began. The young man closed to within about a hundred and fifty yards, but still the lion kept going. At that point, the lord should've let the lion go. But he wanted his trophy. So he closed to within a hundred yards. Now he was on the killing ground. Then, in the flick of an eyelash, the lion pivoted in fury and charged."

I stopped and took another sip.

"Please!" Jon said. "Keep going!"

"Are you sure?"

"Yes," he said in a softer voice.

I set down the glass. "The Englishman had nerve—I'll give him that. He dismounted and slapped his horse away. He put the rifle to his shoulder. He was using a small caliber Rigby—an excellent choice, but only if you're an excellent shot. Which he was not. But it was a gift from his father and he wanted to use it. He waited until the lion was about twenty-five yards away. His shot creased the animal's scalp just to the inside of his left ear. That certainly deepened the lion's love for humanity. The next shot was perfect—straight through the lion's heart. But the cat didn't care. He was atop His Lordship in an instant and ripping him to pieces."

Jon stared at me in silence.

"The old tragic story," I said. "Not enough wisdom, not enough skill."

"But what happened?"

"Hil finished the lion with his pistol with a shot to the brain," Bentley said.

I waved that off. "It didn't matter. The Englishman's left eye and ear were gone and his lower jaw had been crushed in the lion's jaws and wasn't even recognizable as something belonging to a human face. And his shoulders and thighs were mutilated by the lion's claws. We poured carbolic acid into his wounds. He lasted about an hour. And it was a mercy that he went." I took another sip of my drink. "When he woke up that morning, he was a handsome member of a timeless nobility. By the afternoon, he was a mauled and shattered ogre groaning for death."

"Lord have mercy," Jon said. "And the cat had been shot through the heart?"

"It didn't matter."

"But why not?"

"Nothing magical," I said. "Deer and elk hunters see it all the time. Doctors call it hyperadrenia. An enormous charge of adrenaline is rushing through the animal. His brain still has oxygen, and his blood pressure hasn't fallen yet to drop him in his tracks. So he keeps going. Or coming. This day he came."

Jon was quiet a long time. For years, my survival had depended upon my ability to read the expressions of silent animals. Yet, at this moment, the look on his face eluded me.

"Is something wrong?" Bentley said.

"No, I . . . I'm just so grateful to the both of you for sharing this knowledge with me."

"Why?" Bentley tossed off in his customary offhand way. "It doesn't cost us anything."

Now *that* look I did know. It was pure Bentley. He was deeply touched by Jon's remark and, as always, this feeling was mated with a pseudo-cynic's refusal to admit it. I knew him to be one of the gentlest men who ever drew breath, but few others grasped his depths. He had outlawed such knowledge. Bentley was empty of the surface warmth that kindled friendships, and so he camouflaged that with flippancy and wit. He kept everyone at bay. Except, for some reason, me. He had married relatively late, and his young wife had worshipped him, but she died of a cancer. As happens with many who are cut by an inexplicable tragedy, a necrosis of the spirit had drained his vitality. He hunted little now, and the elephant injury provided an excuse. He spent most of his time at the club. Yet he was one of the finest sportsmen I knew. Bentley was a true scientific hunter. His knowledge of spooring—pug marks, scat, everything—was comprehensive and his command of ballistics vast. He was like a baseball player who steps up to home plate and instantly analyzes the pitcher, his delivery, the position of the fielders. I, on the other hand, was more intuitive—something Bentley liked to pretend to snarl about. I grabbed the bat and hit the ball. He had always admired me for that. Yet the reason escaped me. His praise struck me as silly as admiring someone for the color of his hair.

Most affecting of all to me was Bentley's profound love for the animals he hunted. This is by no means true of every hunter, and it is a truth that those who hate hunters always fail to comprehend. Bentley hunted to show his prowess—all hunters do—but that was ultimately a trivial concern. He was known to have a trophy collection worthy of some Eastern potentate, but few had ever seen it. For many so-called sportsmen, trophy rooms are boasting rooms, salons of death. To Bentley, his was a cathedral of life. For more than any other reason, he had taken these animals to freeze them in time, so he could be with them for the rest of his earthly life. "I care nothing for the praise of others," this lonely man had said to me one night after much cognac. "I care only what I am in the eyes of God—and of you." I had laughed and told him he had at least judged it half right.

4

A PECULIAR VIRTUE IN WILDLIFE ETHICS IS THAT THE HUNTER HAS NO GALLERY TO APPLAUD OR DISAPPROVE OF HIS CONDUCT. WHATEVER HIS ACTS, THEY ARE DICTATED BY HIS OWN CONSCIENCE, RATHER THAN BY A MOB OF ONLOOKERS. IT IS DIFFICULT TO EXAGGERATE THE IMPORTANCE OF THIS FACT.
--NATURALIST ALDO LEOPOLD

THE SAFARI CLUB had its own shooting range out in the country. I needed to see how well our Manhattan squirrel slayer could handle a firearm, so we braved the frost and made an excursion. I asked Bentley for the loan of one of his Mausers, as all of my weapons, other than my revolver, were in Africa. To my surprise, he also agreed to lend himself. I was grateful for that. With his drastically linear and methodical mind, he was a peerless instructor.

He began Jon at a range of fifty yards against a paper target tacked to a wooden frame. To the shock of both of us, his first five shots produced an excellent grouping. And this was no squirrel gun. With the Mauser 98, professional hunters have dropped elephants.

I replaced the target and moved it out a further fifty yards. No matter—another fine group from our city boy.

Jon just shrugged. "I've always had a good eye and a steady hand." He laughed. "But tomorrow I'll also have a purple shoulder."

After more shooting, Bentley gave him a refresher on firearms safety and etiquette. Jon was quietly respectful, but I believe he had heard all of this before.

Then Bentley startled me—he invited Jon to see his trophies. "And you, too, Hil."

Even I had not been to Bentley's home in at least a year, and I think Jon realized from the look on my face what a privilege he had just been given.

Bentley had a dinner engagement at the club, so we agreed to meet at his place later in the evening.

My housekeeper, Letty, was the daughter of a freed slave, but she ruled my home like a queen. She insisted any visitor of mine be treated as nobility.

The young woman sipping hot tea before the fire in my study looked the part, or at least played it well. Beneath her chestnut hair she had the fashionable pallor of an existence spent indoors. The elegance of her dark blue satin dress seemed a bit excessive for the time of day, but I put that down to her obvious anxiety at the role of cool detachment she was trying to play. She was, according to her card, Miss Virginia Delamere. She told me she was the fiancée of Jonathan Stratton.

After the customary formalities, she said simply. "I wanted to meet you, captain, after hearing so much about you from Jonathan."

"Your visit is entirely my good fortune."

It struck me as odd that she expected me to carry the conversation. "How may I help you?"

She moistened her lips, not an elegant touch at all, and said, "You may assure me of Jonathan's safety."

"We live in a fallen world, Miss Delamere. I can assure you of nothing."

Clearly that was not what she had expected to hear. "Jonathan says you're a man of the world."

"For what it's worth."

"He says you'll look after him, that I need not worry. He admires you greatly."

"The enthusiasms of youth always pass."

"Captain, I'm afraid."

"Of course you are."

That stunned her. "What do you mean?"

"Each of us is afraid of something. I no less than you."

See seemed suddenly as shaky and delicate as an impala calf.

"Miss Delamere, the kind of assurance you want only God can give. Asking it of me borders on blasphemy."

"I . . . I just don't want to lose my Jonathan."

"More men have been lost by overprotective fiancées than have ever been taken by man-eating leopards."

I regretted that immediately.

"But I've loved Jonny since I was eight years old!" she said as her eyes welled up. "Don't you understand?"

"I do, Miss Delamere."

She seemed barely out of childhood now, elegant satin notwithstanding.

"Please call me Ginny," she whispered.

I smiled at her. A woman whom I had loved, but whom I had lost, had once said to me, "Hil, when you smile, all the world stands relieved." When I smiled at Ginny Delamere, every muscle in her body seemed to ease back into the chair.

"Don't be afraid," I said. "God's grace is more than we know."

She seemed as shocked as a doe who had just seen a wolf smile and wave at her and move on. "That's such a kind thing to say. So tender."

"Don't let it get out."

She smiled and the remains of her tears seeped back whence they had come.

"I was so afraid to come here today."

"As you can see, I'm a terrifying creature."

"Stop it!" she said, and her sudden laugh was magical.

"Well, you must have been afraid of something."

"It was Jonny—the way he described you."

"Ah, yes—Rixton of Africa. The eye patch, the scar, the big-bore rifles."

"That's it!" she said, laughing even more.

Suddenly I had the most absurd and irrelevant thought—that Ginny Delamere's father was a very lucky man.

"As you can see, it's all true," I said.

"I think my Jonny painted you darker than you are."

"Beware—I shoot straight."

"No," she said, gathering her thoughts behind green and pensive eyes. "I'd say you're a man who *sees* straight."

I poured her some more tea.

"Please don't tell Jonathan I came here today."

"Why on earth would I?"

"Wouldn't telling him be the most logical thing to do?"

"As my friend Paul Bentley could inform you, I'm not a logical man."

"What are you, then?" she asked good-naturedly.

"Intuitive to the edge of lunacy."

She smiled again.

I got up and closed the draperies and lit the gas lamps against the dreariness of a winter afternoon. I had never developed a taste for electric light.

"This is such a lovely room," Ginny said. "But very much a man's room," she quickly added.

Paintings of many great cats adorned the walls. The frosted shades of my lamps lit them evocatively. I had taken great care with that.

"I expected to see heads everywhere."

"No, not for me—I can't bear all that staring."

She laughed some more. "But the oils are wonderful."

"Lord Hardwicke."

She looked at me in surprise.

I nodded.

"You must be a very famous man."

"In a circle as big as a teacup. And Lord Hardwicke is a revered friend."

She gazed around at the cats. "They seem so placid and serene. Not ferocious at all."

"That's because they were not."

"I see. They were circus animals then?"

"They were man-eaters."

She looked at me to see if I were teasing her.

"They were simply hungry and they ate. There are no demons here. But I took them all."

She peered into me as deeply as she dared and seemed about to ask something. Yet she apparently thought better of it.

She stood up and walked around the room and studied the paintings. She stopped in front of the fireplace and stared for a long time at the large oil of a leopard above the mantle. Then she turned and just looked at me. Searching again.

"You're wondering," I said, "why no black-maned lion holds the place of honor."

"Yes, I was thinking that."

"Because only one cat can claim that throne. The Man-Eating Leopard of Limpopo."

She came back to her chair and helped herself to more tea. Then she set her cup down and studied me with a slight squint, as if that would somehow sharpen her vision.

"Captain, may I ask you a personal question?"

"Everything is personal."

"Yes. You said that to Jonathan, didn't you?"

"Probably."

She took a deep breath. "When you speak of these animals, I hear something in your voice. Maybe . . . maybe something a little sad?"

I remained quiet.

She hesitated and then said, "You don't like to kill, do you, captain?"

I tried to conceal my admiration for her intuition, but to this day I do not know whether or not I succeeded.

"Captain?"

"Rixton of Africa does not enjoy slaying cats."

Her silence was her encouragement to me to continue.

"When I was young, I took my first lion. It's quite an event, doing that. He was a grand old fellow, and I dropped him with a single shot that even today makes me gasp. And it was a mercy that I took him. He had little time left. Do you know how old cats die?"

She shook her head no.

"They starve to death. Most people feel sorry for the hoofed animals. The poor victims of the bloodthirsty cats. Don't. Save your sorrow for the predators. When they become too feeble to catch a rat or even a man, they just emaciate and die."

She nodded. "I understand."

"So when I stood over the old gentleman, I felt no sorrow for him. I felt sorrow for myself. Something within me I didn't know existed had been violated. And *I* had done the violating."

She held up a hand. "You needn't tell me, captain."

"Every true sportsman has an ethic. He doesn't often think about it, but it breathes inside him like a living being. I'd scalded mine."

"How?" she said in a low voice.

"Man is a predator. It's his job to take prey. But over that dead lion my ethic suddenly told me *it's not man's job to prey upon other predators.* A predator taking another predator isn't a hunt. It's an ambush. A cheat. Maybe even an infamy. Can you guess why?"

She thought for a few moments but shook her head no.

"Because predators don't *know* they're being hunted. True, lions sometimes kill leopards and hyenas, but they compete for the same food. Their battles with one another are natural. But man and lion don't compete. Nor man and leopard, nor man and tiger."

"But why does that mean—?"

"It means there can be no fair chase of an animal that can't even imagine it's *being* chased. Or, if it suddenly realized it was, could never comprehend why."

She looked away as she seemed to be considering that.

"You're still too young to know how unfair life is. Great roiling rivers of unfairness crash through our lives every day until we die, and they bring chaos and pain and despair. I've chosen not to add my own drop of unfairness to that torrent."

"But what about the man-eaters?"

"Cattle killers and man-eaters fall before my guns, but those are all. I do that without remorse. And without pleasure."

"And the rest?"

"Rixton and the big cats have drawn off, signed a truce. An armed truce, to be sure. We never take our eye off one another, but on separate summits now we stand. Until the end."

She stared at me for a long time and then said, "But what about others? Your friends who hunt the cats?"

"I don't judge them in the least. Every man has to find his own ethic."

"Captain, have you ever thought of writing your memoirs?"

"No."

"You should consider it."

"There are already too many hunting tales. And of dubious veracity."

"But yours would be so different. More philosophical."

"The last thing this world needs is more philosophy."

"No, the *first* thing it needs is more philosophy. At least of a particular kind."

"And what kind is that?"

"Yours."

"You'll soften me with your flattery."

"No, captain. That could never happen."

She stood up, and I rose as well.

"I should go now. Thank you."

"For what?"

"For giving me some of your courage."

"I did nothing even close to that. Yours was there all along."

That startled her. "Why would you say that?"

"Because courage isn't the absence of fear—it's the conquest of fear. You've conquered today."

"Such a noble thing to say," she said, shaking her head in bewilderment. "I've never known a man who speaks like you speak. In my world, men barely speak at all. Where does a man like you come from?"

"I thought you knew. I sprang full-blown from the brow of Jove. Or the maw of Satan. Take your pick."

"There you go," she said, smiling. "Painting yourself so dark. And yet you've risked your life to save others."

"Innocent and terrified people huddle in the night, and I pick up my rifle and go to see what I can do. There's no sainthood in that."

"Such a dark portrait. So many shadows."

"Perhaps I should get Lord Hardwicke to execute a flattering one."

I had meant it as a jest, but she leaped at it.

"Yes, yes, do that! A painter sees his subject far more clearly than the subject sees himself. And you can give it to Jonathan and me as a wedding gift."

"You're serious."

"I am. I'll commission it myself."

"You'll buy your own wedding gift?"

"I will. A portrait it will be. And I think, Captain Rixton of Africa, you'll be astonished by what you see."

5

EVEN THE SMALL LEOPARD IS CALLED LEOPARD.
AFRICAN PROVERB

ODDLY, I FELT DRAINED after Ginny Delamere had left. I decided
to nap before changing for dinner. Yet sleep eluded me. I just lay
there in a mental whirl. The fact that I was so tired gave me the
excuse for this inertia, since I knew that mental exertions at this
point were not wise. Many startling things are conceived in
bedrooms, but rarely sane thoughts.

Ginny Delamere was a remarkable young lady. Great
indeed was the fortitude it took for her to come here and ask me
to usurp, if only briefly, the powers of God.

I had no intention of allowing Jonathan Stratton to die in
Africa, but if the Fates proved malignant, what would it matter?
I have always been unmoved by those weepy tales of youth cut
off, the fresh bloom snapped before full flowering. What finer
time for it? Better to be snatched away while full of life and
approaching the summit than swatted to the earth when
tumbling in decrepitude down the other side.

But to a young woman in love, the future was strewn with
rose petals. Ironic and amusing was the fact that it had become
the task of a one-eyed big game hunter to keep the petals fresh.
But how could a man resist? Innocent and alluring and subtly
brave, she was the ideal of the era — the enticing child-woman of

so many men's dreams. So many but I. The sensual swishing of satin skirts crumpled uselessly against my tone deaf ears.

I was of another age entirely. A hardscrabble life at frontier outposts had killed most of my fantasies. After what had seemed to be about a hundred years of fighting heat and cold and Indians and boredom, I had retired on my inheritance and taken to exploring far-flung continents.

I could barely remember a time when I had not thrilled to the chase. It is a curious fact that almost no one takes up hunting as an adult. There are exceptions, but those are very rare. Rather like embalming, hunting for sport is a taste one must acquire as a child, or one does not acquire it at all. But what a quest it is. The boom, the recoil, the harsh reek of the powder. And, above all, that noble beast—at this moment, the only other creature on earth—seemingly surrounded by a corona of light and to be caught at that flashing instant for all eternity.

Mystical musings indeed, preserved and enhanced only by the skills of the taxidermist, unsung artist of the age.

But even the sharpest of spices lose their piquancy, and all fade with time. And now mine were only a memory. Or, perhaps, even less than a memory.

Why in the name of God I would be thinking about all this now puzzled me. I felt strongly, though, that I had come to a marker in the road. Or, perhaps more accurately, a closing of some part of my past, a gate coming down. What baffled me was whether the gate were closing behind me in preparation for a new beginning or clanging before me to bring about an end. But closing it surely was. I had no doubt.

After my non-sleep, I dressed for dinner but found I had no taste for it. However, Letty insisted, so she sliced me some rye and cold beef. I was surprised by how much I enjoyed it. Probably it was Letty's smile of approval that made it taste so good.

Afterward I headed out to Bentley's. In the post the following day came Jon's impressions of that evening. They are worth sharing now in their entirety.

From the outside, Paul Bentley's country house seemed to strike a lonely pose, especially on a gray December evening. Inside, though, was quite another matter. Bentley's servants, crisp and smart, catered to us with enthusiasm. Trays of pastries, along with coffee rich enough to chew, followed by spirits and cigars, improved both body and soul.

Bentley showed genuine joy in our visit. I suspected that entertaining was not something he often undertook, and perhaps he had forgotten how much pleasure it gave him.

But that was all incidental. The trophies were what I had been invited to see.

Holding a very mellow bourbon, I followed Bentley to the back of the house, and Captain Rixton brought up the rear.

We entered a long hexagonal room, and the animals seemed to leap at us from the cream-colored walls. Opposite us, a doorway opened to a room beyond. Above the lintel, the head of a massive African tusker spread his great ears and raised his trunk before us. I got the eerie feeling I could actually hear his trumpeting. To right and left of the door a pair of Giant Sable Antelope stood on platforms like guards outside the gates of some barbaric kingdom. Shoulder mounts of numerous spiral-horned antelope adorned the walls above them.

We crossed the room and passed beneath the bull elephant and through the doorway.

"As you can see," Bentley said, "I have no taste for rectangles."

This room was an ellipse and housed North American trophies. Elk and bighorn and cougar and grizzly greeted the visitor. However, I felt guilty for not being as impressed as I thought I should have been by this startling array of big game. The mounts seemed old and rather faded, the room sparsely furnished and little used. Also, many of the mounts seemed a bit off. Odd musculature here and there and the occasionally distorted face hinted at taxidermists more familiar with animals in death than in life. When a boy, I had spent enough hours at the zoological garden to be able now to recognize the difference between life and an earnest but failed simulation of it.

We did not linger here but went through a doorway in the far wall. I will never forget that moment.

I stepped into an enormous octagon. Across from me a roaring blaze in a black marble fireplace threw out its warmth. Above it hung an immense oil of a black-maned lion. To the left and right of the hearth, a pair of great tusks curled upward from their bronze mounting bases on the floor.

The room was windowless except for a clerestory around the top of the walls. No destructive sunlight here.

57

Gorgeous zebra skins decorated the floor. I noticed that Captain Rixton did not walk across these splendid hides. Unobtrusively but decisively, the old cavalryman sidestepped the horses.

And the astigmatic taxidermist was long gone. The beasts here were alive.

Shoulder mounts of two Black Rhinoceros and three titanic Cape Buffalo jutted from several of the walls on the right, and numerous antelope heads were arranged in order of descending size on either side. Below them, a pair of Spotted Hyena gazed upward in eternal frustration.

Bookshelves on either side of the fireplace and several comfortable chairs showed that it was this campfire at which Bentley spent much of his time.

I was wondering about the absence of predators when I turned to the opposite walls. Captain Rixton later told me with a laugh that he had heard me gasp. That I do not doubt, for there ruled the lions.

No stiff and stilted animals here, and no ridiculous rearing demons that looked less like cats than like men in lion suits. Here in a semi-circular alcove as big as a chapel in a Renaissance church reigned an entire pride of lions. The black-maned male of the painting stood tall in the stubby grass of a recreated African hill. He paused in three-quarter profile from the left, as if he were gazing into the distance beyond my right shoulder.

At the bottom of the slope and to the left another big male lay and stared off to the west. Two lionesses lay to the right. A couple of cubs rolled around with each other, and a third was taking a swipe at the tip of his mother's tail.

In the foreground, two big males, still young and with half-grown manes, were sleeping. One stretched from right to left on his stomach with his head up but with neck slightly bent and his chin resting on his forelegs. The other lay beyond him at an angle and with his chin on his brother's back just behind the mane. If he opened his eyes, he would be looking directly at me and wondering what on earth I was doing here.

Three well-padded chairs were arranged before the tableau. Here in this sacred sanctuary one could sit in silence and ponder the heart of Africa.

I sat, and I could not imagine when I would want to get up again.

Behind the pride, a black curtain had been hung and conveyed the impression of darkness. The single soft gas lamp that illumined the *scene made it seem as if the lions were resting now and waiting for the moon to set before going off on their nightly hunt.*

"Hil," Bentley said, "would you?"

Captain Rixton set down his cigar in a tray beside one of the chairs and made his way around the left edge of the pride. In the back, he pulled a cord and, to my surprise, the black curtain parted in the center and slid to the sides.

An enormous gray rock outcropping loomed behind the lions. Bentley later told me it is called a koppie. *A spotted cat rested at the summit. Smaller than the lions, he nonetheless reclined with an air of primacy impossible to deny. Serene and supreme, he lay there clothed in his favorite raiment, the light of an African moon.*

Captain Rixton slid a tall library ladder out from the shadows and gestured to me.

I walked around the left of the pride and joined him beyond the lions.

He pointed to the ladder. "Make sure you come back alive."

Strangely, he appeared to be only half joking.

I climbed the ladder to see the beast above. When I reached the top, I knew I had been wrong. Now it seemed dishonorable to think in terms of beast, *a word often used as a pejorative. This creature was nothing of the kind.*

The big panther lay there at ease, his daintily spotted right foreleg crossed casually over his left. He lay at about a forty-five degree angle atop the koppie, *so he seemed to be gazing straight at me on the ladder. And when I joined eyes with him, the skin on my forearms tingled, and I could feel the goose bumps form. I swear by all I hold holy that he was staring right into my soul. And yet he was just a remnant, not a living animal. An artifact, a testament to the taxidermist's art. But that, too, seemed heretical and profane. No craftsman could render this. Only a being far greater than man could conceive what I saw. But what kind of being? I recalled Blake's words about the tiger.*

What the hammer? what the chain?
In what furnace was thy brain?

I suddenly felt the urge to touch this great cat. Reflexively, I looked down at Bentley.

He read my mind and nodded.

I ran my hand over the soft fur of the leopard's head. Jolted with atavistic horror, I recoiled. Recovering, I reached out again and stroked him gently.

What the anvil? What dread grasp
Dare its deadly terrors clasp?

The realistic gray boulders on which the leopard rested seemed to be some sort of mixture of papier-mâché and plaster. Embedded in one was a tiny bronze plaque. It was invisible from the floor, so only someone privileged to stand on this ladder could see it. The plaque read simply, The Man-Eater of Limpopo.

I looked at the cat one more time and locked that image in my brain. Then I descended.

"Thank you," I said to Bentley, and I realized my voice was a whisper.

Then I went back to my chair and sat there for a long time.

After Jon's encounter with the man-eater, we retired to a small study I believe had been the late Mrs. Bentley's sitting room. There were no trophies here, and it still retained a few feminine touches that I think gave Bentley comfort in his solitude.

The bourbon and cognac now flowed, and we settled in.

"So tell me more about leopards," Jon said.

Bentley deferred to me.

"First of all," I said, "the leopard is elusive. Lions will occasionally hunt in daylight. The leopard is often a nocturnal hunter, although how often is something many sportsman can never seem to agree on. Add to that the fact that he spends so much time in trees. So unless you're tracking in sandy soil or in mud, here you have an animal almost impossible to stalk on foot. Unless you're lucky enough to be following a blood trail. So you have to sit up in a tree for hours over bait that you placed or over one of his own kills that he hasn't finished yet."

"Very dangerous," Bentley said.

"Why?"

"Because any branch a man can climb to, a leopard can climb to," I said. "Hunters have been pulled from trees. In total silence. And our headman wonders why we're late for breakfast."

"And consider the size of the target," Bentley said. "A lion can go four hundred pounds, but an average male leopard is maybe a hundred and thirty. So you have a small quarry that you have to shoot from a tree. In fading light or in the dark."

Jon looked back at me. "Can you shoot by moonlight?"

"Yes, but if clouds gather and the wind picks up, you're suddenly blind and deaf."

"So what do you do then?"

"You pray. The Limpopo Man-Eater — the only man-killing leopard I've ever shot — almost got me several times before I brought him down."

"How?"

"That's a story for another day."

"And realize, too," Bentley said, "that a man-eating lion isn't half as dangerous as a man-eating leopard. The reason is that a man-eating lion can get incredibly arrogant. Even more than he normally is."

Jon smiled.

"He loses his natural wariness of man," Bentley went on. "You could even say he becomes contemptuous of the little stick figures he's devouring. And that makes the hunter's task much easier. Not so the leopard. Ever."

"That's not to mean the leopard isn't bold," I said to Jon. "He's bold beyond belief. He'll snatch people from their beds. But boldness isn't recklessness. The lion becomes brash and careless. But while the leopard revels in his daring, he stays wary to the end. The lion is the strutting king of the veld, but the leopard is lord of the darkness."

Jon just stared at me for a while. Finally, he said, "But not every big cat is a man-eater, is it?"

"No, but that doesn't mean every one can't be dangerous."

"But why would it be dangerous if it isn't a man-eater?"

"Is your mother a man-eater?"

Jon clearly thought I had lost my mind.

"Well?" I said.

"Hil, I'm at sea here."

"If someone had tried to hurt you when you were a little boy, what would she have done to that person?"

He looked as if were beginning to conclude that perhaps I was not totally mad. "Go on."

"This was back in '96. A friend of mine was walking along a narrow trail near the Sabi with two porters the day he met his maker. Narrow jungle tracks in heavy bush are the worst because they give you so little space to maneuver or shoot in an emergency. One of the porters ahead of him accidentally flushed a pair of leopard cubs. The mother had hidden them in the brush when she'd gone off to hunt. At that moment, she was coming back with a dead guinea fowl for them. She took in the scene in an instant. It was finished in less time than it takes to tell it."

"How did you hear about this?"

"From the porter who survived."

"Did he give you details?"

"The furious mother was on top of the first porter and tearing him before he could blink. Unfortunately my friend was a clergyman who didn't believe in firearms. Faith in God is good, but faith in God and gunpowder is better. All he had was a knife. So he pulled it and just jumped onto the back of the leopard while it was on top of his porter. Can you imagine such a thing?"

Jon shook his head no.

"It might have been stupid, but it was the bravest act I've ever heard of in my life. He managed to nick her once or twice, but the leopard flung him off like a bug. She killed them both. The other porter managed to get up a tree without being seen by the mother. Later he managed to slip away. . . ."

Jon remained quiet.

"But something like that is rare," I said.

"And are man-eating cats rare, too?"

"Very rare in Africa. Much more common in India."

"Any idea why?"

"Probably because there are more people and more big cats in a much smaller area. But all of them have the potential."

"That's the only reason?"

"No, in India they often take to hunting people because of a shortage of normal prey. Due to disease or maybe overhunting by men. That's true of South Africa, too—the Boers are great slaughterers."

"And in the other cases?"

"Usually wounds. Remember, the Garhwal Man-Eater had a bad hind leg and a broken canine. Man was one of the few animals he could catch and kill."

"Yes, I do remember that."

"But there's one last circumstance that's far more ominous than the other two. That's when a normal and healthy cat becomes a man-eater."

"Does that happen often?"

"It's hard to say, but it does happen. Sometimes a big cat will kill a person because of some accidental mischance. Somebody stumbles upon him and startles him and he reacts defensively and kills the person. Most of the time, the cat will just walk away afterward. But not always. . . ."

"And then what?"

"Every now and then, the cat will decide to sample this new item. If he likes the taste or if he decides he likes how easy it is to take human prey—or both of those things—then the nightmare begins. A healthy man-eating cat, complete with all his powers, is lethality incarnate."

Jon looked at Bentley with an uncertain smile. "Maybe I *should* have more insurance."

"And there's one thing more," I said. "The leopard's intelligence. The ability of the big cats to reason things out is staggering. And anyone who's dealt at any length with lions and leopards will tell you that the big fellow has to take a back seat."

"But doesn't the leopard have a smaller brain?"

"Slightly. But it doesn't matter. And people have puzzled over this intelligence for a long time. But I might know the answer."

"And I'm not going to bed tonight until you tell me."

"The most basic rule of nature is that an animal has to be smarter than his food. A wildebeest has to be smarter than the grass he eats, and a lion has to be smarter than the wildebeest he stalks. There's nothing earth-shattering about this. Agreed?"

"Agreed."

"Lions dine mostly on large ungulates like wildebeest. Zebras, too, which are smarter than wildebeest. Leopards prefer impala, a medium antelope and none too smart. But they have another special taste as well. Any guesses?"

"I can't imagine."

"Leopards have a taste for baboons, even though they don't kill them too often. A troop of baboons can be deadly. Males have been known to encircle a leopard and tear him apart with their canines. So it takes an animal of intelligence and skill to pick off one of these very smart monkeys. Do you see where I'm heading?"

"Maybe."

"Well, it gets even better. I have it from hunters up in the Congo that leopards will prey on chimpanzees. I'm sure you know how smart they are."

"Yes, I saw one in a circus once."

"Even more incredible, leopards have been known to take gorillas. Strong as half a dozen men and smarter than an Oxford don but without the snob appeal. Gorillas, for God's sake."

"You know this for certain?"

"Yes. They stalk them and kill them and eat them. Of course, most of them don't make a habit of it. I think if they prey on chimpanzees or gorillas, most of the time it's just a lucky accident for the leopard that the animal happened to be there."

"But not always. . . ."

"No, not always. I know for a fact that leopards prey on gorillas in Uganda."

"I can't even imagine what a battle like that could be like. It must be horrifying."

"Probably."

"And the baboons are just as tough?"

"Maybe more so. Baboons and other kinds of monkeys are as tasty to leopards as grilled beefsteak to us. Some hunters claim leopards eat large numbers of baboons."

"Do you think they do?"

"No. Except in one special case I know of. If they can snatch a baboon they definitely will, but I don't think they make a religion out of it. Facing an angry troop of baboons is like taunting an army of madmen."

Jon laughed. "And what about the special case?"

"Are you sure?"

"Sure about what?"

"That you want to hear it?"

"Why not?"

"It won't help you sleep soundly in the bush."

Jon glanced at Bentley, but he could see from Paul's expression that I was not joking.

"I'd like to hear it anyway."

"Back in the nineties Paul and I were making a little excursion on horseback up into the Waterberg Mountains. That's in Limpopo. After about a day's ride we came across a stone cabin. The owner greeted us as we rode up. He was grizzled old farmer who'd retired to the Waterbergs. He lived by his rifle and his wits. Something of a hermit. Yet he treated us like visiting princes. His name was Pretorius." I glanced at Paul. "Do you remember his first name?"

He shook his head and shrugged.

"Anyway we ate and drank and talked. Paul told him I was a sportsman and—."

"A *famous* sportsman," Paul said.

I waved that off. "Pretorius asked me if I knew anything about leopards and I nodded but didn't elaborate. Then he said there were plenty of baboons there in the Waterbergs to keep the leopards happy. Thinking back later, I realized he did that just to tempt my skepticism. . . ."

"And did he succeed?" Jon asked.

"Oh, yes. I said I never knew leopards to prey much on baboons, even though they favored the taste. Pretorius laughed and said, 'That's true—except in the Waterbergs.' Then he told us that over the last decade he's seen countless leopard kills, and he guessed at least one in five was a baboon. To me, this seemed beyond belief."

"And yet you think he was telling the truth?"

"He had no reason to lie. And he said most of the baboon kills hadn't been females or young ones but adult males."

"While they were sleeping?"

"No, they'd been taken in daylight. This was incredible. He said the most recent kill he'd seen was by a female leopard barely two years old. That means she'd probably just left her mother. And the victim was a big male full in his prime. She ambushed him and struck him down in the middle of the day in the fraction of an instant."

Paul smiled. "Pretorius rewrote the book on leopards and baboons, but no one knows about it but Hil and I and now you."

"And," I said, "it means the leopard is the one big cat nature has produced that's able *routinely* to hunt down some of the smartest animals alive. Which is why a man-eating leopard is the most dangerous predator on the face of the earth."

Jon was quiet for a long time and then finally said, "And Mr. Pretorius? Is he still there? Still well?"

I nodded. "As far as I know. But if a Waterberg leopard ever turns man-eater, all one can do is fall to one's knees and pray for death."

The bourbon and the hour were exerting their effects, and the skin around my eye patch was beginning to itch. It was time to sum up.

"Jon, for your own survival, I want you to remember the differences between the two great African felines. Of course, they're both cats, so they share many traits, but their differences run deep. We know this not just from hunters but from the experiences of people who've raised orphaned cubs."

I paused to gather my thoughts.

"Please go on."

"The lion can be as terrifying as Satan when he's aroused, and the sounds he makes seem to echo from the pit of Hell. But *Ngala* is really a blunt and straightforward sort—as open as the plains he lives on. . . ."

"A hail fellow well met," Bentley said with a smile. "If he were a man, he'd slap you on the back and offer you a cigar."

"Exactly. But the leopard—no. The psyche of *Yingwe* doesn't dwell in the comforting sunshine of the veld."

I sipped my bourbon and gazed off at the memories of a lifetime.

"Captain?"

I looked back at Jon.

"Where then?"

"The soul of *Yingwe* lives in a forest on top of an escarpment surrounded by an abyss."

Jon said nothing but stared beyond my shoulder as if trying to come to grips with what I was saying.

"You don't stroll up to that dark spirit across open grassland," Bentley said.

"No," I went on. "You advance toward it—if you dare—by crossing a crevasse on a swinging rope bridge in a high wind. On the other side, he waits."

"The panther watches your approach with eyes like no others," Bentley said.

"Not the warm gaze of the lion there," I went on. "Hunters love to write in horrified rapture about 'the great golden orbs of the leopard' that 'burn yellow with the fires of bloodlust.' It makes for wonderful reading."

"But it's not true?"

"In bright sunlight the eyes do look like glowing gold, and just about every taxidermy mount of a leopard has golden eyes. But those are just silly spheres of glass."

"Why do they keep making the same mistake then?"

"Very few taxidermists have ever peered into the eyes of a living leopard from just inches away. In fact, very few hunters have, either."

Bentley laughed

"The only way to learn true eye color is to study a breathing animal in indirect light."

Jon smiled. "I don't know that I want to try that."

"Do it and you'll discover that even though the edges of the eyes are often golden, the centers of *Yingwe's* irises are the palest frosty green. Sometimes, very rarely, they're tinged with a hint of aqua. Yet that doesn't soften them—it heightens their intensity. That stare sears into the deepest reaches of your primate soul and assesses what it sees. And you wait at his mercy for judgment."

Jon turned to Bentley, perhaps to see if I were exaggerating. Bentley's face was blank.

"And there's another thing as well," I said. "The leopard doesn't have the big open-eyed gaze of the lion. Even when a leopard is relaxed and completely at rest, he has a subtle natural squint that gives him a haunting and pensive look. Almost a meditative air."

Jon looked away, and we sat in silence for a long time.

"It's those mysterious eyes that baffle taxidermists," Bentley said at last. "That's why most leopard mounts look like bug-eyed monsters."

"And," I went on, "those eyes examine you with a many-layered intelligence as complex as it is impenetrable. Yet a few things have been learned—sometimes at great price—by those who've raised a cub. The leopard—."

"People really have done that?"

"Raise cubs? They've been doing it since ancient Mesopotamia."

"Do you know anyone who has?"

"Yes," I said. "So do you."

"I do? Do you mean at the zoo?"

I gave him a look that told him he was being as obtuse as a dead monkey.

"You?!"

"Yes."

"I never knew that," Bentley said in surprise.

"Really, Paul, do you think I tell you everything?"

"Where did it happen?" Jon asked. "Can you tell us now?"

"In India several years ago. The mother had been killed by a tiger. There were two cubs, and one had already starved to death. I found them in a hollow under a rotted log. A little female was still alive but very thin. I nursed her back to health with goat's milk."

"How long did you keep her?" Bentley asked.

"Until she was about a year and a half. I called her Hirannmaya, Sanskrit for 'Golden'."

"That's incredible," Jon said, smiling. "Did you release her back into the jungle?"

"No, that sort of thing isn't possible. Without her mother to teach her to hunt, she'd have starved to death. And I didn't want to send her to a zoo, so I gave her to a maharajah up north."

"That's amazing. So she lives with him?"

"She has the run of his palace. It doesn't make his servants leap for joy, but maharajahs don't care about small matters like that. When he greets dignitaries, she sits beside him on a leash."

Jon laughed. "Have you seen her since?"

"Oh, yes. Many times."

"Does she recognize you?"

"Haven't you been listening? She's a leopard. Of course she knows me. But even I have to be careful with her. A leopard's psyche is like the sear on a firearm that's been neatly filed and stoned. It takes very little to drop the hammer."

"Then what do you do when you see her?"

"I speak to her and then I let her come to me."

"Does she?"

"Every time."

"I love this! What does she do when she sees you?"

"What any cat would do. She bounds toward me and rubs her flanks against me. Sometimes she stands on her hind feet and drapes her forelegs over my shoulders and rubs the sides of her face against both of my cheeks. Scent marking me as hers."

"I can't believe this," Jon said. "You're an amazing man."

"I'm nothing of the kind. The Almighty is amazing for creating her."

Bentley shook his head. "Hil, you have to write this stuff down."

"But what does it feel like?" Jon asked.

"Her fur?"

"No, no, I mean . . . emotionally."

I had never been asked that before, since no Hindu would have been so vulgar as to inquire, and I had never told the story to any Americans.

"I'm sorry," Jon said. "I didn't mean to pry."

"It's not that. I just had to think about it for a bit." I paused and then said, "When her wise green eyes are just inches from yours and her soft fur is sliding against your face, it's the closest a man can come to strolling the streets of Heaven."

Jon looked away, now seemingly embarrassed by the candor he had sought.

"I have an ivory miniature of her that I keep with me at all times."

"My God. What kind of world am I about to enter?"

"But that's Hirannmaya. Don't be lulled into complacency. The leopard is a creature ferocious in his passions, unforgiving in his hates. And, yet, lavish in his affection—if you earn it. But he has a hair-trigger temperament forever alert to betrayal. If you lose his trust, you won't regain it in this life or in any other."

I finished my bourbon.

"So there *Yingwe* sits at the solitary summit. An incalculable intelligence arrayed in a form of such splendor that simply to watch him ripple and glide has made strong men weep."

"You're not exaggerating, are you?"

"I never exaggerate. Awkward and lowly primates cower in shadows and exist only at his pleasure. Yet, fearsome as he is, the leopard is a gift to us all. A stunning and consummate force of animate nature that could have been born only in the mind of God."

6

THE BEST PART OF HUNTING AND FISHING WAS THE THINKING ABOUT GOING AND THE TALKING ABOUT IT AFTER YOU GOT BACK.
--ROBERT RUARK

JON SPENT COUNTLESS HOURS at the rifle range over the next several weeks under Bentley's exacting tutelage. He had also apparently devoted much time to grunting at the gymnasium. He had lost several pounds, the effect of which was evident in the tightening of his face. His step, too, was quicker, the result of the new energy brought on by systematic exercise.

One afternoon, after a chilly hour at the range, the three of us went home to freshen up and then met later at the Safari Club for dinner. Bentley had sponsored Jon for membership, which delighted the young man and stunned me, for Bentley could never be called the most convivial of companions.

After we had been mellowing out for a while before the fire with cigars and bourbon—or, in Bentley's case, cognac—Jon seemed suddenly pensive. I noticed he had been closely studying the other members relaxing in the sitting room.

"It's so quiet it here," Jon said at last. "So restful."

"This is a men's club," I said. "Not a sorority."

Bentley laughed, and it was nice to hear him laugh for a change.

"No, that's not what I meant," Jon said. "It's just that I expected to hear . . ." His voice trailed off.

"Boasting?" I asked.

"Of a sort, I suppose."

"Why?"

"I don't mean to be disrespectful, but isn't that the reason a hunters' club exists in the first place?"

"To an extent," Bentley said, though he was the least boastful of men.

"But *only* to an extent," I said. "You expected silverback gorillas thumping their chests, but instead you found quiet and modest men trading campfire tales."

"Exactly."

"Of course, there are plenty of boastful hunters," I said, "but you won't find many here."

"They wouldn't be tolerated," Bentley said. "Bad form."

"Paul is being glib, as usual. The real reason is that this club attracts mostly men in love with nature. Not men whose chief thrill is bragging about conquering it. There are a few of those fools here, but most of them won't endure."

"And fools they are," Bentley said and sipped his cognac.

"How so?" Jon asked.

Bentley cocked an eyebrow at me. "Would you care to expound?"

"The swaggering, hairy chested sort of hunter is usually a buffoon. He's ignorant of nature and has no desire to learn unless it helps him reach his bag limit. The ones I've known like that cared little about animals except as dead objects. Scalps on their belts that were really just badges of their own narcissism."

"But aren't they interested in—?

"Animals *per se* aren't their interest at all. They know how to shoot, and that's it. Their knowledge of natural history would slide through the eye of a needle without scraping the sides."

"That," Bentley said to Jon, "is why their trophies are often so poorly done. They don't know how to take measurements of an animal for a taxidermist, and they couldn't tell a good taxidermist from a meat cutter. Or be able to distinguish a lifelike mount from a shriveled corpse. So their leopards and pumas end up looking like rat hounds."

"Paul exaggerates," I said.

"Do I?" He looked at Jon. "I know that sort better than any man here because I once had tendencies in that direction myself. Long ago, before another showed me a nobler way to live."

Jon turned to me and smiled but said nothing.

"How's the shoulder?" I said, changing the subject.

"Much better, thanks," Jon said.

"He's toughening up, Hil. No flinching with the Mauser at all."

"Good," I said. "We'll be sailing soon."

"Before we leave," Jon said, "I have to tender a dinner invitation to the both of you."

"A bachelor who cooks?" Bentley said in surprise.

Jon laughed. "No, at the Delameres."

"I'm honored," Bentley said, "but socializing is not my métier. Hil, on the other hand . . ."

"Ginny would be very upset if you declined," Jon said to me. "She's much taken with you, captain."

"Please just call me Hil."

"*Taken* with him?" Bentley said. "Well, well."

"It's true," Jon went on. "She speaks of him all the time."

"No need to be jealous, though," Bentley said to Jon with mock reassurance. "A wheezing and broken down old *shikari* like Hilton Rixton is truly the ultimate 'safe' man."

Jon tried not to laugh but failed badly.

"Paul, Paul, Paul," I said. "What was the name of that finishing school? The one where you never finished?"

Bentley spread his arms helplessly.

"I'd be pleased to come," I said to Jon. "I promise not to bore Ginny's family with old hunters' tales."

"Quite the opposite," Jon said. "They want you to bring your lantern slides."

"See?" Bentley said. "You'll be the talk of Long Island."

Africa with man-eaters was beginning to look absolutely delightful.

For reasons that eluded me, Jon had neglected to mention that Ginny's father had died long ago. One does not expect a widowed middle-aged matron in New York to be hosting a dinner party the chief feature of which is an after-dinner lecture on shooting a tiger to death in northern India. But there I was, metaphorically reeking of jungle and cordite, in a drawing room of tapestries and old oak and marble busts. And a most appreciative gathering it turned out to be. In addition to Ginny and Mrs. Delamere, the group consisted of three of Ginny's aunts, two with their husbands and a third serene in the comforts of elderly maidenhood.

Ginny sat up close on one of the settees with her mother, while her relatives relaxed in chairs tastefully arranged around the room. Jon managed the lantern slides.

I was unaccustomed to female audiences, so I thought it best to moderate the tone of the talk, to speak less of ballistics and the stalk and the kill and more of the beauty of the forests of northern India. Yet a hunt is most certainly a hunt, and there were a few times that I noticed Ginny slide her hand into her mother's and hold on tightly. When I had finished, the questions also varied from what one would expect from a more masculine assembly. The queries concerned whether or not I thought the tiger had suffered at the end and what the fate was of all those who had been attacked. There was not a single comment on the efficacy of the .400 Nitro Express for the death shot. Frankly, this pleasant change of tone suited me down to the ground.

One of the points I went to a considerable length to explain was the feeling of panic and dread generated in any helpless community by a man-eater in its midst. In crude huts or ramshackle bungalows where the only door locks might be feeble strips of wood, where windows did not latch, and where firearms could only be dreamed about—there terror found its feeding ground.

"A mixture of cancer and paralysis strikes these defenseless people down," I told them. "It eats away at their souls at the same time that it cripples their will. Even people physically untouched by the man-eater become dead while still alive. There's no greater horror than the horror of helplessness."

Perhaps it was that statement that prompted a question from Ginny. It caught me off guard because I had never been asked it. She said, with great seriousness, "Captain, why do you think it is then that people are so captivated by tales of man-eaters?"

I had never even considered that before, though I certainly should have. "Well, I don't know. If I had to offer a quick answer" — I smiled — "which I'd rather not do, I'd say it's because we mentally put ourselves in place of the victim, even though we might never travel to within five thousand miles of jungle or veld."

"I understand," she said. "I suppose being killed by a man-eater has to be the ultimate horror, don't you think?"

I hesitated and then said, "Yes, I do." But my answer was, at best, only a partial truth.

Later in the evening I had settled into the corner of a settee with one of the finest bourbons I had ever been offered, when Mrs. Delamere asked if she could join me. I stood and pointed to the settee and resumed my place when she sat down. She waved aside formality and insisted I call her Marjorie.

"You may smoke if you like, captain."

"I never smoke in a lady's presence."

Ginny's mother had been stunning in her youth, of that I was certain. Her blonde hair had now gone mostly to gray, and she was a bit thick in the waist in a well-rounded sort of way, but no less attractive for that. I guessed she was a few years older than I, but her green eyes revealed an ardor for life that could have overawed the sensibilities of men half her age. It occurred to me that being Ginny's father had by no means been the only pleasure in the life of the late Mr. Delamere.

"We're very grateful you came here tonight, captain. It means so much to Virginia. And to Jonathan as well."

"It's been an enjoyable evening. And rather different, I have to say."

She smiled. "You're not comfortable speaking before a group mostly of women, are you?"

"Was it that obvious?"

"Perhaps only to me."

"It was a challenge."

"And you met it wonderfully."

I smiled a thank you.

"May I be permitted to venture something personal?" she asked. "Personal to me, not to you."

"Of course."

"Did you know that Mr. Delamere passed away when Virginia was only five?"

It puzzled me that she broached this subject. "I learned it just a few hours ago."

"He was killed in a carriage accident. I never remarried, and I have no brothers, so Virginia was reared in a world of women. Most mothers and aunts would cherish having so much influence over a young girl. I did not. Does that make sense to you?"

"I've never been a parent."

"A girl needs a muscular masculine force to help her grow wise and strong and brave in an unwise and fearful world."

"Yes."

"Jonathan is the first man she's ever truly known, and we're so grateful to him."

"He's a sturdy young gentleman."

"But her meeting with you was of another order entirely. It affected her in ways I can barely grasp. And I know her better than anyone does. She says she wishes you were part of our family."

"Well, I can hardly understand that. Our meeting was very brief."

Marjorie smiled. "So is a lightning bolt."

I said nothing.

"I think she was unnerved by men—even a little bit by Jonathan—before she met you. That unease is fading."

"I take no credit for that."

"She said you've lived a life of great danger, and yet there was a calmness about you that she'd never seen in any other man. And that stillness brought her comfort."

"I suppose I affect people in odd ways."

"And also that you spoke with such a delicacy of spirit. . . ."

"It's a mirage."

She smiled again. "Virginia told me of that, too. How you push people away when they say something nice about you."

"Marjorie," I said with a sigh, "if there's a single profound truth I've learned in this world, it's that there's nothing more destructive to a man's character than for him to come to believe he's important."

A look of uncertainty drifted across her face.

"Besides," I said, "if a scar-faced, one-eyed man sets aside his rifle and bends down to pick up a butterfly, impressionable young women suddenly think he's a philosopher."

"Stop it!" she said, laughing. She shed twenty years when she laughed like that.

I sipped my bourbon.

"You're staying the night, of course."

"So Jon informs me."

"Very good. Whiskey that powerful doesn't make a good traveling companion after dark." She looked toward Ginny and Jon conversing. "Captain," she said, "may I—."

"Hil will do."

"Thank you. After your talk, Virginia asked you a question and you hesitated before you answered. She asked about people's fascination with stories of man-eating animals."

"Yes, I remember."

"I sensed you were leaving something unsaid to spare our feelings."

"I was."

"Jonathan is going with you into danger and he'll soon be my son-in-law, so I'd like to know. Can you share it with me?"

For reasons I could not articulate, I felt that beneath the deceptive curves of her maturity lurked a woman of iron.

"All right," I said and set down my glass. "The prospect of being killed and eaten by a man-eater is not the worst thing imaginable. Despite what I told your daughter."

I paused to give her one last chance to wave me off if she wished, but her sharp eyes were hard as emeralds.

"Go on," she said.

"The supreme dread isn't being killed and eaten by a big cat. It's being devoured while still alive."

She stared at me as if she could not believe what she had just heard.

"But can that . . . ?"

She seemed unable to finish.

"Possibly. I know of only one instance of it, and even that's uncertain. In fact, some people who examined the same ground that I did disputed my interpretation."

"But . . . ?"

"I'm a man of many faults and imperfections, Marjorie, but no one who contests my explanation comprehends cats as well as I."

"Can you tell me what happened?"

"It took place in the Almora district in northern India. The victim was a *dakwallah* named Sundar. That's a mail runner in those parts. He was getting on in years, and one day the Deputy Commissioner presented him with a Malacca cane as a symbol of his gratitude to the hard-working Sundar. The old man was very proud of that cane. Lord knows, he didn't own much else. I have no doubt it rested by his bed at night. The Indians are a marvelous people — humble and grateful as Christian monks and with a sly humor that continually surprises you regardless of how long you've lived with them. Sundar always seemed to have a smile. One day he disappeared. Some of his friends went out to look for him. What they found told them that he'd been eaten by a tiger."

I picked up my glass and took a sip of the bourbon as I gathered my thoughts.

"I happened to be in the area at the time and the Commissioner asked me if I'd go with him to examine the ground. We found the place by the road where the tiger had waited in the brush. There had been rain two days before, and the cat's pug marks were easy to see. The brush — ."

"Pug marks?"

"Paw prints. The scrub had been flattened where the tiger lay. The animal had waited until Sundar had gotten very close before it made its rush. Cats have great power but little stamina. They keep their final run as short as they can. Usually a tiger stalks its prey and then pulls it down. But in the odd chance that it sees prey coming, it might just wait in ambush. The tiger pulled Sundar down in the middle of the road—one could see the marks of a struggle in the caked mud as well as a fair amount of dried blood. Then the tiger carried the old man away. And that was it. There was no other trace there that Sundar had ever existed on this earth."

I stopped to allow that to sink in.

After a long pause, Marjorie said, "I think I'm missing something, Hil."

"'Missing' is the right term. Marjorie, where was the cane?"

"My word," she said, staring at me in horror and pressing two fingers to her lips.

"When the tiger carried away Sundar, he must have been alive because he was still holding his cane. The Commissioner and I followed the cat's spoor and we saw places where the ferule had intermittently scraped the ground as the tiger carried Sundar off. About a third of a mile away, we found the spot where the cat had dropped Sundar and eaten him. There were a few bits of cranium and some of Sundar's worn brown teeth. The tiger consumed most of Sundar's bloody clothes as well. And there in the scrub lay the cane. Still wrapped around the shaft was Sundar's severed hand. The tiger had missed it when it was cleaning up the scraps."

Marjorie moistened her lips, as Ginny had nervously done in my study. "But how do you know the tiger didn't kill the man first? *Before* eating him?"

"I don't. I'm not sure. Sometimes a tiger or a leopard will drag a living prey for fifty or a hundred yards before it kills it. But there were signs in the dirt of a struggle where the cat finally stopped to eat."

"I'm not sure I—."

"If the tiger had killed him instantly, it would've taken only a moment and there would've been no scuffle. So I think the tiger just dropped Sundar to the ground and began devouring him. While the poor man pounded on his face with the last of his strength."

Marjorie lowered her eyes and stared at her hands folded in her lap. "Were there any more victims?" she asked, looking up.

"Not as far as anyone knows."

"What happened to the tiger?"

"Vanished. Like a dream when you open your eyes."

Everyone has had the experience of drifting off to sleep and then suddenly jolting awake just a few minutes later with a violent start. These unsettling incidents are unremitting with me. I have often wondered if they are the result of my having sat up so many nights in the forks of trees when waiting for man-eaters, while trying to stifle the anxiety of dozing and falling to the ground.

I lurched to consciousness in one of the guest bedrooms sometime after midnight. At least that was the time my inner clock told me. I lay there for a few moments to allow my heart to stop racing. The fire made the room safe and cozy as a mother's arms, and any normal man would have stayed beneath the warm covers. I peeled off the sheet and quilt and sat on the edge of the bed to allow my head to clear. That is always very quick. My life has long depended on it.

I stood up and slipped on the robe that had thoughtfully been provided and went over and stirred the fire a bit. Then I took my cigar case and some matches from my coat and placed a chair next to the window.

I opened the sash a few inches to draw the smoke out and fired up a panatella. Despite the cold air, I was comfortable in the robe and with the fire to my back. I relaxed with the soothing smoke and stared through the frosted pane at the moonlit garden below.

A gentle tapping barely at the edge of sound was followed by, "Captain, are you all right?"

I went to the door and saw Ginny standing there suitably swathed chin to heel in a maroon dressing gown. Her hair was down to her shoulders.

"I heard you cry out," she said, as though apologizing for some indiscretion.

"I'm sorry. I didn't mean to upend the house. Thank you for checking on me."

"I'm worried about you."

"Worried about Rixton of Africa?" I said with just the hint of self-mockery.

In absolute seriousness, she answered, "If I don't worry about you, what woman will?"

To this day, I am not sure why that touched me so much.

She seemed not to want to leave.

"I can't ask you in, Ginny. You know that. It wouldn't be right."

"I've already told mother that I was checking on you. Besides, I don't think I could be safer than—why are you laughing?"

"I was just thinking about what a friend recently said of my hallowed status as a safe man. It's not really very flattering, you know."

Even in the flickering light from the fire, Ginny's blush was obvious.

I pushed the door open all the way. "Provided you can assure me your mother isn't going to show up with a shotgun."

I put out my cigar and placed two chairs in front of the fireplace.

Ginny smiled and sat down. "Mother is coming with a pot of tea."

I went out to the hallway and saw Marjorie approaching with a tray. I took it from her and we went to my room and I poured for everyone.

There were no more chairs, so I got the tuffet from the dressing table and set it before the fire and sat with them.

"We couldn't sleep either," Marjorie said.

"Don't worry. Jonathan will be fine."

"It's you we're concerned about," Ginny said.

"Indeed. So you think I'm not up to the hunt."

"Oh, for heaven's sake," Marjorie said. "No more talk of wild cats tonight."

"Then what is it?"

"If a gentleman wakes up with a cry in the middle of the night," Marjorie said, "don't you think we should be concerned?"

"It's just a petty foible of mine. Too many long and lonely jungle twilights."

"Are you sure that's all, captain?" Ginny asked.

"Virginia," Marjorie said with a bit of an edge.

"I'm sorry. It's just that—."

"It's all right," I said. "I'm flattered. It's been an elephant's age since I've had a woman lose sleep over me. Let alone two of them."

"Jonathan says you'll be sailing in about two weeks," Marjorie said and sipped her tea.

"Yes. I'll try to have Jonathan back long before June."

"That doesn't matter," Ginny said. "Jonathan and I are postponing the wedding until the fall."

I looked in surprise at Marjorie.

"We've already discussed it," Marjorie said. "We don't want you to feel rushed and perhaps risk your life because of something as insignificant as a date."

I had no sensible response to that.

"So the wedding will be when you return," Ginny said.

"I'll be staying in Africa after the hunt. Jonathan will come back without me. I won't be returning until the end of the year."

"You weren't listening, captain," Ginny went on. "I said we'll get married when *you* return for the wedding."

I just stared at her, and then I turned to her mother.

Marjorie finished her tea and stood up. "It's been settled, Captain Rixton. And all I can say is that you should be grateful you live in proximity to this young woman only a few months of the year rather than twelve." She smiled tenderly at her daughter and caressed her head. "Now you two behave yourselves."

Then she went out of the room and closed the door.

"Ginny, what on earth is this about?"

She looked away and seemed wistful. "I like the smell of the cigar. I don't remember my father very well, but I remember his cigars. There hasn't been such a masculine scent in this house for a long time."

I could not help smiling—she was so persistent in a girlish way. But I knew there was something wrong, and I was fairly sure it was related to Africa.

Suddenly the draft from the window felt like ice on my neck. I went and closed it and refilled our cups and sat back down.

"Let me tell you about hunters," I said. "Real hunters, not weekend buffoons. Most sportsmen will tell you they have a hunter's intuition, that when they're in the bush they have a sixth sense that warns them when they're in danger. They're certain of it—but they're wrong. Can you guess why?"

"No," she said, shaking her head.

"They're sensing something, but they're not intuiting anything. Without noticing, they're absorbing the faint squawk of a frightened bird, the distant alarm call of an antelope or a deer or a jackal. It's so subliminal they don't even realize it—they're inhaling it like the air. I've known hunters who swore they were certain they were about to come upon some cadaver in the bush. And they were right. Swarms of flies in the tropics are so loud that you can't *not* know that carrion lies ahead. But they hadn't been overtly aware of the flies, and yet the subtlest layer of their awareness had been."

I paused.

"Go on, captain."

"Something is buzzing ominously here at the edge of sound, and I'd like you to tell me what it is."

She picked up her cup of tea and sipped it. Her hand trembled as she did so. "When I was a girl, I was very sickly. I almost died several times. It's important you appreciate that. All my life I've barely been able to hold onto life. . . ."

"I understand."

"I had a very close friend at school. We were more devoted to each other than many sisters are. Once, on the last day of the school year, we stopped at a candy store. I'd already told her I didn't have any money, but she insisted and she lent me five cents to buy a bag of candy. I wouldn't see her again all summer, so on the first day of school in the fall I paid her back the five cents. . . ."

"I wish I'd known you as a little girl."

She ignored that. "The following June, we did the same thing. Stopped by the candy store on the last day. This time I had money, but she told me to put it away. She seemed upset about something. She said she'd lend me the five cents and I could pay her back later. I asked her why I couldn't just pay with my own money now. Suddenly she started crying. She said that if I made a promise to pay her back, she was convinced she'd see me again in the fall. She knew I'd never break a promise. So she could be certain that no sickness would take me away over the summer."

What could one say to that? Yet she must have misinterpreted my silence.

"Oh, for heaven's sake, Captain Rixton! Don't you see? If you promise to be at my wedding, I know you'll be there. Then you and Jonny can't die under the fangs of some frightful beast." Her lower lip began quivering, and she tried to hide it with the teacup. "You'd never break your word."

I got up and took the cup from her. I stood next to her and wrapped an arm around her shoulders and looked down at her. "It's all right."

She leaned against me and cried softly. "I'm so scared," she said, trying to strangle back her tears.

I said nothing but just held her in silence and let the terror drain from her.

Finally she slumped in exhaustion.

"This is a special night for me," I said gently.

She looked up.

"This is the first time I've held a young lady half my age in my arms in my bedroom at two in the morning."

She laughed through her tears. "I feel so silly."

"We all have our superstitions."

"Even you?" she said in surprise.

I thought of the tiger claw hanging around my neck. "Even I."

I sat down in the chair her mother had been using.

"Virginia, I've rarely had the special grace of a fine lady worrying about me."

"But why?"

"Where I live there are very few women."

"But why should you have to rely on a naïve young woman for caring? I know it's impertinent of me to ask, but where is Mrs. Rixton?"

"My mother?"

"Oh, stop!"

"There's never been a Mrs. Rixton except for the late Maureen O'Rourke Rixton."

"But there should be!"

"*Should*—the word that haunts us all."

7

DO NOT TRY TO FIGHT A LION IF YOU ARE NOT ONE YOURSELF.
--AFRICAN PROVERB

BARON VON ROON was not the last person I expected to see at the Safari Club on a windy night in March. Kaiser Wilhelm strutting through with his retinue would have been more surprising.

Off the main sitting area there are small office-sized rooms with desks where members can tend to correspondence or just have a cozier private area in which to read. Von Roon had trapped Jon in one of these. The Prussian knew how to pin down his prey.

I walked through the doorway, and Von Roon sensed a predator behind his back. He stood up and turned toward me.

"Good evening, captain. Mr. Stratton has told me he will accompany *you* to Africa—despite my very generous offer two months ago. Evidently you are worthier of a magazine portrait than I."

"I thought you were already in the Transvaal, Baron," I said, ignoring his petty complaint.

"Why try to hunt leopards in the rain? I leave in two days. And you?"

87

"In a couple of weeks. I expect you'll have all this wrapped up before I get there."

"Wrapped?"

"Like fish in newspaper. Finished."

"Perhaps. I have had word that even now there are hunters on the ground." He sniffed. "Englishmen."

"No Huns?"

His permanent half-smile tightened into the grimace of a man having his tooth drilled.

"That word is not to my liking."

"Then complain to the Kaiser. He coined it. During the Boxer Rebellion — don't you remember?"

"Ah, the yellow barbarians. But then you are far more accustomed than I to dealing with the lesser races, *nicht wahr?*" He turned to Jon, who seemed to be enjoying this fencing far too much. "Sir, perhaps we will meet again in the field." He looked back at me. "Keep your weapons at hand."

Von Roon walked past me and was gone.

"And you think *Paul* is abrasive," Jon said with a grin.

"My father was an Englishman," I said, ending the discussion.

"I remember."

I glanced at the book on the desk. "That's Braddon's *Thirty Years of Shikar,* isn't it?"

"I'm almost finished."

"Well done."

"Hil, what do you know about Von Roon? Other than what you've already told me."

I sat across from Jon. "Supposedly he served with distinction in the cavalry in the Franco-Prussian War. I'm told he had a reputation as a brutal martinet. Physically brutal."

"Do you think it's true?"

"I'd be surprised if it's false."

Jon looked to the doorway and out toward the sitting room. "Hil . . . ."

"Speak up."

"What did he mean by that remark about the lesser races?"

"I told you before — I was an officer in the Tenth."

"I don't remember. Tenth what?"

"Cavalry Regiment. One of the two Negro regiments. Finest soldiers in the army. I was posted to Fort Huachuca. A journalist should pay more attention." Inexplicably, that gentle barb seemed to stab him like a hornet in the face. "What's the matter?"

"It's not much, is it?" he said, gathering up his things.

"What's not?"

"Being a journalist."

"Who says so?"

"My father." He slid the book under his arm. "He's from old money and doesn't see the point of my soiling my shirt cuffs with ink. He says journalists do nothing, they just talk about what others have done."

I could not fault the old man for his judgment, but it was rather harsh to snarl it to a well-meaning son.

"We're going to Africa to stalk a man-eater," I said. "Has he ever stalked a man-eater?"

Jon smiled. "Thanks. You always know just what to say." He set the book aside and sat back down. "My God, I'm excited about going."

"If Paul were here," I said, laughing, "he'd say you should be more excited about coming back."

"He gave me one of his Mausers."

"Now that *is* something. I don't know that he's ever done anything like that before."

"Do you think we might see some black leopards?"

"Ah, you've been to the Bronx Zoo."

"Every day for a week."

"A special place."

"Are they a different kind of leopard? I wasn't sure."

"Same animal, just more melanin."

"I never realized they had spots until the light hit one at an angle and then the spots were obvious. Do you think we'll see any?"

"I doubt it. They're much more common in Southeast Asia. Especially Malaya. I've never seen one in Africa."

"So you don't think there are any?"

"Oh, there are definitely some. The place where I know they've been glimpsed most often is in the highlands of Abyssinia. Some sportsmen I trust reported that. A few claim they've seen them on Mount Kenya. That might be true."

"Anywhere else?"

"I'm certain they're in Uganda. An explorer friend of mine actually witnessed a black leopard stalking three gorillas on Mt. Muhavura in the Virunga Volcanoes."

"Did he see a kill?"

"No, he lost sight of all of them late in the afternoon. Then around five he heard agonized screaming from a gorilla and some crashing through the undergrowth. The next morning in a clearing he found the partly eaten body of a big silverback. Leopard pug marks were all around and vanished into the jungle."

Jon turned away and remained quiet for a while. Finally he said, "What chance do we have if even gorillas can go down?"

I had no answer.

"What about the south? Have you heard of black leopards there?"

"Well, there are rumors. . . ."

He leaned forward. "Go ahead."

"In Mpumalanga in the Eastern Transvaal. Near a town named Lydenburg. Some people claim they've spotted black leopards in that area."

"*Spotted* black leopards! Clever turn of phrase."

I could not help laughing. "See, you *are* a writer—an ironist!"

"And where are we going exactly? I want to mark it for Ginny on a map."

"My father built his house on Sabi River." I smiled. "The Eastern Transvaal. In Mpumalanga."

PART TWO

SPOOR

8

THE PATHLESS JUNGLE, THE REED-FRINGED RIVERS
WITH THE WILD CALL OF THE FISH-EAGLE RINGING
DOWN THE LONG REACHES, THE STILL, WARM NIGHTS,
THEIR SILENCE PUNCTUATED BY THE THROB OF THE
LION'S ROAR....

--GAME WARDEN JAMES STEVENSON-HAMILTON

GENUFLECTING BEFORE GOD on the floor of an emerald
cathedral—so Jon whispered to me as Joseph bent down to
examine spoor on the ground ahead of us.

I smiled at the words because of their self-evident truth.
Lush and green from the summer rains, the towering acacias
enveloped us with their own special protection—or threat,
depending upon the moment. The oldest of these giants loomed
over fifty feet and guarded a place uniquely theirs. Unlike the
dank equatorial rain forests, dripping with rankness and rot, the
more open woodland of the acacia jungle radiated an elegant
crispness unknown in those reeking fastnesses of mold and
dissolution and decay.

Yet the seductive draw of the great knob thorns concealed
much that could give pause to the uncertain heart of man. The
immature plants swarming on the forest floor bristled with
spines as formidable as any caltrops devised by the legions of
Caesar. And in the midst of this thornbush lurked predators—

and perhaps one particular predator—who viewed with remorseless dispassion any primates scurrying about and invading this domain.

Thirty yards ahead of us, Joseph was down on one knee with his Holland & Holland .375. My Border Collie, Buc, stood beside him and sniffed the area Joseph was examining. Buc was one of the short-haired and erect ear Border Collies, but I had always suspected his larger-than-average size for the breed hinted at some wily ancestor hidden in the woodpile.

After examining the ground, Joseph held up one finger to me and touched the top of his dark tan bush hat and then stroked his chin. I gave him a brief salute to show that I understood.

Long ago Joseph and I had worked out our own series of gestures in order to maintain silence on the hunt or just to communicate discreetly at a distance.

Joseph stood up and he and Buc moved off farther into the acacias, and Jon and I followed. A local man had reported possibly seeing a leopard in the forest the previous morning, so we were now investigating. I was carrying my Mannlicher, but I had told Jon he need not be armed. I was certain it was not the man-eater, since the leopard would never have allowed himself to be glimpsed in daylight. Yet it was prudent and useful to show all who lived in the area that we were willing to investigate any sightings they brought to our attention.

"Do you have any idea what Joseph saw on the ground?" Jon whispered.

"The pug marks of an old male lion. Probably pushed out of his pride by a young nomad moving in and taking over. The old fellow was lucky. Old males usually end up mauled or killed."

"The hand signals . . . ?"

"Touching the crown of his hat means it's the king—because of the crown. Stroking the beard means it's an old one."

Jon smiled. "It's so simple."

"I shouldn't tell you these things. It destroys my mystique."

Joseph and Buc had stopped ahead of us and we caught up with them beneath an ancient forty-foot acacia.

"That's all, captain," he said with the most beautiful accent in the world.

I nodded and went back and examined the pug marks. Although the rains were more or less over, the earth was still soft and the marks showed as sharply as if they had been chiseled in marble.

"How did Joseph know it was an old animal?" Jon asked as he came up.

I squatted down near the prints and laid the rifle against my right leg, and Buc came over for a second inspection. "Notice how wide the pads are. The feet of the big cats tend to splay as they get older. These are very large. And his stride is long, too, so he's no youngster."

Jon dropped to his knees for a closer look.

"But he's underweight," I said. "These tracks should be deeper for his size." I looked up at Joseph as he came over. "What do you think?"

"About three hundred, captain," he said without needing to examine the marks again.

"He should be about four hundred pounds," I said to Jon. "He's probably not eating well now that he's old and alone and has to hunt on his own. And he might be sick, too."

"With what? Can you say?"

"Probably kidneys. The big cats are like your housecat. If they live long enough, the kidneys go."

"Do you think he's nearby?"

"I doubt he has the energy to move far."

Jon ran some fingers across the tracks. "I'm looking forward to hearing my first lion roar."

"When you do, it won't be this fellow. He'll never roar again."

"But I thought—."

"He doesn't have a pride to protect or a territory to defend. Lions don't create a commotion for fun. They roar to show their primacy. This one will stay quiet. Out of hearing of any younger males in the area."

Jon smiled. "I've read too many fairy tales."

"And if he avoids being torn apart by other animals, when the time comes he'll be like your kitty when he knows he's dying and goes to hide under a table or off in some shadow. He'll find a dark and quiet place and settle down for his long final sleep."

Jon turned and gazed off into the acacia forest. "I thought animals weren't aware of their own death. Or death at all."

"So the deep thinkers tell us. But I stopped listening to them long ago."

"And then scavengers will get him?"

"He'll be shredded and devoured. But his spirit will remain."

Jon gave me a puzzled look. "You act as if they have souls."

"The big cats? If they don't, the Almighty and I are going to have a serious talk."

Jon stared at me for a moment and then said, "You're sincere, aren't you?"

I took my rifle and stood up. "I'm always sincere."

Jon and I had arrived at my farm the previous afternoon, and while he had slept the remainder of the day and through the night with the exhaustion of the innocent, Joseph and I had discussed the situation at hand. Twelve more victims had been claimed by the leopard since Joseph had sent the cablegram, and he was working on a map that charted the locations of the dead. Today I hoped an analysis might give us something more useful than just hope and luck. Yet Joseph had emphasized that he had not seen all the bodies, and so he refused to vouch for the accuracy of every report. What was not in doubt, however, was that everyone in the area now lived in terror of sundown.

"Let's walk on a bit," I said, pointing with my chin, and the four of us ventured further into the thornscrub.

Jon stepped behind me, but I gestured for him to come around and stay on my left as we walked. As was usual, Joseph was on my right checking for sign, and Buc walked ahead of me and slightly to my left, as he always did. Buc was my left eye, and he knew it. If we had been a professional hunting party with a client, I would have had a second tracker behind me looking for any spoor we might have missed as we advanced in a shallow 'T' farther into the bush.

"What is it?" I asked when I glanced at Jon and noticed the hesitant expression on his face.

"I don't feel experienced enough to be walking beside you and Joseph. It's . . . I don't know . . . an honor."

"No, it isn't. I just don't want you sweeping Joseph's back or mine with the muzzle of that rifle."

Jon smiled. "You have such a gentle manner about you."

As we made our way north and away from the river to our backs, the land rose in a series of low green hills. We hiked out of the deep shade of the acacias and up a shallow slope until we had gone about two hundred feet above the level of the riverbank a mile behind us.

"Rest and take a drink," I said, and offered Buc some water from my canteen.

Jon, though, just stood there and stared into the distance.

Joseph came over and sat to my right on the small hillock, and Buc lay down on my left, but with his head up and as alert as Anubis eyeing the Valley of the Kings.

"My God," Jon said, as he set the butt of his rifle against the ground. "I . . ." Then he shook his head in wonder at the endless acacia forest and thornbush that rolled before him. "All this is your land?"

"Well," I said, laughing, "not as far as the eye can see. About five miles to the north and as far east as the Sabi." I pointed to the river off to our right. "That's near the border of the Sabi Game Reserve and the eastern edge of my property."

The view of the river was softened by an early morning mist that hung like a drapery of moist Indian gauze over the valley below. Though the riverine bush lining the banks was still thick from the rains, the waters of both rivers had begun to recede and the usual islands had started popping up midstream.

"You never mentioned you lived near a game reserve."

"You never asked."

"I guess I didn't realize they even had game reserves here."

"The only one in South Africa."

Jon looked over his shoulder at me. "And you expect me to go back to Manhattan?" He turned back to his own slice of Eden. "I want to bring Ginny here."

"She's always welcome."

He came and sat next to Buc and laid his helmet on the grass. "That's not the big rifle you were telling me about," he said, pointing to my weapon.

"Sometimes this old *shikari* gets tired of hauling around the Jeffery. And I certainly don't need it for a leopard. This will more than do."

"Is that the military weapon?"

"It is. The 95 Mannlicher I mentioned. Eight millimeter. The carbine version."

"That's a very short barrel."

"Just under twenty inches. I prefer it in dense bush. A newer Mannlicher came out a year or two ago. Called the Schönauer. It has some improvements, but I'm comfortable with this one."

"May I shoot it?"

"I'd rather you didn't. It's only about seven pounds, so it bucks like a zebra hurling a kick at a lion's head."

"I can take it."

"That doesn't matter. I don't want you to develop a flinch. Stay with the Mauser. It's heavier."

"Isn't Mannlicher a German name?" he said with a bemused look. "I thought you didn't like Germans."

"Prussians," I said and took a sip of water. "Besides, Mannlicher was an Austrian. And that's almost like being a Bavarian. And they're the salt of the earth."

"You know, Hil," he said, laughing, "your fancy footwork would do a prizefighter proud."

I smiled but said nothing.

"It's cooler up here," he said, looking off toward the north and wrapping his arms around himself.

"It always feels cooler when a leopard is on the prowl."

We sat in silence for a while until movement in the distance caught Buc's eye and Jon followed his gaze.

"Impala," I said as we watched the herd make its way through a break in the thornscrub several miles below.

"They seem as vulnerable as little chicks out there in the open."

"Not as much as you might think. They're wary. That's lion country."

"And it's your land?"

"It is. And there's little shooting here, so the lions are even more brazen than usual. They're always bolder where they don't have to worry about trophy-happy Englishmen or Portuguese slaughterers from across the border."

"Do animals go back and forth between the game reserve and your property?"

"All the time."

"You said little shooting, but there's some?"

"There has to be. The people on my property need to eat."

"Other people live there? On your land?"

"When my father bought it, there were quite a few small Shangaan settlements on it. Squatters really. They're still here. He didn't move them off and neither will I. And they can hunt provided they're sensible about it."

"Meaning they haven't always been?"

"As sensible as drunkards in a brewery. Look out across the land and tell me when you see an elephant or a rhino. You won't."

"There are none at all?"

"There are a few black rhinos around, but the white rhinos haven't been here since the seventies. And the elephants were shot out long ago."

"For trophies?"

"The English do that, but the Shangaan and the penniless Afrikaners kill for meat and hides. Who can blame them? I'd do it, too. And they're lethal with traps and snares and dogs. It's these biltong hunters that really had the biggest effect."

He looked embarrassed. "I'm sorry, but I don't know what a biltong is. Is that an antelope?"

I smiled. "It's a form of jerky."

He still looked confused.

"You've never been to the West?"

"No, I haven't had that chance yet."

"A type of air-dried meat. Jerky is just the American version of biltong. Real biltong is more flavorful though. Spicier. The

Shangaan like to use roasted coriander and black pepper to give it some punch."

"What does the word mean? Hippo or something?"

I laughed. "It's Dutch for a strip off a hindquarter."

"I'm looking forward to trying it."

"It's a bit of an acquired taste."

He gazed off into the distance. "It's good of you to keep those people here."

When I remained silent, Joseph said, "The captain is as modest as he is generous. That's why my people revere him."

"Revere?" Jon said with mock seriousness. "That's a powerful word."

"My people usually give nicknames to others based on their appearance or their character," Joseph said. "With the captain, they — ."

"Remember that English farmer near Nelspruit?" I said to Joseph to change the subject.

"Oh, yes," he answered with a smile. He looked back at Jon. "A big man of much self-importance. He believed the people referred to him as *Nyarhi*, which means buffalo and would be a term of respect."

"But?" Jon said.

Joseph glanced at me.

"Feel free," I said.

"They called him *Mfenhe*. That's the chacma."

Jon looked puzzled.

"A type of baboon," I said.

"I see," Jon said, laughing. "And what do they name the captain, Joseph?"

"*Nkawu*," I answered.

"And that is?"

I smiled. "A cute little monkey called a vervet."

"Please don't laugh, sir," Joseph said to Jon as he chuckled. "The vervet is cleverer than you or I."

"How is that?"

"Many ways," Joseph said. "An example is his alarm calls. He has a special call for leopards and lions and hyenas. When he shouts it, all the other monkeys know there's a big killer on the ground. Another call is for eagles, so the other monkeys search the sky. And there's a completely different one when a vervet sees a snake." He smiled. "A smart monkey, *Nkawu*."

"I see, but that doesn't mean your people call the captain that, does it?"

Joseph remained silent.

Jon tried to fight back a smile. "So is the captain lying?"

"The captain never lies," Joseph said with the solemnity of a monk, "but he does sometimes decorate the truth."

"And if we undecorate it?"

Joseph looked at me, and I spread my hands in surrender.

"The Shangaan call him *M'Dabula*."

The rumble of gunfire rolled in like distant thunder from the east.

"That sounded like it was on the reserve," Jon said in surprise.

"Probably was. They've been thinning out the carnivores there."

"Why would they do that?"

"The butchering of the grass eaters was so great that when the new warden came here a few years ago he knew he had to do something drastic. This was probably the only place on earth where the meat eaters outnumbered the grazers. Because of the biltong hunters."

"So he's killing the carnivores?"

"Just culling to bring their numbers down to something approaching what's normal. He's afraid if he doesn't, they might wipe out their own food supply."

"Could that really happen?"

"I don't know. Maybe not. But he doesn't want to take the chance."

"But how will he know when he reaches the right number?"

"I have no idea. But he told me over a dram or two one evening that he was going to restore what he called 'the balance of nature.'"

"I've never heard of that."

"Nobody has. I think he might have coined it himself. But if anyone can do this, he might be the one. It's a bold move, but he's a Scotsman, so you have to expect that."

Jon laughed.

"His name is Stevenson-Hamilton." I smiled. "Naturally, he's an ex-cavalryman. He was a colonel in the 6th Inniskilling Dragoons during the South African War."

"But thinning out the lions won't bring back the rhinos and elephants."

"No, but if he makes a haven for them in the reserve, they'll start moving down from the areas in the north where they haven't been wiped out yet. There are still Shangaan who live on the reserve, and he's hired some as policemen."

"The people who killed off so much of the game?"

"There are no better guardians of the chicken coop than the former foxes. They do yeoman work."

"But didn't some of the people in authority complain about it?"

"Squawked like wet hens. But his success shows the wisdom of picking a Celt for the job. An Englishman will do what's reasonable, but a Scotsman will do what's right."

Jon laughed. "Ginny told me your mother was Irish, but Rixton isn't a Celtic name, is it?"

"Norman."

"Ah."

"But you have to understand that the Normans are simply the blessed issue of Celtic maidens who opened their loving arms and tamed the Norsemen."

"You have an answer for everything, don't you?"

I could hear Joseph laughing softly off to my right.

Jon shook his head and took a drink from his canteen, and we sat together in silence for a long time.

"Let's go look at your death map," I said to Joseph as I took my rifle and stood up. "Maybe we can make some sense out of this."

As Joseph reached for his rifle, he suddenly seemed as serious as a hangman.

"What's wrong?" I asked.

"The captain will not like what he sees."

"Is the map finished?"

"Yes, late yesterday afternoon."

"Why didn't you show it to me last night?"

"After the captain's long journey, I wanted him to be able to get at least one full night of rest."

"And you thought a chart of the dead would keep me awake?"

"Yes, captain."

Gunfire sounded from the east, and Jon looked at me. "Could the leopard be on the reserve?"

"I doubt it. Even if he'd been there, the noise of the guns of Hamilton and his police would've caused him to move off."

Jon turned toward the forest just as, in an eerie coincidence, a cloud drifted before the sun and threw the area into shadow. "But it's quiet here."

I said nothing because nothing needed to be said.

"Do you think he's down there then?" Jon asked as he stared at the darkening acacia forest.

"No way to know," I said. "But like all cats he'll move from more disturbance to less. And my land is the most peaceful of all."

"So you think he'll show up here eventually?"

I glanced at Joseph.

"Sir," he said to Jon in that operatic baritone that was a gift from God, "we would be unwise to believe that he will not."

9

... LIKE SHAKESPEARE'S DRAGON, IT IS MORE FEARED THAN SEEN ...
--NATURALIST DESMOND MORRIS

THOUGH WE HAD ENJOYED a glutton's breakfast before starting out, tea and coffee and lemon biscuits were waiting for us when we got back to my modest A-frame fifty yards above the bank of the Sabi. Miriam, Joseph's wife, must have been watching for us, because on the dining table everything was already arranged as neatly as chess pieces on a board by the time we crossed the porch and came through the door. We set down our hats and weapons and relaxed at the table as Buc slid next to me and rested his chin on my left foot.

Miriam stood off to my right, waiting to serve. Yet she was no servant in anything but the most superficial sense and was less like someone attending us than a sentry watching over us.

Miriam also happened to be the most hauntingly beautiful woman I had ever known. Lean like Joseph, she was as black as obsidian, with understanding eyes over sharp cheekbones that looked like they were cut from volcanic glass hard enough to deflect a rifle bullet. Her age was indeterminate. As anyone who has been to the continent knows, black Africans can have lived half a century and still look thirty. My guess, though, was that she was perhaps thirty-five, like her husband. But whatever her age, there was no question she was the center of this home and, along with Joseph, the bedrock of my life.

"That'll be all, Miriam."

She smiled the smile I lived for. "Welcome home, sir."

I grinned and she went off to other tasks.

Joseph took a sip of tea and then went and got a manila folder and pulled out the map he had put together of the leopard's depredations. He laid it onto the teak as reverently as if it were a mediaeval parchment, and a single glance told me we were in trouble.

Joseph had made fourteen small triangles in pencil on the map. Inside four of them was an "X" written in green ink.

"Over two hundred square miles? Are you sure?"

"Yes, sir."

"These are all confirmed victims?"

"Only the ones in ink, captain. The others are possible victims."

"You confirmed the four?"

"I confirmed three of them."

I turned to Jon. "Most male leopards have territories of fifty square miles or less. So this is a big problem. If he had his own territory, we'd know where to search. But this. . . ." I looked back at the map. "I have no idea."

"Is a territory the same thing as a home range?" Jon asked.

"Yes and no. A home range is where an animal lives. A territory is a home range, too, but it's one he defends. Some types of animals defend their home ranges and some don't. Leopards do. They'll keep out other males but let as many females in as want to come in."

"But how can one leopard defend two hundred square miles?"

"That's the point—he can't. He's been pushed out of his territory by a younger leopard. So he's roaming. Far." I looked back at Joseph. "Are you sure about this one?" I pointed to the mark he had made near The Dragon's Tail. "Did you go up there?"

"No, captain, not all the way to the *Draak*. I—."

"What's that?" Jon asked.

"Northeast of here," I said, "is the northern part of an area called the Drakensberg Escarpment. Drakensberg means Dragon Mountains. Before you get there, you pass through a lower region of beautiful ridges and deep ravines. It's about a thousand feet high. Long ago one of the *voortrekkers* called it *Die Draak se Stert*, The Dragon's Tail."

"Sounds ominous."

"It's a stunning place. Nowadays you'd be hard pressed to find any Englishmen who still know that name, but some of the Afrikaners remember it."

"It's not too high for leopards?"

"Nothing is too high for leopards. And there are plenty of antelope. Chacmas, too. Leopards can thrive there."

"I didn't want to leave our people here without protection, captain. That kill was confirmed by a sportsman who reported it to Sir Alfred." He pulled some more papers from the folder.

"Who's that?" Jon asked.

"The magistrate in Barberton," I said.

Joseph had taken four sheets out of the folder. "The hunter made these sketches of the pug marks. Sir Alfred told me to give them to you. There are written reports here, too. On the deaths. He wants them back when you're finished with them."

"Why did he send them to me?"

Joseph smiled. "Because he knew the captain would take the field without being asked."

"These are beautifully done," I said as I looked them over.

"I heard the hunter was an engraver for *The Illustrated London News*."

"These front pug marks must be four inches long."

"Four and one-quarter, captain."

"Do you know if these are actual size?"

"I was told they are."

"A big leopard," I said to Jon and handed one of the sheets to him. "An old male. Past his prime but not past his power."

"They match the pug marks near the three kills closer to here," Joseph said. "The ones I examined."

"Size?"

"Possibly a seven-footer, captain. About a hundred and forty pounds."

"This artist is a good observer," I said to Jon. "Look at this one." I pointed to the sketch of the right forefoot.

Jon examined it but looked up at me in confusion.

"See that little notch out of the pad?"

He examined it again. "I hadn't even noticed that."

"Probably from a snare long ago. There won't be any mistaking this cat's spoor for another animal's." I looked back at Joseph. "And the other ten kills?"

"I believe they were by the leopard, too. Based on what I was told. But I didn't see the victims or the spoor myself."

"I want to talk with this engraver. Do you know if he's still here or if he went back to London?"

Joseph reached across and placed a finger on a green "X" on the map.

"He's dead?"

"Yes, captain. He returned to the field. One last time."

"Did you see the corpse?"

"I did."

"The leopard?"

"Yes, sir. The ground was damp that day, and the pug marks were clear. There's something odd about *Yingwe's* stride, captain." He paused and seemed to be searching for a word.

"Asymmetrical?"

"Yes. The right hind foot turns in."

"He's hurt?" Jon asked.

I shrugged. "Probably an old wound. Maybe from a snare, but more likely from a bullet long ago. Which makes this even more of a bad dream, because now he knows firearms. He's what sportsmen call an 'educated' cat." I examined the mark on the map. "How close is that spot to the old Hawthorne place?"

"About two miles, captain, but the farm isn't abandoned anymore. The heirs sold it to a gentleman named Vanderveer. About a month ago."

"Has he been over here yet?"

"No, sir."

"I'll speak with him when I get a chance to see if he knows anything. How many hunters are on the ground now?"

"At least six."

"Oh joy," I said, shaking my head. "Already."

"Yes, sir. Mostly amateurs, I'm told."

"And the baron is back here I assume."

"Yes."

"Is it true there's a reward?"

"Fifty pounds. I was told Sir Alfred was against it, but he was overruled."

"I'll probably end up getting shot by one of those fools." I had a sip of coffee and broke a biscuit in half and took a bite out of it.

"I told Miriam you'd say that and she scolded me. She said no bullet could ever strike down *M'Dabula*."

I could not help smiling. "You know, Joseph, you're the luckiest man in the world."

He grinned. "My good fortune, captain."

"And don't ever forget it."

He gestured with a nod toward Jon.

"What's wrong?" I asked, looking at his grim face.

"Is it hopeless? The hunt, I mean. Two hundred square miles. That can't be done, can it?"

"Depends."

"On what?"

"Luck and skill. And more on the former than the latter."

"You're still going after him? Even with all that territory to cover?"

"If I don't, my people will live in terror and some will die in agony."

"Then I'll be going along, right?"

"What do you think?" I asked Joseph.

He smiled. "I don't believe the captain brought him all this way just for the boat ride."

"See?" I said to Jon. "Besides, that pith helmet is far too cute to be wasted."

Jon looked away.

"What's the matter?" I asked.

"It doesn't seem right to joke when we're talking about people being devoured."

"Should we weep and wail?" I said. "Or should we act like men and see what we can do?"

"You're right." He pulled the map in front of him and looked it over again. "What can we do?"

I smiled. I liked that "we." He was beginning to see himself as part of the team.

"Well, we can't track him with too much hope of success," I said. "Not in this terrain. This isn't the edge of the Kalahari. The spoor we're most likely to find here would be blood spoor after he's wounded. And maybe some hair."

"That's not much, is it?"

"Almost nothing. On the other hand, we might get lucky. Leopards are very careful of their feet. Their pads are softer than you might think, and they try to stay on game trails. And those are quieter, too. So we might be able to find some pug marks on the trails. But we can't count on that."

"So what options are there?"

"We have three. After we learn where he's prowling, we can stake out a live goat or calf and sit up over it. Then we—."

"I don't understand. If he's a man-eater, why would he want a goat?"

"Man-eaters never eat *only* people. They take down or steal whatever they can get."

"I didn't realize that."

"Or we can put a dead prey animal like an impala in a tree fork and sit up over it and hope the leopard thinks it's another leopard's cache and a free meal. In that case, though, the leopard would be even more cautious than usual, which makes—."

"Why?"

"Because he'd think another leopard was somewhere in the area. So he might avoid the bait altogether if he's especially wary."

"I see. What's the third option?"

"The best one of all," I said, taking a sip of coffee. "And the most unpleasant. Sitting up over the remains of one of his own kills."

"One of his kills? Do you mean a half-eaten person?"

"I mean what used to be a person."

Jon gazed out the window toward the riverbank where the great saurians basked as they contemplated life and death. "This isn't like I imagined it would be."

"Nothing is what we imagine it will be."

He looked back at me. "Do man-eaters have any preferences? I mean about prey."

"That depends on what cats you're talking about. With tigers, no. Even the biggest man is a paper doll compared to a tiger, so a tiger doesn't care how big he is. A man-eating leopard is another matter."

"Because of his size?"

"Even the biggest leopard is lighter than most men, so he's much more careful about prey than the tiger is. But, then again, *Yingwe* is more careful about everything."

"And in this case that means size?"

"If they have a choice, leopards who've decided to dine on people almost always choose a woman over a man. And a child over either. It's a question of the most manageable prey for an animal that doesn't weigh much more than a hundred pounds."

"I guess that makes sense."

"Everything *Yingwe* does makes sense."

"Not always to me, though."

"He doesn't have to make sense to you. He has to make sense only to himself."

Jon nodded, although he seemed reluctant to agree.

"And when leopards do attack adults, the victims are usually sleeping or bending over and gathering wood or something like that. Small and vulnerable."

"But you said they'll attack male hunters. They're not small or bending over."

"That's a different situation. There the leopard isn't selecting dinner. He's being attacked. He's in a rage and defending himself. I once saw a leopard during a beat in India run straight up the trunk of an elephant and pull the hunter right out of the howdah."

"My God. Did he kill the hunter?"

"Before anyone else could even react. And the elephant panicked and bolted and left a hole in the line, and the leopard flew through it and was gone."

"But he wasn't a man-eater?"

"No.

After a long silence, Joseph said, "Captain, I told everyone I met to send word here of any more deaths."

"Good. What's the feeling out there now?"

"Great fear, captain. But I saw some smiles when I told them *M'Dabula* is back."

I sighed and nursed my coffee and stared out the window to the forest beyond.

10

HE WHO SWALLOWS A LARGE STONE HAS CONFIDENCE IN THE SIZE OF HIS THROAT.
--SHANGAAN PROVERB

I SPENT THE REMAINDER of the day and part of the evening going through the written descriptions Sir Alfred had acquired of the remains of the leopard's victims. Yet one can do this for only so long before the smell of death seems to waft up from the paper and one must set it aside. Sounds in the kitchen that caused Buc to jump up and bolt to the back of the house were a welcome distraction. I left my study and found Miriam placing a plate of biltong and a glass of lemonade in front of a handsome Shangaan boy of about sixteen seated at the kitchen table. He was sweaty and ragged and exhausted, although Buc was trying to make him feel at home. A half-tied bundle of clothes lay on the floor next to him. He stood as I walked in, but I told him to sit back down.

"This is Peter, captain," Miriam said. "He worked for Baron Von Roon but has run off."

"Tonight? In the dark?"

"Yes, sir," Miriam said.

"Why?"

"His best friend was killed." She hesitated. "By the baron."

I heard footsteps and turned to see Jon coming in from the parlor.

"Tell me, Peter." I slid out a chair and sat down.

He looked at Miriam.

"Go on," she said.

"He beat my friend, captain. With a *sjambok*. And he died."

"Why did he beat him?"

"He found leopard spoor but he forgot to tell the baron."

I glanced at Miriam and looked back at Peter. "Why was that worth a beating?"

"He wants *Yingwe*. He wants the man-eater. Before the captain gets him."

"How did your friend die?"

"His wounds, sir. They festered. And he died."

"Have you told anyone else?"

He seemed horrified. "No, captain."

"Sir. . . ."

I looked over at Miriam.

"Joseph said he can use help with the horses now. Since Martin went to work in that shop in Nelspruit."

"Do you know horses, Peter?" But it was a pro forma question, for I had already decided.

"Yes, captain."

"Joseph is cleaning up the groom's quarters right now," Miriam said.

"Is he? The sergeant anticipates the captain?"

Miriam smiled a smile that could have melted a Kimberley diamond.

I looked at Peter. "Do you have family nearby?"

"I have no family, sir."

"Now you do."

I let that sink in as he just stared at me.

"Now leave that food for the time being and go help Joseph in the barn."

The boy grinned and ran out the back door toward the stable with Buc right behind him.

I stood up and saw Miriam still smiling at me.

"Yes?" I said to her.

"*M'Dabula* is a very great man."

"It must be the female company he keeps."

Then the oddest thing happened. She started to answer me, but suddenly her voice began to crack. I had never heard that before in all the years she and Joseph had been with me. She seemed as surprised as I was. She turned quickly away and whispered, "Thank you, sir," and hurried out to help the men in the stable.

"Hil . . ."

I turned toward Jon.

"If Ginny loves me half as much as that remarkable woman loves you . . . ."

I brushed it off. "It's just respect."

"Oh, yes. And I'm a Dutchman."

"Let's go onto the porch."

We went outside into the cool night air and I sat in my rocker and Jon eased into the one beside me. He was learning when it was wise to be silent.

I propped my feet up on the rail and gazed toward the black jungle half-lit by the crescent moon.

After several minutes, Jon said, "May I ask something?"

I murmured a yes.

"What's that weapon he was talking about?"

"A whip made out of hippo or rhino hide."

"It's for beating people?"

"No, the *voortrekkers* made them to drive cattle."

"So what do you think?"

"A whipping with a *sjambok*? Murder. No matter how you shade it."

"Do you think he meant to?"

"He was probably indifferent—which is the worst kind of murder."

After a short silence, Jon said, "You seem so calm about all this."

"Should I stammer?"

"It's just that . . ." He looked away. "I don't know."

"Shocking, isn't it?"

"What?"

"That this isn't some salon on Long Island."

"Do I sound that bad?"

"This is the lowveld. Life stripped down to the muscle. Accept it."

"I won't be the same man when I get back to New York, will I?"

"No."

He turned back toward the forest. "I wonder if Ginny will recognize me."

"She might not."

"So what's going to happen now?"

"To the baron? Nothing. No black boy will speak against a white man. And a German aristocrat at that."

"And the other people who work for him?"

"The same."

"Why do they stay with him? His workers, I mean."

"I'm told he pays double what others pay. To poor people, money is always a dangerous drug. But who can blame them?"

"Then can't *we* do something?"

"No."

"So he'll get away with it?"

"No. There'll be a reckoning. There always is in the bush."

"But — ."

"The veld has its own laws. Greater than the edicts of man. And they'll be enforced."

"How, though?"

"In ways most white men can't comprehend."

"You mean the witch doctor you talked about? What's he called . . . ?"

"A *Sangoma*."

"Yes. Him."

"You're learning."

Jon jumped at the sudden burst of noise from the forest. "What's that?"

I said nothing as the eerie two-note vibration, like the sound of some jungle goliath dragging a giant saw blade back and forth through a fallen acacia, rolled out of the forest.

"My God, is that something alive?"

"It's a male leopard calling in the night."

"*Our* leopard maybe?"

"No."

"How can you be sure?"

"I know the individual calls of all the leopards in the area."

"That's really possible? Or are you joking with the New Yorker?"

"No magic. Live here long enough and have an attentive ear."

"Can he see us?"

"Possibly."

After a long pause, the leopard's call began again, but this time farther off.

"He's moving on," I said. "And even if I didn't recognize his voice, I'd know it wasn't our friend. He'd be more cautious. He's an interloper now. A wanderer. He'd never call and draw attention to himself from a younger leopard."

"I'm going to write all this down. I've started a journal."

"Excellent."

"I want my children to know of this someday. And Ginny."

"Tomorrow we'll take to the field to see if we can learn more about our opponent."

We sat quietly for a while, and then Jon said, "I have a strange question. . . ."

"No need to apologize. What is it?"

He hesitated and then said, "Who has the advantage here, him or us?"

"Who do you think?"

"I've been trying to decide, and I'm not sure, but I believe we do."

"And why do you think that?"

"Because we have a human brain." He smiled. "And we have rifles."

"Very good."

"I'm right for once?" he said, laughing.

"Ah, no, I didn't say that. You're completely wrong. But it was a good try."

"Well," he said with an exaggerated sigh, "I think I'll leave this out of my journal then."

When I smiled and turned away and said no more, he seemed surprised.

"Aren't you going to tell me why I'm wrong?"

"You didn't ask me."

"You're a strange man, do you know that?"

I said nothing.

"All right, Captain Rixton, tell me why."

"Yes, we have advanced brains, but they're really just monkey brains with a bigger hat size."

"But we have guns."

"Yes, we have technology, but that's no rabbit's foot. Now consider this cat. *Yingwe* doesn't live in the veld, like we do. He *is* the veld. Its purest essence."

"I don't . . . I'm not sure I understand what you mean."

"He's the spirit of the forest brought to life. The soul of the jungle itself infused within a predatory and incisive intellect too complex even to begin to be grasped by a bumbling fruit-picking ape."

Jon lost his smile and turned away toward the forest.

"When we step into that woodland again tomorrow, I want you to remember one thing above all else. Remember it when you swagger with the arrogance of a monkey walking on its hind legs and holding a metal tube with a little explosive powder. . . ."

I paused and he turned toward me.

"I want you to remember the leopards of the Waterbergs — and never to forget that this implacable creature was stalking simians and killing them and devouring them a hundred centuries before you were born."

11

THE FORCE OF TERROR AND DESPAIR THAT ASSAILS A GROUP OF DEFENSELESS VILLAGERS WHEN A MAN-EATER MOVES IN ON THEM . . . IS NOT UNLIKE A DISEASE EPIDEMIC FOR WHICH NO KNOWN ANTITOXIN EXISTS.
--WRITER MAITLAND EDEY

A crowd had bunched around the rondavel where the leopard had paid his terrifying midnight call. Jon and I were in a village of about two dozen families on my land west of the border of the Sabi Reserve and trying to make some sense of what had happened the previous night. Rondavels are single-room circular huts with thatched roofs, and these structures were made of stone, although that is not always the case. Everyone seemed to be talking and gesturing at once. Most of the men were questioning the young man whose home this was, but nothing he answered could be heard above the noise. His wife, a lovely young woman about twenty years old, was large with child and sat on the ground beside him. She was shaking as if she were freezing, which was unusual, since the shakes rarely last so long, and what had occurred had happened many hours before. Yet fear had swept across this village like a cold wet wind. The woman failed to see me beyond the mob, but I recognized her immediately. Her late father had worked for me many years earlier when she had still been a little girl, and I had not seen her since she was about seven or eight. Now no one was paying the slightest attention to her, except Buc, who was licking her face as she trembled.

"Quiet!" I shouted. "Move away!"

Everyone in the crowd jumped as if startled by a thunderclap and leaped away from the rondavel.

"Stand aside," I said to the husband as he came toward me. He stopped like he had been hit in the face.

I handed my rifle to Jon and went up to the woman and knelt beside her. "Hello, Lucy," I said gently.

The last time she had seen me I still had two eyes, and so the patch was throwing her off. But when I smiled, a look of recognition and joy lit her sweet face.

As I slid an arm around her, she whispered, "*M'Dabula*," and melted against me.

"Were you hurt?"

"No," she murmured and squeezed me as tightly as she could.

"All will be well," I said and slid a thumb across her cheek. "Do you believe me?"

She looked up. "Yes," she said, smiling. "*M'Dabula* is here."

The trembling had fled.

I went over and bent down to examine the gashes on the wooden door of the rondavel as Buc sniffed them. The leopard had slashed with his powerful claws for what I judged to be about fifteen minutes—the most terrifying minutes in the lives of his young prey. Then he had given up and moved on. His pug marks had long since been obliterated by the crowd.

"Tell me what happened," I said, standing up and looking at the husband.

"*Yingwe* came in the night. He tore at the door for an hour. We screamed and made noise but he had no fear. He kept trying to get in. Finally he left. We don't know why."

"Does the door have a latch?"

"Yes, sir."

"And the others?"

"Some do."

"We'll check them before we go," I said to Jon. "We'll fix any that need it."

"Do you think he'll come back here?" Jon asked.

"Possibly."

I looked around. Toward the edge of the village was a corral holding about three dozen goats.

"He took not even one *mbuti*, sir," the husband said, anticipating my question.

It made no sense. The leopard could have snatched a goat with no more effort than drawing a breath and have walked away and dined at his leisure. And, naturally, he did not. Such was the nightmare of confronting man-eating cats. Or, indeed, *any* big cats. They refuse to read the books we write about them, and they laugh at all the tales we tell.

"*Hi wena mani vito?*"

"Michael Indaba, sir."

"*M'Dabula . . . ,*" Lucy said and came and stood beside her husband. "Please don't be angry with him. He was very brave."

"Never ignore your wife like that when she's afraid. Understand?"

"Yes, sir."

"Good," I said, nodding. "You did well last night, Michael."

"Thank you, sir."

I turned around, and the cluster of people parted like I had spit them with a wedge. Buc and I walked across the village toward the forest and I studied the ground as we went. At the eastern edge of the village I found what I had hoped for.

A game trail skirted the village and leopard pug marks were still fairly clear, not having been erased yet by careless human feet.

"This is our rogue," I said to Jon as he came up next to me and we both bent down to examine the marks. "Look." I pointed to the healed gash in the pad of the right forefoot.

"Do you think he's still nearby?"

"He could be on Mars by now." I stood up and gazed off into the forest. "Or he could be lolling on a branch thirty yards from here and watching us groping around like fools."

"You're so reassuring."

I pointed to the pug marks. "Look at the uneven stride. That right hind leg is damaged, but it's a firm stride, so it's an old wound."

"A bullet?"

"From someone too scared to follow him up."

We walked on, but there was no spoor to see in the tangle of underbrush. "Let's head back after we check the doors and locks on the huts."

We had walked for a half-hour to get to the village and now we had the return trek ahead of us.

"Hil, do you really think he could be watching us?"

I smiled. "I just said that to wake you up. I doubt he's nearby."

"Why?"

"Listen. What do you hear?"

He looked confused.

"Well?"

"Birds singing."

"But no squawking. And no alarm calls from jackals or monkeys. Or buzzing of flies around a kill. The jungle sentries are silent."

Jon stared off at the massive wall of green. "It feels threatening anyway. Even in silence."

"That's because it *is* threatening. And will be until the end of the world."

"Then what?"

"Don't you know? A New Heaven and a New Earth."

"You're sincere, aren't you?"

"I'm always sincere."

He smiled. "I now have another entry for my journal."

A commotion in the village grabbed our attention. We hurried out of the forest to the nasty spectacle of Von Roon questioning Lucy's husband as if he had been a coward in the face of the enemy. I was surprised to see that Von Roon's gun bearer was a white man.

"Roon!" I shouted.

He spun around. He loathed it when I left out the "von".

"Captain," came his cold reply.

"Step away from that man."

He took a slow step backward.

As always, he was as impeccable as a papier-mâché mannequin in a shop window, although his companion was another matter.

I gestured to Lucy and Michael to stand beside me.

Von Roon looked appalled at my treating them as equals rather than menials, and I relished his shock and disgust. I had commanded a company in The 10th, and each of those Negro soldiers was a far better man than I could ever hope to be.

"Have you seen our quarry?" Von Roon asked.

"I see what you see."

"Can we believe him?" his companion said.

The big man's accent was indeterminate but seemed to be from one of those Middle European backwaters where the Prussians enjoyed recruiting their serfs.

"Herr Kuskarohr, Captain Rixton."

"*Hauptmann*," he mumbled without enthusiasm.

As powerful looking as a large chimpanzee, Kuskarohr was adorned with sweat-stained bush clothes that dated from around the time Stanley found Livingstone. I suspected Von Roon approved, on the theory that the surest way to appear elegant was to be seen with the hideous. Kuskarohr's blotched face hinted at some familiarity with distilled spirits, and his reddish nose was one of those meaty affairs with splayed pores deep enough to catch rainwater. Several black hairs thick as bailing wire coiled boldly out of the surface without even the half-justification of a mole to shame an observer into tolerance.

"But he *was* here," Von Roon said, pointing to the scarred door with the pointless self-confidence that was one of his nobler traits.

"If you say so."

"Have you heard the rumor about this cat?"

"No."

"A story floats through the jungle that this is a black leopard."

"And you believe that?"

"*Warum nicht?*"

"Because it's ridiculous. Nobody has ever seen any black leopards in this area."

He shrugged.

"Where did that tale start?"

"Someone saw it."

"Who?"

"No one knows."

"Then why believe it?"

"Because it pleases me to believe it. And are not the black ones the most savage of all?"

"That's just a child's fantasy."

Von Roon clearly did not like that remark, and Kuskarohr saw his expression.

Evidently Kuskarohr was accustomed to wielding his bulk to intimidate, and he looked like he might be about to take a step toward me, as he probably did with everyone.

Ever alert, Buc sprang between us with a growl and a baring of teeth.

"Unwise," Jon said to Kuskarohr as he looped around Buc and casually swung the muzzle of the Mauser until it swept Kuskarohr's belly.

"*Sehr mutig,*" Kuskarohr said with a sneer but continued eyeing the rifle.

Without taking his eyes from Kuskarohr, Jon handed his weapon to me and stepped closer to the big man.

Kuskarohr appeared suddenly confused and possibly even frightened by the American's obvious indifference to his menacing mass.

"Enough of that," Von Roon said, and Kuskarohr seemed grateful to reconsider and sign a truce.

"It's time to move on, don't you think?" I said.

Von Roon glanced around. "*Ja.*" He gestured to Kuskarohr and they turned away and rushed off into the forest to search for the leopard that was not there.

By early afternoon we were still several miles from my house when we stopped to rest and sat Indian-style in the shade of a big acacia. I gave Buc a drink, and Jon and I sipped from our canteens and enjoyed the silence of each other's company, as only men can.

Ordinarily I would have stayed in the field after a sighting of the leopard, but I was not going to take Buc further into the bush. He was too tempting a meal for our foe. Also, we had rushed out so quickly that morning when we had been told of the appearance of *Yingwe* that I had no time to speak with Joseph about my plans for the days ahead. And since there was no trail to follow and no kill to sit over, there was no point in wasting time and wandering around like dazed guinea fowl. Hunters who trusted in luck, and I had foolishly done so myself on occasion, were like poker players who chased bad cards across the green baize. They died broke. Now I had a chance to get back quickly and settle a few things with Joseph before returning to the field.

"Hil. . . ."

I looked over at Jon as I scratched Buc behind an ear.

"I'd never seen such fear in human eyes as I did today. I wouldn't have thought terror like that was possible."

"They're completely helpless."

"It's the greatest of all the horrors, isn't it? The horror of being devoured."

"They have no guns. No recourse."

"Except for you."

I said nothing.

"That young girl . . . when she saw you . . ."

"I knew her when she was a child."

"It was far more than that. Her fear just vaporized."

"Thanks for your keen eye on Von Roon's bootlicker back there," I said and tilted my canteen for Buc so he could drink some more.

Jon laughed. "He *was* stunned, wasn't he?"

"Could you have taken him down?"

"Oh, yes."

"Boxer?"

"I was captain of the wrestling team at Columbia. I'd have tied him in knots in thirty seconds."

"Well, well. Even I can be wrong."

"About what?"

"I was thinking with the wisdom of an aging, one-eyed *shikari*."

"Thinking what?

"That you were just a pasty-faced wastrel lolling in the fleshpots of Manhattan."

"Well, I'm ecstatic I could disabuse you of that, sir," he said, smiling. "But I didn't face him down to defend you."

"Indeed. . . ."

"I faced him down to protect *him*."

"From?"

"From Captain Rixton."

"Meaning what?"

"You're an insightful man, Hil. In all sorts of ways I'd never have guessed. But even you can't see everything."

"And . . . ?"

"Even Rixton of Africa isn't able to gaze into his own eyes."

"Eye. And if he could . . . ?"

"He'd see the look in them I saw when that boy told him about the death of his friend from the *sjambok*. And then when you explained to me the law of the veld . . . then this wastrel began to understand things you never even hinted at to Ginny at a soirée on Long Island."

"Such as?"

"Things about you . . . dark things that civilized men could never comprehend."

I sipped my water and remained quiet.

"I knew . . . knew beyond knowing that if Kuskarohr had kicked Buc out of the way, you'd have smashed his head to a jelly with your rifle butt. Done it without a second thought. Maybe without a first."

I said nothing.

"And we can't have that, can we?" He reached over and rubbed Buc under the chin. "Now please tell me what you think about what Von Roon said."

"About what?"

"A black leopard."

I took a deep breath and my exhale lasted about a week. "I don't know. It's an absurd story. Leopards hunt mostly at night. And every man-eating leopard I've ever known or heard of has hunted *only* at night. How could anyone have seen him well enough to know he's black?"

"I can't imagine."

"And, for that matter, who could've seen him under any conditions at all? Leopards rarely let themselves be seen. And man-eaters never do."

"So you think someone just made it up?"

"No, and that's the eerie mystery of the thing. Why bother to invent something like that? What would be the point?"

"I don't know."

"Neither do I. And one certainty I've acquired from a life around the big cats is that some bizarre stories aren't too strange to be true, they're too unbelievably strange to be false."

He smiled. "That line goes into my journal."

Gunfire rumbled in the distance as we sat and sipped from our canteens. Finally I said, "Are you ready now for the business at hand?"

"Yes."

I pulled Joseph's map out of my pocket and unfolded it and handed it to him.

"Examine this and tell me what you can deduce."

He laid the map on his lap and studied it.

"Keep drinking even if you're not thirsty," I said.

He did as I ordered as he continued analyzing Joseph's handiwork.

"What's this area?" he asked, pointing to the upper right corner of the map where circles indicating four victims were clustered just this side of a more or less vertical border.

"Portuguese East Africa."

"And this east-west line?"

"The Limpopo River."

"Well, based on what I've learned from you and from this map, I'd say he might've come over the border from the

127

Portuguese side. Especially since his first victims are grouped near there. And you mentioned Portuguese hunters, so I guess there's disturbance on that side. . . ."

I smiled. "Go on."

"Since you said he's old and was probably pushed out of his own territory by a younger leopard, he's skimming the edges of the territories of other leopards down here for prey. Is that right so far?"

"Accurate as a Swiss watch."

"And the marks on the map for the other victims show he's moving south. Probably because there's less shooting on your land than anywhere else."

"See? You're a prodigy."

After a pause, he said, "And now I'm waiting for the 'but'."

"No buts."

"What will he do eventually, though? I mean now that he's probably heard the gunfire."

"God alone understands the ways of *Yingwe*."

"Can you make a guess?"

"Well, he can't stay in one place. That's too dangerous for him. Because of the other leopards as well as the guns."

"Then what choices does he have?"

I laughed. "Did you hear what you just asked?"

He seemed as baffled as a vervet monkey trying to fathom calculus. "I'm not following you. It's a simple question."

"It's a philosophical question, and it's not simple at all."

"Do you exhaust all your friends like this?"

"Only the special ones."

He seemed genuinely touched. "Thank you. Now explain what you mean to this fellow in the dunce cap."

"Admit it, when you came here you thought of animals in a different way. Just as most people do. Like furry or feathered machines. Even brilliant animals like the big cats. No different from the automatons at the carnival."

He hesitated. "I'm not sure I ever thought about it. But I suppose that's true."

"Nobody ever thinks about it. They assume it. But now you're asking me about this animal making *choices*. Considering a range of complex options and making shrewd decisions about them. *That's* the philosophical leap you've made. And it's enormous."

He then turned away, apparently uncomfortable with what I had just said.

"Well?"

"You unnerve me. Do you know that?"

"How?"

"I don't know. I can't explain it. But you have the opposite effect on me to the one you had on those people today. With them you were like a sip of Mrs. Winslow's Soothing Syrup. But with me it's different. . . ."

"How?"

"You're always challenging my outlook on things."

"Outlook? You mean your biases."

"It's exciting to learn these things, but somehow it's disturbing, too. And it never ends."

"When it does, you'll be dead."

"Every day I'm with you I'm like a virgin bride hearing from her mother about some new terrifying delight to expect on her wedding night."

"Welcome to Africa," I said, laughing.

He turned back to me with a smile. "I've been here about ten minutes and I already need a rest."

"Sleep under the stars in the man-eater's domain and you'll get a nice long one before the sun rises."

"All right. Tell me what this feline sage with a soul is likely to do."

"Because of the sound of gunfire, I think he'll make a wide loop in the direction he came from. Back up toward The Dragon's Tail. Especially if the pickings were good and he could catch them. But he won't go back exactly the way he came down."

"Why not? "

"Well, it would make it easier for us if he'd just use the same trails, wouldn't it? But he won't. He'll swing around and make a loop, more or less."

"That doesn't make sense."

"You mean it doesn't make sense to you. But you're just an ape with a nice tailor."

"All right," he said, laughing. "Explain."

"Even though he doesn't have his own territory anymore, he's still a leopard. His instinct will be to sweep wide as if he's patrolling his own terrain. And add to that his natural caution to avoid places he might have been seen or heard or scented. . . ."

"What I don't understand is how he can avoid all the other leopards he might see. Or even how he did it the first time. The young ones with the territories they're defending."

"He's *Yingwe*."

"But how can he sneak in and snatch prey and get out without being seen by them?"

"That's not difficult at all. Male leopards mark the edges of their territories by scratching tree trunks and by rubbing against them and by urinating on trees and bushes. Our friend checks out these signals as he moves along the borders."

"So? How can he be sure the younger leopard isn't waiting for him right there behind a bush?"

"He can figure out by smelling the old urine. He can sense how recently the resident cat was there and get some idea how far away he probably is by that point."

"Oh, come on. He's that sophisticated?"

"He's that sophisticated."

Reflexively, Jon glanced at his rifle and then looked back at me. "And you're sure he's capable of that?"

"The leopard is capable of everything. Except sin."

12

IT IS WORTH REMEMBERING THAT IF A LEOPARD IS LOVINGLY HAND REARED WITH GREAT KINDNESS, IT WILL GROW UP TO BE A LOYAL AND FRIENDLY COMPANION.
--NATURALIST DESMOND MORRIS

JOSEPH WAS LEADING a saddled chestnut thoroughbred away from the front of the house when we arrived home. He turned when he heard us, and I spread my arms in a question.

"The owner of the Hawthorne farm is here, captain."

"Perfect," I said and looked forward to hearing if there had been any more sightings of the leopard.

I crossed the porch and went inside, with Jon right behind me.

A woman was down on one knee in the center of the parlor and rubbing Buc behind an ear. He wagged his tail when he saw me but was not about to move and end these delights.

The woman turned and stood up and faced us, and I was confronted by one of the most striking creatures I had ever seen, in a jungle or out.

"Captain, this is Mrs. Vanderveer," Miriam said as she came in from the kitchen with a tray holding a pitcher of lemonade and glasses. Miriam seemed to be enjoying my surprise.

"Madame," I said, removing my hat and setting my rifle against a wall.

"My pleasure, captain," she answered and crossed the room with an athletic stride and shook my hand.

"This is Mr. Stratton."

"Make it Jon," he said with a smile.

"Sir."

She was almost as tall as I was, and a sweep of hair as red as a blazing acacia that had been struck by lightning was swirled and pinned tightly to the top of her head and made her seem even taller. She wore a green plaid shirt and khaki trousers and high riding boots. A hunting knife with a handle carved from impala horn hung at her left hip. She looked to be in her late thirties.

"Let's relax," I said, and we all sat in my comfortable chairs while Miriam served us lemonade.

"Thank you for seeing me, captain. I want to —."

"Hil will do," I said.

Buc settled against the front of her chair, and she reached down and stroked him as she spoke.

"I'm Valeria Vanderveer. I just bought the Hawthorne place and I have to speak with you about something very important."

"Well, it doesn't have to be important. I'm pleased to meet you in any case."

She seemed surprised.

"I don't have guests very often. Will Mr. Vanderveer be joining us?"

"I'm a widow."

"I see. Please go on."

"I need to speak with you about my leopard."

At the right edge of my vision I could feel more than see Jon turn and look at me.

"Very well," I said, faking a calmness at her "my".

"I'm told you're here to hunt down the man-eater." Her tone was as cool and clipped as a colonel facing a shavetail.

"Well," I said, "why I'm *here* is God's own mystery, but I'll hunt down the man-eater if I can."

"Then if you listen to everyone else, you'll be committing a murder. So if — ."

"How is that?"

"My leopard hasn't harmed anyone."

"Has anyone says it has?"

"Everyone."

"You'll have to explain what you mean."

"Haven't you heard the rumor of a black leopard in this area?"

"Yes."

"It's not a rumor. He's here and he belongs to me. And he's not the man-eater, though some *windgatte* claim he is."

"How do you know he's not?"

"I nursed him as a cub."

"I'm sorry, Mrs. Vanderveer, but that doesn't prove anything."

"It proves it to me!"

"But if you have him at your home, why do people think he's the man-eater?"

"He's run off because of all the gunfire from these lunatics who couldn't hit a baobab at three feet."

"Where is he now?"

"He's been glimpsed north of here. Toward The Dragon's Tail. And I'm told you're here to track him down and butcher him and I'm here to stop you."

"How?" Jon asked.

She glared at him. "With my word of honor that he is not the cat."

"And you're certain he hasn't killed anyone?" I said.

"I already told you that!"

She had little skill at concealing her impatience. And her anger, too. Yet, unless I understand nothing at all about women, anxiety lurked beneath.

"And do you think raising your voice to me will get you what you want?"

My guess is that the silence lasted a few seconds, but it seemed like a month.

"My mistake was in thinking I could ever get anything from an Englishman." She stood up and took her tan bush hat from the table next to her.

"Or even an Englishman once removed."

She looked at me in confusion. "What does —?"

"It's not important." I turned to Miriam. "Have Joseph bring around Mrs. Vanderveer's horse."

"Yes, captain," she said, and went out through the kitchen.

This fiery woman looked at me one more time. "Thank you for your trouble."

I nodded.

She seemed for an instant to be about to relent, but then she appeared to force herself to turn away and she walked across the parlor and out.

"Stay, Buc," I said as he followed her to the door.

"What on earth was that?" Jon asked, standing up and staring after her.

"Oh, you have to understand gingers," I said with a smile. "They're a separate subspecies of the human race. Beyond all calls to rationality."

He turned toward me. "Doesn't anything ever make you mad?"

"Courage sheathed in careless beauty cuts a lot of ice with me."

Miriam came back in and made little effort to soften her look of disappointment.

"Really, Mrs. Mpunga, what would you have me do?"

She poured me another glass of lemonade and looked down as she handed it to me.

"Hil . . . ." Jon said.

I set aside the glass and went to the front where he was staring out the window.

She was standing by her horse and leaning her face against his neck. Her tall form had lost its tautness and she seemed limp against her animal.

"She looks adrift, Hil."

"A woman like that is never adrift."

"Even when she cries against the neck of her horse?"

I took a deep breath and let it out slowly and suspected my life would never again be the same. "Always be wary of the sincerity of a woman who weeps in front of you." I turned and looked Jon in the eye. "And always—*always*—trust a woman who weeps alone."

I walked out onto the porch, and she turned when she heard my boots against the planks.

She quickly straightened, obviously embarrassed, and cleared her throat. "I wasn't crying, so don't even think it."

"Did I say you were?"

"I'm just tired. Goodbye, captain."

Before she could slip her left foot into the stirrup, I stepped around her and placed a hand on her horse's chest.

"Captain is too formal. My name is Hil."

"Yes," she managed to whisper.

"Valerie was it?"

"Valeria."

"Yes," I said, smiling. "I know."

She stared at the saddle in front of her. "I'm sorry. I'm surrounded by swaggering men and childish fools. I don't know where to turn."

"But you did somehow know to turn here."

"Yes." She looked at me. "And I didn't mean to be rude to you."

"Do you think I don't know that?"

"I've lived alone for so long, my manners aren't. . . ." She hesitated and then said, "Will you forgive me, captain?"

She seemed puzzled that I just gazed at her for several long moments. Finally I said softly, "Yes."

"Thank you."

"*Jy is welkom.*"

I was surprised by how touched I was by her sad smile.

"Can you help me?"

"I have to deal with the man-eater first. Or he deals with me, depending on the roll of the dice."

"I understand that. But then? Can you help me then?"

"To find your leopard?"

"Yes."

"If Rixton of Africa cannot, who can?"

"You believe there's hope then?"

"Of course. A fallen world isn't a hopeless world."

She lowered her eyes and for a moment she seemed lost in silent thanksgiving.

"Do you have a trustworthy headman?"

"I do."

"A good shot, too? One who can protect your people?"

"Yes."

"Then why don't you stay the night here and we can discuss these matters?"

"Would that be all right?"

"I'll have Joseph ride over to your place to tell your headman. He has just enough time to get there and back before dark."

She turned away. "I don't deserve your kindness after the way I acted."

"I agree. You don't."

She looked at me like I had just poked her with a pin.

"So what?" I said. "If each of us got what we deserved, we'd all be croc meat, don't you think?"

She stared at me for a moment, and then said, "You're an unusual man."

"Now write a note for your headman telling him to give Joseph what you need for the night, your nightclothes and whatever else, and we'll have a peaceful evening on the Sabi."

"My nightclothes?"

"Well, Valeria Vanderveer, take this as formal notification from Captain Hilton Rixton, Englishman once removed, that you're perfectly welcome to sleep without them."

For the first time, that field of freckles began to soften and bend, and then suddenly the pink ceramic mask cracked and she burst out laughing.

"And what in the world is an Englishman once removed?" she asked, still laughing.

"My father was English and my mother American."

"I'm sorry for what I said about the English."

"Oh, he'd have just waved it off. He had the Englishman's flawless sense of indifferent superiority."

She smiled. "And Mrs. Rixton?"

"A wild Montana cowgirl."

"Where's that?"

"The American West. Just south of Canada."

Her bemused look was captivating, but I tried not to let her realize its effect on me.

"So you're half wild and half tame...."

"Well, every woman I know says I'm perfectly safe."

She considered that for a moment. "In most ways, perhaps."

"But not all?"

"Oh, no, definitely not all," she answered with an almost invisible smile. "And what woman worth her steel would prefer anything less?"

13

THE LITTLE I TAUGHT THE LEOPARDS WAS AS NOTHING COMPARED WITH THE ABUNDANCE OF KNOWLEDGE AND WISDOM WHICH THEY IMPARTED TO ME.
--NATURALIST BILLY ARJAN SINGH

LIKE MOST FINE JOURNALISTS (of whom there are three or four), Jon could intuit people's feelings from even the subtlest facial or verbal hints. So he entertained our ill-at-ease guest at dinner with tales of New York that made her smile and even laugh and kept the conversation miles away from the horrors of a predatory cat terrorizing the helpless and a tame cat rushing headlong to its doom.

We fed like delighted hyenas on warthog *spit braai* cooked by Miriam on the massive grill out back and supplemented by baby marrows and broccoli and sweet peppers grown in my garden. Mellowed by a rich Montepulciano sent to me by a generous Italian count and sportsman I cherish as a friend, we were as relaxed as any people could be who were about to contemplate the mystery of mortality. Following that was one of Miriam's specialties, a malva pudding drowned with a buttery syrup sweet enough to crack your teeth, and then washed down with coffee that could have peeled the paint off Admiral Dewey's cruiser.

After we finished, we went into my study. Miriam lit some lamps against the growing darkness, and I told her to have Joseph join us. I noticed that seemed to surprise Valeria.

Joseph was a teetotaler, but I poured the rest of us small glasses of Vin Santo, also shipped to me by my Tuscan friend. Then it was time to settle down to the riddles of uncertain life and violent death.

"We have two strategies with the man-eater," I said. "We can go out and look for him blindly or else wait for him to strike and then we can proceed from there. If we try to track him hither and yon, we'll find nothing, and if we wait, people will die while we're waiting."

I paused.

"So we don't really have a choice, do we?" Jon said.

I deferred to Joseph.

"No, sir," he said, "we do not."

"Valeria, Joseph has already put out word for us to be notified of any deaths caused by a cat." I noticed Jon's skeptical look. "Trust me," I said to him. "The jungle telegraph is as efficient as anything contrived by Morse."

I looked back at our guest. "Any thoughts?"

"I completely agree. You have to wait."

"Once we hear of another victim, we'll take to the bush. And we'll walk. I don't want to risk any horses."

"Leopards will attack horses?" Jon said in surprise.

"No, but lions will. To a lion, they're just big zebras."

"Have you ever seen an attack on a horse?" he asked.

"No, but I had one described to me. A couple of years ago, one of the rangers over at Sabi was riding in the dark with his dog and was ambushed by a pair of young males. They were actually going for the horse, but he got caught in the melee when he fell from his mount."

"Was he killed?" Valeria asked.

"The horse bolted with one of the lions running after him, and the ranger's dog chasing the lion. What a dog. The other lion grabbed the ranger by the shoulder and was dragging him when the ranger managed to get out his knife and stab him. Stabbed him more than once. The cat dropped him and staggered off. The ranger managed to climb a tree, and it's a good thing he did. He found out later that his horse had escaped, and now the other lion came back for him. But the ranger's dog ran back, too, and kept the lion at bay until some of the ranger's men came looking for him. They had dogs of their own, and they kept the lion away while they rescued their friend. He survived and is back in the saddle. Tough as they come."

"What happened to the first lion?" Valeria asked.

"He'd already died groaning in agony before the other lion got back."

Jon looked puzzled. "Wasn't it odd for a pair of males to go out hunting alone together like that?"

"Oh, no. They were probably brothers pushed out of their pride by the dominant male and looking to take over another one. Lions can form friendships that last a lifetime." I reached down and stroked Buc lying on the floor next to me. "And we'll be going without this fellow, too. He's much too tempting as leopard bait. He'd give his life for me, and we can't have that."

"And going without me as well," Joseph said, relieving me of the duty of saying it.

"Why?" Jon asked.

"Because I need Joseph here to protect my people. He's a better tracker than I am, but I need him here."

Jon looked confused. "I'm not following what you're saying. You told me the leopard would probably sweep around and head north again."

"That's right."

"Well?"

"I have to allow for the fact that I might be wrong."

Jon just stared at me.

"Does that shock you?"

"No," he said with an odd look, like he was struggling with some great tension, and then he exploded in laughter. "It shocks me that you'd admit it."

Valeria tried to hold back, but it was hopeless and she began laughing, too, and I saw that even Joseph was fighting to suppress a smile.

"Ah," I said, shaking my head at Jon and Valeria like a disappointed parent. "So little respect. It must be the wine."

"I'm sorry," Valeria said, looking down and wiping away tears of laughter. "Jon Stratton is an evil man."

"Now at last you're beginning to understand the depth of depravity of a squirrel slayer from Long Island."

"Manhattan!" Jon shouted.

"Worse."

"Stop it!" Valeria said, still laughing and drying her eyes.

We sipped our wine in silence for a while, and our guest eventually turned away and her gaze seemed to drift far off.

"Valeria. . . ."

She looked back at me.

"Shall we talk about the black leopard?"

She set down her glass. "My husband and I had a farm in the *platteland* near Lydenburg. I found two starving cubs one day at the edge of our property. They looked very bad. Their mother had been killed by a lion."

"And you raised them yourself?"

"One of the cubs died later that day. She was spotted. But the black one held on. I named him Dusk. I have a *Rifrug* who'd just had puppies, and she had a few teats to spare and she nursed him like he was one of her own."

"Is that a dog?" Jon asked.

"We call it a Ridgeback," I said.

Valeria smiled. "It was beautiful to watch. And I think that's why Dusk never looked on my pups as food, only as brothers. Even my other ones who weren't related." She laughed. "I think he's the only leopard in the Transvaal who has no interest in devouring dogs."

"How old is he now?"

"Four. He's the first proven case of a black leopard in Mpumalanga."

"Did anyone ever write it up?"

"I don't believe so. When my husband was killed in the war, Dusk was my rock. He was there for me always." She looked away toward the front of the house and out to the dark forest beyond. "I don't make friends easily. . . ."

"Is that right? I had no idea."

She turned toward me with a half-sad smile. "I'm trying to fix that."

"And then?"

"I needed to get away from Lydenburg. Too many ghosts. So I bought the Hawthorne farm."

"And you've been here how long?"

"Four months. And now my whole world has been flipped upside down." Suddenly her walls collapsed. "My God, Hil, I'd do anything to get him back. I'd give my life for that cat."

As with all very guarded people, it was always rock and steel and locked gates, or else naked intimacy. They had no idea of the golden mean. And yet I doubt there had been many other times in her life when she had been as starkly open as she was at this moment.

I reached across the table with an open hand.

She looked down at it as if it were a leg-hold trap.

"It's all right," Jon said with his customary casual reassurance. "Rixton of Africa is quite the sentimentalist."

Embarrassed now, she gently placed her hand in mine, and I closed my fingers around it and smiled. "We'll do what we can."

She fought to hold back tears, and the embarrassment that went with them.

"That's all right," I said. "I know you're not crying. You're just tired."

Then she managed to laugh through her misty eyes. "Thank you." She turned and looked directly at Joseph. "All of you."

"Madame," Joseph said with a nod. "It is my pleasure."

"How long has Dusk been loose?" I asked.

"About three weeks."

I said nothing but just looked down and swirled my wine around in the glass.

"What?" Jon asked.

"That's not good," I said. "He was hand raised. So he doesn't know how to hunt for himself."

"Yes he does," Valeria said. "I taught him. But I never had to show him how to climb trees. He did that on his own when he was about three months old."

After all I had seen in life, I was not easily surprised, but my look of blatant astonishment must have shocked her. "How did you train him to hunt?"

"With plenty of hard work."

"Well, you're not going to bed tonight until you tell us how you did it."

"Weaning him was easy. But after that it got harder. I started feeding him small pieces of meat and he did well on that. But I wanted him to learn about prey. So one day I gave him a dead squirrel." She smiled. "Can you guess what happened?"

"He just stared at it," I said.

"Exactly! He did pat it around a little, too, but then he looked up at me like he was saying, 'Well, *nou wat?*' So I sliced it open and pulled out some of the intestines and let them hang there. Then he lunged at it and ate the whole thing."

"Success," Jon said.

"We weren't even close to that. Now every time I gave him an animal, I opened it a little less, and I was glad to see he still grabbed it and ate it. I was worried, though, that he might ignore something I didn't slice at all. So one day on a lark I trapped a live rabbit and just stunned it and tossed it to him while it was still alive and twitching to see if that would be enough. If it would excite him without the dangling intestines." She paused and smiled.

"And?" Jon said.

I smiled because he seemed to be struggling with her unusual accent. He had certainly never spoken with an Afrikaner before.

"He pounced on it and shook it and broke its neck, and then ran into the house and jumped onto a table and devoured it. He was five months old."

"Success?" Jon asked.

"Not yet. Even though he'd started chasing prey when he was only five months, he wouldn't kill it. Even if he caught it. He'd just press it to the ground with one paw, and release it and let it run off and then catch it again. Like a housecat with a lizard."

Here she paused for effect. She clearly loved telling stories about her leopard.

"Come on, Valeria," Jon said, smiling. "You're such a tease."

She glanced quickly at me. "Sometimes."

"Well?" Jon said.

"I began running ahead of him and dragging a half-dead squirrel or rabbit on a piece of twine. So he'd get the idea of chasing *and* killing."

She smiled, but this time it was at her own expense.

"Yet I'd been too optimistic. I thought it would be as easy as everything else had been. It wasn't. But I never stopped. Week after week. . . ."

"Oh well," Jon said with fake petulance, "I'm not even going to ask again if you succeeded."

"All right," I said with a smile. "Then I'll ask."

"To be honest, Hil, I don't know if I did or not. I don't want to take any credit I don't deserve."

"Take it anyway," I said.

"One day I found the remains of a rabbit on my bed. And it wasn't one I'd give him."

"He might have scavenged it," I said.

"I know. So I wasn't convinced. I kept training him with the animals on the twine. It was fun at first, but eventually it got to be exhausting. . . ."

"I can imagine," I said.

"Then one evening I came in and I heard a loud buzzing coming from my bedroom. I ran in, and there was Dusk lying across the top of my bookcase six feet above the floor and feasting on an impala calf. And it was freshly killed." She grinned. "The sound was the buzzing of the flies fighting for a taste."

"He'd found his own tree!" Jon said, laughing.

"How old was he then?" I asked.

"Eleven months."

"You dragged half-dead animals around in front of him for six months?" Jon said.

"I did."

"Well, Valeria," I said with a smile, "you have the patience of a saint. Uncommon for gingers."

She gave me a puzzled look.

"American slang for redheads. Usually ones who are" — I had to smile — "a little *wilde*. In a good way."

She stunned me by seeming very touched, and I suddenly had the thought that it was not so much for the compliment about her persistence as for the fact that I was already fond enough of her to give her a nickname.

She returned to her wine and sipped it and stared off at something only she could see.

"Valeria . . ."

She roused herself from her reverie and looked at me.

"Sorry. I was in a little bit of a *dwaal* there. . . ."

"Does Dusk have any experience with other leopards?"

"Yes. Why?"

"In case he runs up against another male out there. Including the man-eater."

"When he was young, I walked him on a leash and kept him in a large wire enclosure at night. But as he got older, he started to get restless. Especially in the evenings. So—."

"Lord of the darkness," Jon whispered to himself.

"I'm sorry . . . ?"

She looked puzzled.

"Please go on, Valeria," I said.

"So I let him have the run of my place."

"Did that work?" I asked.

"Beautifully. Sometimes he'd go off into the forest at night. But he'd always come back. And then when he was fully mature, he'd go to look for romance. And I wouldn't try to stop him. So he definitely came across females, and maybe a few males."

"That's good."

"He's smart and tough. He'll be all right. Except against rifles. That's why I can't sleep at night."

"I'll put out the word that anyone who harms the black leopard will have to answer to me."

She hesitated and said, "Will that be enough?"

"For everyone except Von Roon."

"Why?"

"Because," Jon said, "he's too foolish to fear Rixton of Africa."

"I've heard of Von Roon. I didn't like what I heard."

"He's a murderer," Jon said. "He whipped one of his boys to death."

"And he's still free?"

"Not ultimately," I answered.

"I don't understand," she said.

"I have a *Sangoma* involved. Adjudicating the law of the veld."

"But a *Sangoma* is a healer."

"Among other things. Mine is also versed in the darker arts. One day a spiritual foot will be thrust forward into the path of Von Roon, and he'll totter and tumble into the precincts of Hell."

After that, no one said anything for a long time until Joseph broke the silence.

"Captain . . ."

"Speak freely."

"Madame, will the leopard come if you call him?"

"Oh yes. He knows my voice. He even knows my footsteps."

"But he ran away anyway?" Jon said.

"I wasn't home when it happened. He's usually not bothered by gunfire, but one day there was so much shooting by those *domkoppe* looking for the man-eater near my farm that he must've panicked. My headman tried to call him back, but Dusk comes only for me."

I went to my desk and got the manila folder with the drawings of the man-eater's pug marks.

"What do you make of these?" I spread them in front of her.

"An old male," she said as she examined the drawings with the intensity of a jeweler appraising precious gems. "Large, too. Slightly bigger than Dusk." She tapped the sketch of the right forefoot. "This looks like an old wound from a snare." She picked up another drawing. "And this hind foot is wrong. It's angled in. He might have been shot at least once."

"How big would you say he is?"

She thought for a moment. "At least seven feet between pegs. Maybe even a little more."

"All right," Jon said. "Help me out. Where are a leopard's pegs?"

Valeria smiled like a patient schoolteacher. "Some hunters like to exaggerate about their trophies, so they put the skin onto the ground and measure it that way. But that's fake because they stretch out the skin before they measure it. The only honest way is to lay the animal out right after it's been killed and drive a little peg into the ground in front of the nose and one at the tip of the tail and then measure that distance. That's what we mean by 'between pegs'." She slid the sketches back into the folder and handed it to me. "So, captain, did I pass the test?"

I smiled. "I'm as transparent as glass."

She returned my smile. "Smoked glass maybe."

"Hil . . ." Jon said.

"Mmm?"

"Back in New York when you were talking about shooting charging leopards and all that, you didn't say much about getting a straight clean shot if you can. But I assume that's possible once in a while, isn't it?"

"Anything is possible."

Valeria went over to the desk and came back with a pencil and sat down. She started sketching on the cover of the manila folder and in about a minute had produced an amazingly textured profile of a leopard walking from right to left. His right foreleg and right hind leg were going forward, and both his left legs were moving toward the rear.

"That's odd — I never noticed that before," Jon said.

"What?"

"That they move both legs on one side of the body forward or backward at the same time. Dogs don't do that, do they?"

"No, they alternate. Only cats, camels, and giraffes move like that at a normal walk."

He shook his head and smiled. "Funny I never realized that before."

"Now pay attention. If you draw a — what's the matter?"

He was still staring at the sketch. "That's beautiful."

148

"My mother was an artist," she said with a wave of the pencil. "Can you pay attention now, please?"

"Yes, teacher."

She drew a horizontal line along the side of the leopard about a third of the way up the torso. "Some hunters like to imagine an invisible line halfway up the body instead of a third. But if you're trying for a heart shot, I like to say a third because that's closer to where the heart is. Does that make sense?"

"Yes."

"Halfway will work, too, most of the time, but you can miss the heart. The reason some hunters say halfway is that it's easier to judge half the body. Estimating just one third is much harder for the human eye to do at the usual range. At least on a small animal like a leopard. It's your choice."

"All right."

She drew a vertical line running up the back of the cat's left foreleg where it just grazed the flexed elbow and then crossed the horizontal line. At this juncture she printed an "H".

"That's where you want to hit," she said, pointing to the intersection of the two lines. "That's a heart shot. If you do it right, you'll hit his pump. He'll usually drop right there and be dead instantly. *Verstaan jy?* Do you understand?"

"I do."

"The heart is back farther than some people think who've never cut open a cat. And that's most hunters."

"It looks like about nine or ten inches."

"That's a good average, but it can vary because adult leopards come in all sizes. Some hunters just say, 'Shoot behind the shoulder,' and that's good advice but not enough. Can you see why?"

Jon studied the sketch. "I'm not sure."

"It's like someone asking you where the Sabi River is and you say, 'Below the equator.' What good is that?"

Jon laughed.

"Some people who've been lucky to shoot one cat in their entire lives will tell you to shoot behind the elbow. But that's meaningless, too, because it depends on where the elbow is. What they mean is shoot behind the elbow when it's as far back as it will go during a normal stride." She gestured at the sketch. "The way you see it here."

Jon examined it.

"And you're right," she said. "That's usually about nine or ten inches. But if the leg is moving forward, then the elbow is in a different place. If you shoot there, you'll miss the heart completely."

"I understand."

"If you hit a little bit higher or behind or in front of that point, that's all right. That's a lung shot." She printed an "L" at each of those three points. "It's not as quick as the heart shot and he'll run after he's hit, but he probably won't go more than fifty yards before he collapses and dies."

Jon nodded.

"Some hunters look at it completely differently than I do." She shrugged. "They like a shoulder shot instead of what I'm telling you, and that's fine."

"Is there a reason you don't do that?"

"I try to avoid major bone if I can. Too many things can go wrong. I've seen it."

"But it can do the job?"

"Most of the time."

"But not always?"

"Nothing is always. But it's usually effective."

"Nice to know."

"It won't get the heart, but if the bullet hits the shoulder, it'll penetrate it and go through both lungs and probably the other shoulder, too. If it does, he'll drop and you've got your man-eater. Or your trophy." She ran the palm of her hand softly along the drawing. "But I don't hunt for trophies."

"Neither does the captain."

She looked at me in surprise. "Truly?"

I remained quiet.

"Another advantage of the shoulder shot," she went on, "is that it stops the cat right there. Sometimes an animal will still run a short distance even after it's been shot through the heart. It's called — ."

"Hyperadrenia," Jon said.

She hesitated and glanced at me.

"What?" Jon asked. "You don't think I know that word?"

She looked back at him, "No," she said with a smile.

He burst out laughing. "Well, I didn't until recently."

"Now that's a shock," she said, laughing with him.

"Thank you for explaining all this," he said.

She waved it off. "Just always remember that if you're really precise with the heart shot behind the shoulder and have a good cartridge, you can hit the heart and one or both lungs at the same time." She set down the pencil. "Then your fiancée will see you waving and smiling with all your limbs intact as you're standing by the rail when the ship docks."

"You've done this before," Jon said, and it was not a question.

"I've had to put down a few cattle killers over the years. So I staked out a calf and took them down."

"With one shot?" he asked.

Valeria glanced at me and then looked back at Jon. "It's not polite to ask, but yes. What did you expect?"

"Sorry."

"What did you use?" I asked.

"A .275 Rigby."

"Hil, wasn't it a Rigby that the English lord used? The one who was killed by the lion?"

"It was, but he wasn't as good a shot as he needed to be to use a small caliber like that. Mrs. Vanderveer is."

"Valeria," she said.

"Or Ginger."

"That, too," she said with a smile.

I smiled back, but my thoughts were already drifting off as I finished my Vin Santo and gazed out the window at the forest beyond.

"Now all we can do is wait. It won't be long."

I sat at the far end of the porch in the dark with Buc sleeping on the decking beside me. I had to be wary, since leopards were happy to snatch dozing dogs from their masters' feet before their owners even realized what had happened. My revolver rested on a table next to the arm of my chair. The eye patch lay on my lap after I had removed it so I could scratch my evening itch. I leaned my head back and slowly inhaled the cool air and listened to the comforting sounds of the hippos coming ashore for their nighttime feeding.

Buc snapped his head up, and I was reaching for my revolver before I realized he was looking toward the doorway. Valeria came out wearing a white terrycloth robe and stood there by the door. Her hair was down and she shook her head as if limbering her neck and stretched her arms toward the sky, like a butterfly bursting from a cocoon. It was a moonless night and she failed to see me, but when Buc ran over to her she realized she was not alone.

"Have a seat."

"I'm sorry. I didn't mean to disturb you."

"I couldn't sleep either." I got up and slid one of the rattan rockers closer to mine. "Relax." I picked up my eye patch.

"You don't have to put it back on. I'm not frightened by the scars of men. Outside or in."

I smiled to myself but said nothing.

She sat beside me, and Buc lay in front of her with his head on her bare feet.

"Heaven, isn't it?" she said as she gazed across the river.

"If Heaven is lucky."

"Thank you."

"For what?"

"Just thank you."

"This is the second time in the last few months that an unmarried woman has visited me in the dark."

I could just make out her smile.

"And who might that other woman have been?"

"All I'll say is that she wasn't someone who could handle a Rigby."

"I'm sure," she said, laughing.

For a while we sat in silence and listened to the night sounds.

"Jon told me you commanded black troops in the cavalry."

"I prefer to say we served together. How did that topic come up?"

"Jon said he saw a surprised look on my face when Joseph joined us at the table. So he explained your background."

"Ah."

"I'd never seen a black man sit and eat with whites before."

"And now you have."

"And I never saw a white man treat a black man as an equal."

"And you still haven't. Joseph isn't my equal. And he never can be."

"But what—?"

"Except in terms of formal education, Joseph is my superior in every way imaginable."

She turned away. "Now I feel ashamed. He was so kind to me when I arrived and he took care of my horse."

"Which is why you looked him in the eye at the table and thanked him personally."

"Do you notice everything?"

"Yes."

She seemed not to know what to say.

"Don't worry. Joseph isn't just a wise man, he's a charitable man. One time he was clawed by a lion and his leg swelled like a rotting rabbit—and in his pain he carefully explained to me the point of view of the lion."

"I'm privileged to be here. I want you to know that. Privileged to be that man's friend. And yours and Jon's."

I said nothing.

"I've never made friends in one day before. Never."

She seemed astounded at herself.

"Well," I said, "there's no accounting for folly."

"Or amazing luck."

We both remained quiet for a few minutes and then she said, "I need your advice. . . ."

"It's free."

"Do you think I should go look for Dusk alone and then you can join me after you get the man-eater, or—."

"Or he gets me?"

"Stop it. I was going to say or should I wait for you?"

"Neither. When Jon and I hear of another attack, you're going to be with us."

"I am?" she said in surprise. "When did the captain issue those orders?"

"Suppose Jon and I come across Dusk while we're looking for the man-eater. You said Dusk was headed in the same direction. What can we do? We won't have any way to trap him. And he won't come with us. Only with you. You have to be with us."

"And you'd trust me in the hunt for the man-eater?"

"Of course. Why not?"

She looked away. "I don't know. I guess I'm not accustomed to people trusting me. Trusting my judgment."

"Maybe it's because you're too quick to show them the back of your hand."

She turned toward me but remained quiet.

"Instead of a corner or two of your heart."

A cool breeze had begun blowing, and she pulled up the thick collar of her robe, but I doubt it was really against the wind.

I reached across and turned the collar back down. "No defenses are necessary here."

I was surprised when she still had nothing to say, although her silence said much more.

"Trust is a great gift, isn't it?" she finally asked.

"Greater than love."

"Why do you say that?"

"Love is easy. Even cowards and criminals are loved. But trusted?"

"I was right. You *are* an unusual man."

"That's why remarkable women insist on visiting me in their nightclothes."

She turned away, but not before I could see her trying to hide a smile.

"When you go home tomorrow, get everything in order at your place and be ready to leave with us on short notice. It'll be abrupt. It always is."

"I'll do that." She stood up. "Now I'll leave you alone. I feel better now. I think I'll sleep well."

"*Goeienag en soete drome.*"

"*Dankie,*" she said with a look of surprise. "And sweet dreams to you, too." She stopped halfway across the porch. "You know, captain," she said, still staring straight ahead toward the door, "you were right. About every single thing you said about me." Then she turned and looked at me over her shoulder. "Except one. . . ."

"And that is?"

Slowly and melodramatically she tightened the belt on her robe. "The nightclothes."

Then she smiled a spectacular smile and turned away and disappeared like a phantom into the darkness.

PART THREE

PREY

14

YOU KNOW YOU ARE TRULY ALIVE WHEN YOU'RE LIVING AMONG LIONS.
--WRITER KAREN BLIXEN

"THE OLD MAN IS DEAD," Joseph had said, and I knew exactly what he meant.

Valeria had left immediately after breakfast, and Joseph had been doing his usual early morning reconnoiter when, with that lowveld instinct at which most can only marvel, he sensed something amiss in the bush.

He and Jon and I were now standing in the cool shade of a massive acacia in the dense forest about fifty yards from my house and gazing down at the departed monarch.

I dropped to one knee and ran my hand across the flank of the old lion.

"Still warm," I said.

He was in slightly better condition than I would have expected but was quite thin. About three hundred pounds, as Joseph had judged from his pug marks. The cat's reddish tan mane was still handsome but partly thinned out now, since he had been failing and losing condition for at least several months, and probably longer.

Jon pushed his helmet back and knelt beside me. "He's magnificent."

"Even in death."

"Do you think it was what you said? Kidneys?"

"Probably. A doctor friend of mine told me that when they begin to shut down it starts a massive organ failure he called a cascade. Then the end comes fast." I looked up at Joseph, "Ten?"

"At least, captain."

"Ten what?" Jon asked.

"Years."

"You can tell that by looking at him?"

"There are plenty of clues. All those scars on his face didn't get there in a day. That took years."

"Are the scars from fighting with his prey?"

"No, mostly from battling other male lions. And these spots at the base of his whiskers — see how faint they look?"

Jon nodded.

"They're easy to see when the animal is young but not now. That's because the hair on his face thinned so much as he got older. It takes eight or nine years to reach this point."

Jon ran his fingers along the lion's whiskers.

"Look at the color of his nose. When lions are born, their noses are usually pink. Once in a while gray. When they're about three, they start to get black speckling on them. The nose doesn't get fully black like this until they're about eight."

I opened the cat's mouth and pulled down his bottom lip. All the teeth were as yellow as antique ivory. Both lower canines had had their tips broken off long ago. Two of the lower incisors were gone, and the rest were now little more than stumps. I stretched the lip open some more. The cheek teeth were heavily worn and thin, and several of the cusps were either missing or smoothed down to knobs that looked no sharper than tiny thimbles.

"Run your finger along the back of one of the bottom canines."

Jon did so without hesitation.

"And?"

"There's a groove there."

"That's a wear groove." I felt the deep channel at the rear of the tooth. "It takes at least eight years for a deep groove to develop, but this is even deeper. Ten years at least." I pulled down the front of the lip. "Look at the incisors."

Jon bent down to examine them.

"Get closer. What do you see?"

"Dark spots in the middle."

"Those are the pulp cavities. And these are really exposed. We're beyond ten now. I'd guess he's thirteen or fourteen."

"And that's very old?"

"For a wild lion? And one without a pride? Ancient." I released the lion's lip and smiled down at him. "A grand old fellow. And he didn't get ripped apart or starve to death. He just came here to this cool spot on my land far from the gunfire to lie down and take his final rest." I ran my hand softly along his side. "And he fulfilled his role in this world far better than either of us ever will."

"Hil, you always insist on confusing me. . . ."

I looked over at him.

"Just when I think you doth bestride the world like an arrogant colossus, you suddenly act as humble as a nun. You baffle me."

"I baffle myself. Why should you be exempt?"

Jon stroked the lion's head, and I noticed goosebumps on his arm as he did so.

"What an experience," he said almost reverently. "I wish I'd seen him in his prime."

"You will. Someday."

He looked at me as if I were sucking on an opium pipe. "Come on. Not the animals with souls again."

I just smiled.

"If I write that in my book, my readers will think I'm crazy."

"No, they won't. They'll think *I'm* crazy. But leave it out if you like."

"Well, I didn't mean to say — ."

"In fact, definitely leave it out. Let the godless be surprised on the last day."

Jon shook his head. "The Almighty tossed away the mold after he made you."

"There was no mold. I was carved by hand."

"Now *that* I believe!" He turned back to the lion and slid his fingers through the mane. "It's sad to think he'll be gone soon."

"The hyenas will have the last word about their old foe."

Jon kept petting him. "I know."

"But it doesn't have to be."

"What, more miracles?" he said in exasperation.

"Of a sort."

"What do you mean?"

"Would you like to have him?"

Jon looked at me as if the opium had finally entered my bloodstream.

"The finest taxidermist in Pretoria is a friend of mine. We'll take some measurements, and I'll get my *KODAK* and we'll take some photographs of this old gentleman and then get him into the salt right away" —I turned toward Joseph— "thanks to a master skinner I know."

"Yes, captain."

"And my friend in Pretoria will work his wizardry."

"I don't know what to say, Hil. That would be incredible."

"And *Ngala* will be there waiting for you when you get back to New York."

"My God, I . . . . Thank you."

He looked down at the lion and would have been surprised, and probably disturbed, to realize that he was now gazing at the great cat as if he still breathed. And maybe even had a soul.

15

LIFE IS SLOW BUT DEATH IS NOT SLOW.
--SHANGAAN PROVERB

OVER THE YEARS, I had seen more than one of my troopers disgorge a meal that had marinated too long in the Arizona heat. Frontier army slop being what it is, this was not particularly noteworthy. However, I had never witnessed anyone vomiting merely at the sight of something. But now Jon spun away from us and hurried farther into the forest where he could no longer be seen, although, probably to his embarrassment, could still clearly be heard.

We were standing beside a small stream deep in the acacia forest just outside a tiny village several miles northeast of the larger one where Lucy and Michael had barely escaped the grasp of the man-eater. Valeria had set aside her rifle and, without hesitation, had bent down and pulled a piece of old cloth off the remains of a little Shangaan girl, now lying on her stomach about ten feet from the bank of the stream. She was about five years old. Her clothes had been torn off in pieces with the same precise skill a leopard uses to pluck the feathers from a guinea fowl before he devours it. The flesh of the girl's back and buttocks was gone, and her ribs and pelvis showed brightly even in the shaded recesses of the forest. Her upper arms and thighs had been stripped of flesh as well. Although leopards usually relish the viscera, these had been partly pulled out but lay uneaten beside her. A pair of holes showed where the leopard's upper canines had pierced the back of her neck and a second set revealed where the lower ones had sunken into her throat. Yet, in a macabre irony, her sweet little face endured untouched. Her eyes were open and she seemed simply to be resting. Which, of course, she was, but not on this earth.

Yingwe's deep pug marks taunted us from the softened soil around her and continued down to the stream, where the leopard had paused to drink. His spoor resumed on the other side and disappeared into the forest.

When we had first reached the spot, the parents, whom I did not know, were sitting on the ground near their little girl. I thought of going over to them and offering a few words of comfort but decided not to when I considered the uselessness of that. They were now slumped over and holding each other and seemed as empty as the dead husks they no doubt thought themselves to be.

"Do you think they'd let us sit up over her?" Valeria whispered.

"It doesn't matter. The leopard isn't coming back for her."

"How can you be sure?"

"He wouldn't have left her out in the open like this if he were coming back."

"You're certain?"

"Certain. He'd have taken what's left of her and hidden it in some brush. He's didn't. He's done with her."

It had been shortly after three in the afternoon, and Joseph had just finished getting the lion into the salt, when Michael Indaba, breathless and tired, had arrived at my home to tell me of the latest attack, this one at the little village. Even though it would be late before we could get there, I was determined not to wait and told him to go to the Hawthorne farm and to ask Mrs. Vanderveer to meet us in an hour and a half at the old lightning-struck jackalberry just north of her property. Everyone in the area knew well this stricken jungle giant with the split trunk and referred to it as Nightstorm. Then I told Michael to get some refreshment and rest before Joseph escorted him back to his village.

Miriam stuffed a big knapsack with what must have been a half-ton of biltong and dried fruits and other nourishment, along with razors and tooth brushes and a first-aid kit, and Jon volunteered to be the pack horse.

Buc knew, as he always did from my manner, that he would not be going. He sat obediently at the front door and whined when I bent down and pressed my lips to the top of his head.

"I'll be back soon, Buccaneer," I said and caressed him on the black patch of hair around his left eye that had awarded him his name.

I always promised him the same thing, and he always believed me. And it had always been true.

Valeria was waiting for us at the old acacia. With her rifle slung over a shoulder and her impala-handle hunting knife on her left hip, as well as her own small knapsack on her back, she seemed an utterly natural and unaffected daughter of the veld.

"She definitely has a way about her, doesn't she?" Jon said.

But it was a question requiring no answer.

Since I had no details of the attack, the three of us walked along in silence. In view of the circumstances, pointless chatter would have seemed faintly obscene.

Simon Dumayavo, a member of the village and an old friend of mine, had met us on the trail. Tall and white-haired and lean as a leather strop, he was the village elder to whom everyone turned in a crisis. He took us directly to the body.

About a dozen people from the village were sitting on the ground around the dead girl and, presumably, waiting for us to inspect the area before they moved her.

"You're right," Valeria now said to my remark about there not being enough of the girl left to lure the leopard back for more.

Valeria stood up and walked toward the small stream and gazed into the forest beyond it.

Simon joined us, and I could hear Jon coming up behind.

"Simon, do you know about what time the leopard took the child?"

"Around midnight, *M'Dabula.* Her father says he heard a soft swishing sound about that time but thought nothing of it. When he woke up at dawn, the child was gone."

"Too much time," I said. "Common sense tells us he's far away. On the other hand, he might be fifty yards from here watching us and thinking about coming back tonight for another easy victim."

Valeria ventured more deeply into the forest to where the pug marks vanished in the undergrowth. She reached down and plucked something from a thorn bush and handed it to me without turning around. It was a yellowish tuft of leopard hair. I gave it to Jon.

"A souvenir," I said to him. "In case this is all we ever see of *Yingwe.*"

"Hil," Valeria said, still peering into the dense woodland, "he's out there. I'm sure of it. Listen."

But I heard nothing. "My ears aren't as good as they used to be. Too much shooting over the years."

"Alarm calls. Red-billed hoopoes. Drongos, too. About a quarter-mile away."

"Those could be for another reason, though."

"*Ja,* they could be. . . ."

But her tone told me she was unconvinced. And I knew better than to try to convince a redhead of anything.

"Trust me, Hil."

"Val, I do trust you."

She gave me a look of pleasant surprise and then turned back toward the forest.

"There—you heard that, didn't you?"

I had. An alarm call from a jackal. And I hated it. Jackal calls always sounded to me like the heartbroken wails of a lost child.

"He hasn't gone, Hil."

"There's nothing we can do tonight. We'd have to bait him with a goat to draw him out, and we have no idea where to stake it."

She was about to say something but stopped.

"Val, he's not going to come back to this kill. Right now he might as well be on Mars."

"*Ek weet*," she said with a sigh, as she lapsed into her native tongue. Then she just shook her head in resignation at herself. "Sometimes I think with my heart and not with my head."

"No, you don't. You think with your spirit. The spirit of the veld. Don't ever stop."

She smiled.

"Besides," I said, "thinking with the head is overrated."

I heard a rustling of paper behind me and saw Jon rapidly writing notes.

"Hil . . . ," he whispered.

"Speak up. This is nature, not a soirée on Long Island."

"What did the father mean about hearing something at midnight? Did the leopard take the little girl right out of their hut?"

"Possibly."

"How?"

"Let's go see."

The village was much smaller than the one where Lucy and Michael lived and was completely surrounded by a gated palisade of vertical thornbush trunks about six feet high, like a Zulu *kraal*. Of course, even with the gate closed, that barrier would no more deter a leopard than it could frighten off a jungle breeze.

Simon led us to the thatched-roof rondavel of the stricken family.

"Do you know if this door was locked last night?" I asked Simon.

"It was open, captain."

The door was a collection of about a dozen thornbush limbs lashed together with twine and swinging on a couple of crude hinges. It had no latch other than a small piece of wood on a string that could be dropped through a little loop of wire pinned to the wall. A determined chacma baboon could have easily torn through it. A hungry leopard would simply have laughed.

A pair of tiny windows with a lattice of rough branches flanked the door about four feet off the ground.

I followed Simon inside, and Valeria and Jon came in behind me. Two narrow wooden beds covered with woven matting sat in the center of the single room with about two feet of space between them. A brass water pitcher and a couple of clay drinking cups for slaking a midnight thirst had been set on the floor between the beds. A few other crude furnishings, including a small table with an oil lamp, were situated around the circular walls. The rear third of the round interior had been separated by a pair of brown curtains hanging on a cord. Through the opening between them I could see the dead girl's sleeping area.

As Simon was about to take me to the back, I held out an arm and stopped him and then dropped down on one knee to the dirt floor at the foot of the beds.

Yingwe's pug marks had been obliterated near the front door by human feet, but here they were as sharply etched as cut glass. He had walked straight in toward the beds and then probably had heard the gentle breathing of the little girl in the rear. Without pausing, he had slipped between the beds and, with the delicacy of a ballerina, had stepped over the pitcher and cups without disturbing them and then swept like a mist to the rear of the hut and killed the girl in her sleep and in silence. He had picked her up and, with his remarkable strength, had held her like a little doll completely off the ground to avoid all sound as he again glided over the pitcher and cups and slid between her sleeping parents and vanished into the night.

I stood up and returned to the doorway and gazed outward at nothing — but inward at things no man should ever have to see. I knew now beyond all doubt that we were far beyond an "educated cat" accustomed merely to the hapless chattering of humans or the blast of gunfire. Some of the man-eating tigers I had pursued had astounded me with their cunning, and the wisdom and elusiveness of the man-eating leopard of Limpopo had almost made me despair. But now we had entered another realm. Never in all my stalks through the most menacing jungles had I confronted so fearsome a fusion of wariness, audacity, and intellect as I did now. Compared to that, the powerful eight millimeter rounds in my Mannlicher were no more than the cheap talismans of a credulous fool.

16

WHILE THE LEOPARD WILL LEAVE YOU WITH PAINFUL SURFACE WOUNDS, IT IS ALWAYS THE DEEPER SCARS, THOSE WITHIN YOUR HEART, YOUR SOUL AND THAT PLACE WHERE EGOS PRESIDED THAT CAUSE THE MOST PAIN AND SUFFERING.
--HUNTER PETE SWANEPOEL

SIMON ASKED US TO STAY for the night, and I was happy to do so in case the leopard returned. Simon was a widower, and the three of us joined him for supper in his rondavel. Valeria, however, excused herself shortly after finishing her meal and said she had something to attend to.

After deliciously grilled kudu steaks, we settled back against cushions on the ground and relaxed for the first time that day.

"Simon, have you heard the rumors of a black leopard in the area?"

"I have, *M'Dabula*, but I have no personal knowledge of it."

"Well, there is one, and he's tame. He's not the man-eater."

"A man rode through this morning and told me about it."

"This morning? Who? A white man?"

"Yes. A big man with a strange accent. He said he works for the baron."

"Kuskarohr," Jon said in disgust.

"Where did he go?"

"Off into the forest, but I don't know where."

"Did he mention where the baron is now?"

"No, captain."

"What exactly did he say about the cat?"

"That a pet black leopard ran off and has now become a man-eater."

"The cat belongs to Mrs. Vanderveer, but he's no man-eater. He was scared by all the gunfire and ran away. If you see the black leopard, don't approach him, but could you get word to us as soon as possible?"

"I will. Are you leaving tomorrow?"

"We have to. I'm assuming *Yingwe* is heading north, but I don't really know."

"We have a hut for you here tonight. And a separate one for the young lady."

"Thank you. Is there one anywhere near the center of the village?"

Simon looked puzzled. "Yes. Why, captain?"

"I'm going to sit up for a while in case our friend returns. I need a wall to my back and a clear line of fire to the gate. Was the gate open last night?"

"No, it was tied shut."

"Leave it open tonight."

"Do you think he might come back?" Simon asked.

"Might—a word I've always hated. I don't know."

"A guess then?" Jon said.

"I doubt he's hungry enough yet to risk it. But the girl was easy prey, and so it's possible. *Yingwe's* logic is never a man's logic. For at least one night I don't want to leave these people at his mercy."

"Thank you, *M'Dabula*."

"May I ask a question?" Jon said to Simon.

"Of course."

Jon glanced at me with a conspiratorial look and then turned to Simon. "I've been trying to find out what the captain's name means. The name you call him. But I haven't been able to."

"Did you ask him?" Simon said with the elegant simplicity for which the Shangaan are well known.

"I did. He says it's some kind of monkey."

Simon smiled.

"Well?" Jon said. "Can you tell me? So I can die as only a *semi*-ignorant man?"

Simon turned to me.

"All right," I said.

"A few years ago, four Portuguese bandits came across the border. They had escaped jail and fled into the Transvaal and made their way south. Every time they found a village, they would scream and fire their guns and terrify everyone. And then they would rob and rape. One day they reached this village. It would be the last day of their lives."

Simon looked at me.

"Go on," I said.

"The captain was passing through the area and heard the noise and hurried to help us. One of the villagers had already been shot. He was lying wounded on the ground when the captain got here. He ran over to him and set down his rifle and checked on him. At that moment the four bandits were dragging three young girls out of one of the rondavels. When they saw the captain, they released their prey and the girls ran back into the hut. Then the bandits pulled their pistols. The captain stood up and straddled the wounded man and drew his revolver and fired. All in one smooth motion. The bandits shot back and he was hit twice but he never moved. He stood there bleeding and firing as calmly as if it was a shooting match—one, two, three, four. And all four dropped like slaughtered curs. From that day, we've called him *M'Dabula*—The Man Who Shoots. And all wise men in the Transvaal know him by that name."

After a long silence, Jon said, "The wounded villager?"

"I recovered completely."

"Thank God for that. And none of the bandits lived?"

"Of course they did," I answered. "They're living in Hell."

Jon gazed at his friend who had slain four men, and then turned back to Simon. "Thank you."

He got up and went to the doorway and gazed out into the twilight.

"He's a good man," Simon whispered to me.

"Oh, yes. He needs some seasoning, though."

"Yes, he doesn't seem very long out of the egg." Simon stood up. "Mr. Stratton."

Jon turned around.

"We haven't finished our meal."

Jon came in and sat down, while Simon went to a small table at the back of the rondavel and returned with an unlabeled bottle of a clear spirit and three cups. He poured about two fingers of the drink into them and handed one to each of us.

I held up my cup and smiled and said, "*Geniet jou drink.*"

Jon took a sip and coughed as savagely as if I had kicked him in the throat.

"You're a madman!" he gasped, tears running down his face.

Simon smiled but remained silent.

"Some Manhattan wastrel you turned out to be."

Jon sniffed the drink in his cup.

"Try another taste," I said.

His eyes tried to bargain with me.

"Don't go civilized on me now."

This time he managed a sip without bringing up a lung.

"My God, Hil, what is it?"

"It's called *mampoer*. It's distilled from peaches. Sometimes other fruits."

"How long is it aged? Seven or eight minutes?"

"It's South African moonshine. Aged in the cup."

"What's the proof?"

"Well, out here that's not an exact science, but probably about one fifty. Give or take a liver."

"And I thought *man-eaters* were dangerous. Do you think we should dare share this with Valeria?"

"Dare? That half-feral redhead would throw back this firewater without a flinch."

Jon gave me a mock glare. "And you don't think I can keep up with the half-feral redhead?"

I smiled. "Nobody can."

Several of the village boys followed us at a distance as Jon and I walked around the inside of the fence. Samuel, a boy of about twelve, was wearing my hat. We had about two hours of light left and I was looking for any opening the leopard might have used to enter the previous night. I expected to find none. Jon was shocked when I told him that.

"Then how did he get back out?"

"How do you think?"

"But with the girl in his mouth?"

"One time I saw a young giraffe that a leopard had cached in the fork of a tree—and you're wondering about a little child and this pathetic fence?"

I walked along examining both the ground and the fence and soon found what I expected. I pointed to the spot, easily seen, where the leopard had gathered his hindquarters beneath him and had sprung over the thornbush trunk palisade. A few dried drops of the girl's blood were visible in the dirt for those with eyes to see.

"Tonight we're going to make it even easier for him," I said.

"By leaving the gate open?"

"You're sharp as a cat's claw. And I'll be waiting."

"I was a good student in school, but half the time I feel like my head is underwater."

"Why?"

"How do you know he won't just jump over the fence at some other spot where he comes out of the forest?"

I turned to my eager followers. "Time to go boys," I said with a smile and took my hat back from Samuel. "I'll see all of you again before I leave."

They grinned and a few said, *"M'Dabula,"* and then ran off home.

"Let's find Valeria," I said as we crossed the village and I checked the sinking sun.

"What about my question?"

"One of the most important things to know about predators is that they're innately conservative. They have to be. They can't just bend over and eat. They work for a living."

"Yes, but even—."

"Unlike ridiculous humans, no cat exerts himself for no reason. If you could explain to a lion that people take walks just to take walks, he'd look at you like you were insane. So there's your answer."

"Where?"

"Cats have to save their energy in order to be stalkers and killers. They don't sleep fifteen or sixteen hours a day because they're lazy. They do it because they're wise."

"Meaning what then?"

"Meaning the same is true when they hunt. They'll use the smallest effort that gets them the most food. And so they always pick the easiest path as long as it's also the safest."

"And that's why you think he'll come through an open gate instead of jumping the fence like he did last night?"

"He'll take the way that needs the least effort as long as he sees no danger in it. And he sees no danger in an open gate."

"You're certain?"

"Don't take my word for it. Think about what *Yingwe* did last night."

"All right, I'm thinking about it but . . . I don't know."

"When he slipped into that hut, I can guarantee you he was originally going to take one of the parents. Probably the woman. But then he heard the little girl in the back, and she was the safer prey. So what did he do?"

"He went straight in and got her."

"That's the point—straight. You and I are clever primates. We'd have seen the pitcher and cups between the beds and ruminated on it for a week and then circled around one of the beds and slunk to the rear that way. And then congratulated ourselves. But he didn't do that. Cats never take the long route if they can avoid it. Never."

"But what about the things that were in his way?"

"*Yingwe* saw that walking between the beds was the shortest and easiest path, and in a fraction of an instant his agile brain made the decision to risk stepping over the cups and pitcher instead of meandering around the beds."

"But if —."

"Think about what a housecat does if he wants to cross a counter that has objects scattered across it. He doesn't walk around. He very carefully steps over and through the things and doesn't disturb them in the slightest."

"I didn't know that. I've never had a cat, so I've never seen it."

"To clumsy apes in trousers and boots what the leopard did last night seems crazy. Dangerous and crazy because he might have knocked those things over."

"I figured he was just lucky."

"No. With his nimbleness, it was nothing. Less than nothing. He wouldn't have given it a second thought. *Yingwe* rarely has second thoughts, because his first one is almost always right."

"No wonder every day I feel less safe."

"What can I say? Maybe you are."

"Here we have a cunning cat lounging —."

"Cunning? That's like saying the Mona Lisa has a cute little smile."

"All right. He's brilliant and he's lounging on a limb somewhere and hoarding his energy. And then there's me — trudging through the forest to the point of exhaustion like some silly holiday sightseer."

"When you stop and think about it, that's a good way of phrasing it. We're going about this the wrong way. . . ."

He gave me a wary look. "How's that?"

"If we really want to bring *Yingwe* to book, we don't need rifles. We just have to tell him there are such creatures as human hikers." I smiled. "Then he'll die laughing."

As we crossed the open area in the center of the village, I heard Valeria's voice drifting from the rondavel where the little girl had been killed. I approached it quietly and peered inside. Valeria was seated on one of the beds with the young mother in her arms. She was leaning against Valeria's breast, and Valeria was caressing her hair and speaking to her soothingly.

175

I gestured to Jon to back away, and we slipped off in silence.

17

THE LEOPARD MAY RESPECT YOUR WEAPONS, BUT HE DOESN'T FEAR *YOU*.
----HUNTER LOU HALLAMORE

SIMON HAD PREPARED a rondavel for us, and it was almost perfectly situated facing the gate and just a bit off center to the right. When sitting up and waiting for a man-eater, I like to be nestled in the fork of a tree, or high up on a *machan* as I would have been in India, but there was no possibility here of the former and no time this night to build the latter. So in these compromised circumstances I prefer to sit cross-legged on a firm flat surface with my back against a wall. I had placed some woven matting on the dirt for padding and had propped up more behind me against the rondavel. A large pitcher of water and a cup had been set on the ground beside my cushion.

Simon had told me that Valeria was going to spend the night with the couple who had lost their daughter, and so I was surprised to see her come out of their rondavel now and walk toward me. She approached with a stride that looked more like hurled exclamation points than leg movements, always a danger to the unwary male. Yet since redheads boast as many volatile moods as they have freckles, all the intended victim can do is flick off the safety of his rifle and wait for the pounce.

"I understand you're going to sit up for the leopard all night," she said in a tone as pleasant as a whetstone being drawn across the blade of a rusty knife.

Her hat was gone and her hair unpinned and that flowing flame was now blowing in the breeze, so she looked even wilder than usual.

"Yes, but only if I'm granted permission from the Princess of the Amazons."

She was standing with her hips cocked to the left and with most of her weight on that leg and her hand resting by the impala-handle hunting knife.

She glanced down at herself, and when she looked up again she failed to hold back an embarrassed smile. "Am I that bad?"

"Oh, no, not 'bad'."

"What then?" she said, trying not to laugh.

"I'm armed with only a rifle, so I dare not speak."

"I'm sorry, Hil," she said and dropped down beside me. "You know how I am."

I had no answer for that.

"You can't expect to sit up the whole night and then take to the bush tomorrow morning, can you?"

"I'll steal a few hours before dawn."

"No, the Princess of the Amazons says you can sleep now while she stands watch and then you can relieve her after midnight."

"Does she indeed?"

"I've sat up waiting for leopards before."

"I know that." I gestured toward the rondavel of the young parents. "How are they?"

"Still in shock. I'm doing what I can."

"I know."

"Their names are Sarah and Philip. I've asked them if they'd like to come and work for me."

"You still need help?"

"No, but they do."

I smiled but said nothing.

"Too many ghosts for them here. So they'll be coming to Hawthorne if they want to."

"You know," I said with a smile, "you're in danger of softening my judgment of you."

"Please don't change the subject."

"Which is?"

"The night watch."

"All right. Go ahead."

"Go ahead what?"

"Go ahead and get your Rigby."

"You can be such a nice little *bokkie* when you try," she said, smiling, and squeezed my shoulder and was gone as quickly as she had come.

"I'll be away for a while," I said to Jon as I poked my head into the hut. "Keep your weapon to hand."

He looked up from the chronicle he was writing. "Will I be safe?" he said, smiling.

"With Valeria no one is safe, but she'll keep the leopard off your face."

"*M'Dabula*," he said as I was turning away.

I looked back.

"Why didn't you use your rifle?"

"When?"

"On the Portuguese bandits."

"Is that finding a way into your deathless prose?"

"Possibly."

"It was lying on the ground and it would've taken a few extra seconds to get it into action. The main reason, though, was that those eight millimeter rounds would've sliced through them like a knife through paper and maybe hit the girls in the rondavel behind them."

He nodded. "I hadn't thought of that."

"So take that to heart. If a cat ever jumps me, don't shoot him until I get him off me. Otherwise even if you hit him, you'll probably end up killing me, too."

"I understand." He went back to his writing and then looked up again. "Should we mention that to Valeria?"

"No. She already knows it."

When Valeria returned, I told her I was going to air my soul before wrestling with Morpheus and that I would be back shortly.

"I'll be here," she said, settling in against the wall. Then, perhaps with more meaning than she intended, she added, "I'll always be here."

About an hour of daylight remained, and I slung my rifle over my right shoulder and walked out through the gate and along a game trail into the forest.

The summer rains had obviously been heavy and yet the mystery of the acacia woodland was that, no matter how dense, it never oppressed but, rather, liberated. After only a short time, even the flimsy little village had begun to strangle me, but now among the trees I could breathe deeply again.

The shadows seemed about a mile long as I broke through the forest into a more open area. A herd of impala caught wind of me before they saw me and bolted and vanished through the thornscrub in what seemed little more than an instant. Far too quick were these succulent antelope for the bullet-slowed *Yingwe*, who now had to resort to lesser fare.

Deprived denizens of cities who had never been to a forest before, let alone to an acacia woodland on the Sabi, were always stunned by how much sound there can be. The terms "peace and quiet" have been shackled together so long in everyone's mind that people assume the former can come only from the latter. But peace can arise by other means.

On this late afternoon, the cool wind had picked up, and as it rippled through trees of all sizes and densities, the subtle differences in sound created a unique blend at that moment that would never again be heard by anyone else on earth. The experience always called to mind what a conductor had once shared with me about the way in which the unintentional variations and even the tiny imperfections of twenty violinists create the "sheen" of an orchestra, the sound of which would have been flat and dull had each musician performed identically and perfectly.

And there were other players in this symphony as well. The humming and buzz and metallic clatter of insects established the background to everything, although old hands in the lowveld were often oblivious, like fish that never notice the water because it is never absent. Birds jostling for their roosting places in the trees now chattered and squawked. Among the loudest was the magpie shrike, whose less than soothing sounds made the similarity of his name with "shriek" seem especially appropriate. And, as always, vervet monkeys could be heard arguing with each other, as only primates can.

The lightly wooded area ahead and to my right was no denser than a drapery of green gauze. I raised my field glass and I could easily make out a magnificent kudu bull watching over the four ladies of his harem browsing contentedly on the leaves of the lower branches of a marula tree. I dropped to one knee and leaned forward against my leg and just watched.

Then, after a few minutes, as if rolling down from some Olympian height, rumbled the far-off roar of a lion. I smiled, as I always did at that sacred sound, and again thanked God for making me the richest man on earth.

I circled around the kudu so as not to disturb them and pressed more deeply into the forest.

Now I had fully invaded the leopard's domain. If he was almost invisible in the thornscrub, he was truly a phantom here. All the advantages were his. Nonetheless, the still voices of the jungle sentries conveyed the assurance that I was safe. Yet sometimes silence can mean simply that the sentinels have already fled. There was never a way to be sure.

I made my way along a narrow game trail in the darkening woodland until it opened onto a small shadowy clearing. Fallen branches and the corpses of collapsed shrubs matted the ground, and I wandered over to a thirty-foot high jackalberry at the edge of this ancient citadel. Sitting as quietly as I could on the twigs and dead grasses, I took off my hat and leaned back against the trunk and laid my rifle across my lap. Then I simply breathed the freedom few men can know. While the cool evening air flooded me with life, I recalled the words of the poet, as I often had before, and felt *as free as nature first made man, ere the base laws of servitude began, when wild in woods the noble savage ran.*

On my last day of life, this was the only place where I would want to be. The bier on which I would choose to lie and take my final breath. My only other wish would be that Buc and Hirannmaya and my horses could live as long as I and lie here with me, for there can be no Heaven without them. There are locales beyond number where one might decide, perhaps foolishly, to live, but it was to me beyond question that this was the finest place on earth to die, enshrouded and ennobled in a verdant cathedral buried deeply within the heart of the world.

Growling far off in the forest jarred me. I stood up with my rifle and turned toward the east. That it was an angry leopard there was no doubt, and when a deeper growl engaged it, I realized a battle for primacy might be about to arise. A roaring duet of pantherine rage crashed through the woods but then ceased as quickly as a brief and sudden burst of thunder. Rarely were these contests fought to the death, since male leopards, for all their coiled fury, were usually too sensible for that. My guess here was that the deeper growl was from an older animal, perhaps the man-eater himself, and that the younger resident chieftain had caught sight of him first and decided to inform the aging wanderer, in the frank leopardian manner, just whose pug mark was imprinted on the deed to this land. The wise old leopard knew this, of course, but his glands were still lively, and so he roared out his own lordly rebuke before moving on.

I picked up my hat and walked more deeply into the forest despite the failing light.

I had gone about a quarter of a mile when a bizarre cacophony that often reminded newcomers to the bush of the horrors of a Victorian madhouse told me in advance what I would find. I veered off the game trail and at the edge of it I stood in the shadows and watched. Five spotted hyenas paced beneath a huge jackalberry and alternately circled and glared upward with the hooting and tittering half-lunatic frustration for which they are famous. I raised my field glass. The remains of an impala lay draped across a fork in the branches about twenty feet above them. Drooping beside it was what appeared to be a spotted rope, until it twitched and swished with an occasional flicker of emotion. Sprawled along a branch, a young male leopard, fully in his prime and power, gazed down at the hyenas with the sort of bemused contempt that is the leopard's alone. It was an incomparable moment. About a six-and-a-half-footer, he was probably a bit smaller than the man-eater, but no less stunning for all that. Some sound behind me in the forest snared his attention, and when he swept his gaze around he caught sight of me. I was still looking through my field glass, and our eyes locked. From his shadowed perch, he took my measure with a surety and comprehension that no other cat on earth has mastered. Civilization now had vanished and normal time had ceased. Across eons we stared at one another through the deepening twilight. Finally I honored our silent bargain and took a step backward and relinquished to him his jungle realm.

Darkness was beginning to envelop me with all the reassuring warmth of a winding sheet, and so I started back. As I made my way through the forest, consciousness of my surroundings began to fade. This lapse in attention was unwise, but I seemed to be losing control of my own awareness as my mind insisted on speaking to me over and over again of the half-eaten little girl, and of countless others to be devoured in the future. And that it was to stop this agony that I now had to bring a magnificent and majestically savage life to an end.

The smell of a campfire drifted toward me on the breeze as I walked back toward the village. I could hear the crackling, and I followed the sound and the scent to a tiny clearing where a man sat staring into the flames.

"Good evening, sir," he said as he looked up. A rifle lay on his bedroll. "Pardon me if I don't rise from the tomb. Rather too tired for that. Please join me for tea."

"Thank you."

I sat across from him and laid down my rifle.

"Captain Rixton, I presume?"

I laughed. "Right you are, Stanley."

He smiled back and offered me his hand. "Cyril Lloyd."

He was about a decade older than I with silver hair and a generous moustache and spoke with the cross-bred accent of a rusticated Englishman who had lived in South Africa since around the Pleistocene. He seemed powerful as a bull croc and twice as fit.

"I'd heard you'd be tracking the leopard, and so I visited your place but you were already gone. I spoke with your headman. A remarkable fellow." He pulled a black metal pot from the edge of the fire and poured me some tea into a tin cup.

"Thank you," I said and sipped the brew. "Why are you out here alone like this?"

"Why is any man alone?" he asked like some weary Greek Stoic and gazed back into the fire.

I knew better than to try to answer that.

"Have you seen the cat?" he asked.

"Only one of his victims. A little girl."

"Is it true he's black? I heard that rumor, but I don't believe it."

"He's not," I said and told him the story of Valeria's leopard.

"Then I made the right decision," he said with obvious satisfaction, but I had no idea what he meant.

"You'll have to explain."

"I've seen the black one."

"When?"

"I had a chance for a clean shot at him just before sundown, but I wasn't sure he was the man-eater, so I let him go. I won't kill for nothing. He—."

"Where?"

"Not far from here. He seemed headed toward The Dragon's Tail."

That was good news. It was quiet up there and had plenty of game. If Valeria was right and Dusk was clever enough to avoid the resident leopards, he would be all right for now.

"The man-eater is down here," I said.

He nodded and sipped his tea. "Then here I'll stay."

"For fifty pounds?" I asked, hoping I might be able to annoy him out of his cryptic speech and into being more open with me.

"That won't buy me salvation." He picked up the pot and topped off my cup. "Do you know the history of this leopard, captain?"

"No."

"He's come down from up near the border, but he wasn't born to speak Portuguese. His cradle was the Sabi."

"How do you know this?"

"Four years ago a young sportsman down here shot him in the leg. I was present. Shot him not for a trophy or to protect cattle. Not for any sensible reason. Mindlessly. Like a boy who blasts the head off a rabbit simply because it shows itself. That sportsman was my son. . . ."

He paused and waited for an acknowledgement.

"Please go on."

"Naturally, an offhand shot is a blind man's shot. The leopard vanished."

"Why didn't your son follow him up?"

Lloyd gazed at me in the flickering light. "He did."

"Ah," I said. "I'm sorry."

"My son was probably the first person that cat ever killed. Eventually the leopard moved on and established a territory in the north."

"You're sure of that?"

"Oh, yes."

"But how can he have killed people up there for so long and we'd never heard of it down here?"

"It was in a very remote area. Few knew except the families of the victims."

Four years of perfecting the stalking and taking of human beings. Now I had more reason than ever to worry about a would-be bride on Long Island and whether or not her Jonny would be coming home in a box. And about the safety of some windswept redhead who prowled my thoughts more often these days than I wanted to admit.

"I tried to track him once," Lloyd went on, "but I had no talent for it and so I had to surrender to his wiles. Yet now he's come back to me like a heretic's lost faith, and I have one final chance."

"Chance for what?"

"Redemption for so many deaths."

"You blame yourself?"

"Of course. After his mother died, I coddled my son into what he was."

I remained quiet so he would continue.

"A self-centered, thoughtless child even long after he became an adult. Someone who could shoot an animal without cause, without thought. Even without pleasure."

"He paid the price."

"But what about all the others who paid? Paid for a stupid and callous act? What about the little girl?"

I had no answer, and we sat in silence for a while.

"Have you ever tracked a leopard before?" I finally said.

"Alone? Only briefly that one time."

"And not alone?"

"Once with a forestry officer friend in Bechuanaland. He had an interesting way of sitting up over a kill or a bait if there were no trees nearby, so we used that to—."

"Was he successful?"

"Yes, he was. And I was there. So—."

"And was the cat a man-eater?"

He hesitated. "No."

"And yet you think that applies in this case?"

He seemed not to know what to say.

"I'll help you break camp." I finished my tea and stood up. "Where do you live?"

"Nelspruit."

"Family there?"

"Alas, just some cousins in England."

"There's a village nearby where my friends are waiting for me. We can—."

"The village where the little girl lived?"

"Yes."

"The village didn't help her. What difference does it make where I sleep?"

I thought of Valeria with her back to the wall and the Rigby in her lap. "Believe me, it makes a difference now."

"No, thank you."

He took off his boots and tossed them aside.

"I'd keep them on."

But he ignored me as he rubbed his feet.

"It's madness to sleep out here alone. Come in with me."

"I have a fire."

"No leopard is afraid of a campfire."

He looked skeptical.

"Trust me," I said. "That's just a story foolish amateurs mumble in the night to make themselves feel safe. If *Yingwe* comes to pay his respects, he'll look at this fire and smile."

I turned away and had taken just a few steps toward camp when I suddenly turned around on a whim. "Do you happen to know Baron Von Roon?"

"The Prussian murderer? Oh, yes."

"You've heard about the boy then?"

"Sir Alfred started an investigation, but no one will talk, so it already died. Faster than the boy under the *sjambok*."

"Do you know if the baron is back in the field?"

"I believe so. The story I got was that he thought the man-eater might circle north and east. Toward the southern edge of the escarpment. So that's where he's probably heading."

"Smart man," I said as I turned away.

"Captain."

I looked back.

"There's no justice in this world."

"There's more justice than you could ever dream of," I said, reflecting on the sad fact that age had brought him little wisdom.

"The boy is gone."

"And the jungle will bring a reckoning."

Then I tried again to get him to come in, but there was no reasoning whatsoever with Cyril Lloyd of Nelspruit.

"What's wrong?" I said to Valeria standing with her rifle at the open gate of the village.

"What do you think?"

I was sure there was no other woman on earth who had so perfected the look of infinite exasperation.

I spread my arms in a question.

"There are about ten minutes of daylight left."

I fought back a smile. "And you were worried about Rixton of Africa being struck down in darkness?"

"Oh, dear God," she said, turning and walking away, "why do I try to live a life like this?"

"Val."

She stopped and turned back around.

"Thank you."

Her entire body seemed to relax. "You're aging me. Do you know that?"

"Dusk," I said and smiled. "He's well." Then I told her Lloyd's story.

"Oh, Hil," she said and ran up to me and looked beyond my shoulder. "Where's Mr. Lloyd?"

"He says he's sleeping out there tonight."

"Alone? Doesn't he know how dangerous that is now?"

"He does. But unless we drag him in by the feet, he won't come."

"But that's no way for a man to leave this world."

"It's his choice, not ours. But he might come in on his own if we let him. That's all we can hope for."

"We'll leave it to God then," she said, staring off into the dark forest.

I smiled. "You care more about people than you like to let on."

"I don't understand people at all. I never have."

I had no answer for that.

"And he's sure he saw Dusk on the way to the *Draak*?"

"Yes. We'll go up there and get him after dealing with our friend down here."

She bit her lip and seemed unable to speak.

"And if *Yingwe* gets us and we don't make it," I said, "Dusk can live a nice life up there on The Dragon's Tail."

Tears filled her eyes. "Thank you," she whispered. "And God bless Mr. Lloyd for not harming my boy."

I decided it would do no good to tell her that Von Roon was heading up there.

"I've never understood why women cry when they're happy."

"Lord, give me strength. Haven't you ever had tears of joy?"

"Never."

She looked suddenly serious. "Truly?"

"Truly."

She smiled through her tears. "Maybe someday you'll meet someone who can cure that."

We walked across the village together and I told her about hearing the leopards sparring in the distance and then seeing the young male laughing silently at the laughing hyenas.

"The man-eater won't be back tonight, will he?"

"Probably not."

She shrugged. "I'll sit up anyway."

"And I'll relieve you at midnight the way we planned."

She touched my shoulder gently. "Sweet dreams, *kaptein*," she said with a smile.

I dared not even imagine what those dreams might be.

Hoofbeats behind us flattened any plans of dreams in the immediate future.

I turned around and saw Kuskarohr riding into the village in the last of the fading light.

"Do you know who that is?" Valeria asked.

"Von Roon's serf."

For some intuitive reason I still cannot fully explain, I gently took Valeria's rifle from her and laid it against the wall of the hut. Jon was just coming out, and the three of us walked over to where Kuskarohr was dismounting his chestnut Thoroughbred in the center of the village.

People started gathering, and Simon was carrying a lantern.

"I need shelter for the night," Kuskarohr demanded with his usual grace.

Simon nodded. "You're welcome here, sir."

The couple who had lost their daughter came out of their hut and stood beside us. Valeria slid her arm around Sarah in unconscious comfort and affection.

"Where's Von Roon?" I asked.

"Barberton. Talking with the magistrate. Some little matter about one of our boys who died."

"How?"

"Cut himself and got blood poisoning."

"Cut himself with what?"

He shrugged. "Who can say?"

"Philip," Simon said to the young husband, "water the gentleman's horse."

Philip went over to his mount and began to lead him away, but stopped as Sarah joined him and she began stroking the horse. A tiny smile managed to light her lovely face as she slid her hand along the sleek neck.

"Is the baron going to be out here again soon?" I asked.

"Very soon."

"Tell him to be careful. Those *sjamboks* can be dangerous."

Kuskarohr looked at me with surprise and perhaps a hint of fear. Then, to change the subject, he turned and glared at Philip.

"You were told to water that horse!" he shouted and went to take back his animal. As he did, his bulk pushed Sarah aside, not so much deliberately as indifferently, and she lost her balance and fell to one knee.

A lifetime of wandering the wildest places on earth has scorched into me a thousand memories never to be smoothed away. And yet that night I witnessed something I could not have imagined and that will stay fresh and alive within me until my final day.

With the swiftness of *Yingwe* himself, Valeria sprang at Kuskarohr. Her left arm shot out and the heel of her hand slammed into his right shoulder and spun him toward her. Then with a fist of iron she fired a right cross straight into the center of his face and dropped him like a brain-shot elephant.

Kuskarohr's head crashed into the ground as he hit, and, half-dazed, he pushed his hands against the dirt as he struggled to get up. With a feline pounce, Valeria leaped over him and straddled his torso and her right boot smashed his left hand into the ground. He howled in pain as she whipped her knife from its sheath.

"Never touch one of these people again! Never! *Verstaan jy?*"

"*Ja,*" he managed to gurgle.

His nose was shattered and bleeding and his upper lip crushed.

"So help me God, I'll open you up. I'll drop your intestines right here!" She pressed the knifepoint against his gut. "And when the hyenas are finished grinding you up, you'll be gone *sonder 'n spoor.* Understand?"

He was so stunned he could barely nod.

"And no one will ever know. No one except Valeria Vanderveer and God. And *that* I can live with."

She pulled the blade away and swept it upward and flicked it against his chin and sliced the flesh, and blood trickled onto his throat like the stain of permanent sin.

"Now water your horse and get out!"

She leaped to the side with the grace of a panther and with one arm scooped Sarah up onto her feet.

Once again I was reminded how often I wallow in error, for "*half*-feral" hardly covered it at all.

18

IF YOU'RE GOING TO BE SUCCESSFUL IN YOUR PURSUIT OF THE SPOTTED CAT, IT'S BEST TO REMEMBER THAT A LEOPARD, ANY LEOPARD, IS NOT SO MUCH A QUARRY AS AN ADVERSARY, AND A WORTHY ONE AT THAT.
--SPORTSMAN BRUCE WOODS

NORMALLY I CAN SLEEP lying on the edge of a razor blade, but this evening I dozed fitfully and woke up about eleven-thirty. I was surprised to see Jon still awake. Before settling in, I had made a gentle joke about the wild woman in our lethal trio, but Jon failed to respond and seemed troubled and preoccupied with his own thoughts.

Now he was sitting with his back to the wall of the rondavel with his legs up, his arms around them, and his body leaning forward with his forehead resting against his knees. The oil lantern was still lit and several sheets of writing paper lay on the ground beside him.

"Would you believe I can feel you staring at me?" he said without raising his head.

I smiled. "The school of the lowveld is working well."

He looked up. "Isn't that what the squirrel slayer thought right before the man-eater invited him to dinner?"

"Could be," I said, laughing.

"I just finished writing ten minutes ago. I'd like you to read it."

He picked up the papers and handed them to me.

"I'm thinking of inserting this as some sort of interpolation, but I'm not sure. Maybe I won't even include it at all. I'd like your advice."

"What's this all about?"

He gestured at the sheets. "It's in there."

UNTITLED

Over the last few weeks in the African bush, and perhaps during just the last few days, I have felt as if the world has changed. Of course it has not. I have changed. Two great shifts in my thinking have shaken me, and with not even a single professor to tell me what I should think or how I should think it.

The first seismic upheaval concerns my conception of justice. People who have never seen more than three trees together in one place, people who have never smelled the scent of a lion or heard the call of a jackal, often speak with a sneer of "the law of the jungle." These people know nothing. But I do know. I lack the philosophical sophistication to explain it with Aristotelian eloquence, so I will simply provide an example.

Today I saw a brutish white man push aside a delicate little African woman and she fell to the ground. Instantly a white woman who cares for her came to her aid, and not with a disapproving word or a censorious shake of the head but with a six-inch steel blade. Why? Is knocking someone down a capital offense? No. There are no felonies here, but, then, there are no misdemeanors, either. Why is that? Because in the real jungle, the noble jungle, there is no one shaving the truth as if peeling the skin off a rancid grape. There are no elegant attorneys armed with deceptive speech like beautiful flowers flush with lethal toxins. There are no relatives weeping and wailing for the "fine man" who stepped out of line just this once. No credulous juries, no exhausted judges. There is life and there is death. That is enough. Had the woman opened up the man with her steel, it would have horrified me just a few weeks ago. Today it would have meant nothing. Or, as my friend Captain Rixton might say, less than nothing.

The second shift in my thinking has been even more subtle, and I doubt my ability to explain it with even a hint of the lucidity it deserves, but I will try.

I described earlier the circumstances of the killing of the little girl by the leopard and her appearance as we found her. I did this not to shock but to instruct. Yet my depiction of that scene as we saw it is its least important aspect. Its profundity lies elsewhere.

If a person is beaten senseless by thugs in an alley near Five Points, reporters refer to that person as a victim. This is customary. Likewise the little girl we examined today might be labeled by the thoughtless as a victim of the leopard. I have come to realize that this is not true, cannot be true, and never will be true. The reason is that there can be no victim where there is no crime, just as there can be no crime where there are no criminals. The child was not a "victim" of the hungry cat any more than oxygen is a victim of my lungs. She is a uniquely vital essence in this rolling cycle of birth and maturation and dissolution. And life here, as well as its passing, occurs not in the squalid streets of what I once foolishly believed was some sort of progress over the primitive. The little girl fulfilled her destiny in the depths of an eerie and blameless netherworld of light and darkness, with no gray areas between. A month ago I had thought that I had merely taken an excursion to another continent. As spectacular as that venture has been, it is also far more, for my journey now is infused with a philosophical dimension I could never have imagined. Captain Rixton has pulled aside for me an enchanted curtain and encouraged me to pass not simply into a forest, but into the infinite purity of the primeval. From its embrace I both fear and hope there can be no escape.

After I finished reading, I set the papers down beside him. "You'd be wise not to change a single word."

I picked up my rifle and left him alone with the night.

"You're early," Valeria said with a smile as I went outside and joined her. "Here, lean against the cushions."

"Stay where you are. I'm fine." I sat against the wall and laid the rifle across my lap with the muzzle pointing in the opposite direction from Valeria.

"Very quiet tonight," she said.

"What do you expect?"

She gave me a puzzled look.

"Who'd dare rouse your ire? Neither civilized man nor jungle beast."

"Oh, stop," she said, turning away, but I could see she was trying not to smile. "Anyway, I let Kuskarohr stay the night."

"After his invigorating session with you, I hope he has a change of underwear."

She laughed in spite of herself. "Was I that bad?"

"I already told you you're not bad at all. Just untamed."

"Then beware, *kaptein*," she said with a fierce squint.

"Why do you think I'm sitting with my back to the wall?"

She smiled. "Jon and I were talking about you."

"I know. I was feeling some gas pains."

"You're a terrible person. Has anyone ever told you that?"

"A woman did once. But she was ambivalent, I think."

"Don't change the subject."

"What subject?"

She laughed again. "The one I'm thinking about."

"Oh, that one."

"Jon said you're a mystic."

"What could anyone from New York know about mystics?"

"Is he right?"

"I don't even know what he means."

"He said you told him animals have souls."

"Oh, that. Of course. And there's nothing mystical about it. Common sense if you've lived with them for a day."

"But isn't it strange to believe such a thing?"

She seemed uncertain, testing me.

"A famous saint named San Juan de la Cruz said that all creatures are traces of the passing of God."

"And do you believe that?"

"Yes."

The last remnants of her ice wall finally melted away. "I believe it, too. Dusk convinced me. I'll always believe it."

"And does that make you feel mystical?"

She sighed and smiled. "It makes me feel happy."

"Me, too."

After a short silence, she said, "Hil, have you ever been married? Jon and I talked about it, but he didn't know."

"Don't they teach etiquette in this country?"

"I don't know that word."

"*Etiket.*"

"Oh," she said, smiling some more. "That one. Apparently not."

"No, I've never been married. Close once, but that's all."

"Close?"

"My love called it off three days before the wedding."

"Oh, Hil," she said, and laid a hand on mine. "I'm sorry for asking."

"Long ago. It doesn't matter."

"I don't understand how someone could do something like that."

"What? Marry me or call it off?"

"Will you stop it, please? You know what I mean."

"Well, better three days before than three minutes after."

"Yes, and we won't talk about it anymore," she said and turned away.

I kept staring at the side of her face until she looked back.

"Can you see inside my head?"

"Certainly. The untamed are my business."

"Why, Hil? Why three days?"

"She'd suddenly regained her sight like the blind healed by Christ."

"You mean she was right?"

"Of course she was."

Valeria looked out across the darkened village and did her best not to ask anything more.

"And I'll tell you why," I said, "because if I don't, I know you won't sleep tonight."

She shook her head and laughed. "Is there a window on the side of my brain?"

"Every woman has one. But not every man knows how to peek in at the correct angle."

"Waiting for a cattle-killing leopard over a staked-out goat isn't half as demanding as having a conversation with you. *Weet jy dat?*"

"Yes, I know."

"So why was she right?"

"A few months later she wrote to me and told me why . . . the most disturbing thing anyone has ever said to me. She said that the qualities she found most attractive in me were the same ones that frightened her the most."

Valeria seemed bewildered. "What qualities? Did she say what she meant?"

"My faith in primitive laws beyond the decrees of man. Those were her exact words."

"Did you answer her?"

"I told her that God created the true laws—the laws of nature—but most men have done everything they could to pervert them."

"And she was afraid of that?"

"She said she was embarrassed to admit that what I said was so raw and brutal it excited her. But it terrified her at the same time."

After a long silence Valeria said, almost angrily, "She was a coward and a fool."

"We're all of us cowards in our own way." I smiled. "Except the Princess of the Amazons."

"Your virtues aren't your vices. Only an immature woman would believe such a thing."

"Possibly."

"What became of her? Do you know?"

"Harriet Martindale didn't lack for suitors. Very dark hair and almost violet eyes. Quite attractive, though in a rather severe way."

"You didn't answer my question."

"She married a Quaker schoolteacher from Pennsylvania."

"Oh, Good Lord. From a captain to a Quaker. . . ."

"Time for you to get some sleep, isn't it? *Yingwe* is on the move."

She turned away and gazed off toward the forest beyond the gate. "Not yet. I'm not tired at all."

We sat in silence for a while. Finally, still looking into the darkness, she said, "Your fine qualities don't frighten Ginger. They never will."

Nothing frightens Ginger, I thought.

She seemed rigid as marble and still angry at a woman she had never met. "I want you to know that. Always."

"And my vices?"

"When I start tripping over them, I'll let you know."

We sat quietly for a few minutes, and then she said, "Hil, may I ask you something?"

"More about my autobiography?"

She hesitated. "No, I don't think so. But it's something I've been wondering about since the day I met you. It's probably not important but . . . I don't know . . . it just keeps fluttering around in my mind."

"Well, we can't have any fluttering when we're on the trail of a man-eater. So what is it?"

"When I apologized for being rude to you that first day, you got a strange look on your face. Then you said something, I don't remember what, but it was your facial expression I can't get out of my mind. I didn't understand it."

"It was admiration."

"For apologizing?"

"That's the point. You didn't apologize."

"But I did. I—."

I held up my hand. "No, what you did was far deeper. When a person says he apologizes, he's actually saying he's still in charge. And he's making sure the other person knows it. 'I APOLOGIZE.' I've never been impressed by that. He's just flashing his own ego. Do you see what I mean?"

She hesitated. "I'm not sure."

"But when a man or woman asks for forgiveness, as you did, that's very different."

"How? I don't understand."

"You're laying yourself open to the other person's rejection. You did exactly that when you said, 'Will you forgive me, captain?'."

"But what—?"

"It's trusting. And an act of bravery. I might have slapped you down. Or tried to."

"But you didn't."

"How could you have known that in advance? When people say, 'I apologize', they expect a medal for it, but they've done almost nothing."

"Yet all I did was—."

"When the Princess of the Amazons asked, 'Will you forgive me?', she opened herself up. Bared her breast." I smiled. "So to speak."

For several long moments, Valeria was quiet. Then a slow smile spread across her face. "I was right, that woman *was* a coward and a fool." A breeze swept across the village and she turned up the collar of her jacket. "It's cool tonight."

"It's foolish for two people to be cold if they're together," I said and invited her toward me with a welcoming arm.

She smiled as she slid against me, and her muscular body instantly softened beneath my arm like a cuddled lamb. Then she murmured something so quietly I could not make it out, and in about two minutes she was sound asleep.

19

THE NIGHT HAS EARS.
----MASAI PROVERB

"Well," I said as I dropped to one knee and examined the pug marks just outside the game trail.

Valeria came up to me with Jon right behind.

"*Yingwe.*" I gestured to his tracks on top of my boot prints and smiled.

Jon looked at me as if I were mad.

"It's not the first time a man-eater has covered my backtrail. I doubt it'll be the last."

Jon bent down and examined the tracks. "Do you think he followed you?"

"No, he wouldn't have shown himself in daylight. I'm sure these were made long after I was back in the village."

"Well, I'm concerned about you anyway."

"I'm touched."

"Oh, it has nothing to do with you."

I raised an eyebrow at him but said nothing.

"I just worry that if I let anything happen to you, Ginny will never forgive me and won't marry me."

I heard Valeria laughing softly behind me.

"Seriously," Jon said, "why did he turn around?"

"Who can say why?"

"And that saved Lloyd's life," Valeria said as she examined the ellipse the leopard had made as he had returned to the denser bush.

"True enough," I said. "If he'd kept going, he'd have run into him dozing by his fire."

After our light breakfast of coffee and biscuits, Simon had wished us well, and we had ventured off in our search for *Yingwe*.

Valeria was as fresh as a blossom, as she was every morning, but Jon seemed fully as lively as a withered vine. What he had written the previous night had shown that he was learning, to the detriment of his sleep, that the risks to his flesh posed by a man-eating leopard were far less perilous than the lethal rebuke the forest primeval hurled at his once-comforting metaphysical delusions.

Valeria looked off to the south. "I hope Lloyd went home."

"Hard to say," I answered. "It seemed to me like he was asking for martyrdom."

She turned and followed the leopard's trail back toward the trees.

"We'll lose that spoor soon enough," I said to Jon and pointed to the faint pug marks Valeria was following into the jungle. "But I'm assuming he'll keep on in that direction, though one never knows. Swinging northeast in his loop."

"And then?"

"There are a few small villages that way. He might not know that yet, but his keen ears will hear any activity. So he might be drawn there for an easy meal."

"They're at risk, too, then?"

"We'll head that way now. Though I'm sure he'll get there before us."

"Hil!" Valeria called, and I quickly joined her at the edge of the forest.

She nodded at the marks on the ground. "Somebody cut the leopard's trail."

Boot prints overlay the leopard's pug marks where the cat had vanished into the woodland.

"Lloyd?"

I nodded in disgust. "He's determined to die."

Jon came up next to me. "You know Lloyd's tracks?"

"Nothing special about that. I make it a point to check everyone's boots so I recognize them if I see them again in the bush. Common sense."

We walked along the game trail in silence, and after about twenty minutes Jon said, "May I speak?"

"Why not?"

"I didn't want to alert the leopard."

"If he's interested in who's following his backtrail, he already knows. So talk."

"I was wondering if we can camp out in the open if we have to."

"We can as long as one of us is always awake to stand watch."

"Makes sense. And I guess we'd better be sure we have a big fire, too."

I noticed Valeria smile and turn away.

"What?" Jon said

He looked, as the Afrikaners like to say, as baffled as a monkey on a stick.

"Cats aren't afraid of fire," I answered.

"But I thought—."

"Why should they be? They see fire all the time. It's part of their lives."

"I've read, though, that—."

"You've read campfire tales from once-a-year hunters. Naturally if cats are in the middle of a blazing forest they'll be scared. Who wouldn't be? But a campfire? Or a burning torch? It's nothing to them."

Jon seemed disappointed. "I don't think my readers are going to believe me."

"What does that matter?"

He should have remained quiet but chose not to. "I have my reputation to protect."

Valeria snapped around like he had just splashed her with scalding water. "*So wat?*" She stared at him with the glare of

Medusa. "Have any of your readers ever been brave enough to track a man-eater?"

"Is that a rhetorical question?"

She looked at me in confusion.

"Retoriese vraag," I answered.

"No," she said to Jon. *"Antwoord my!* Answer me!"

"No, I guess they haven't."

"But *you* are. So stop worrying about the opinions of people you'll never meet."

"I have an obligation to make sure — ."

"And don't dare question a man of iron who was facing tigers when your *kak* was still yellow and wet."

Stunned, Jon stared at her as if he were trying to decide if Valeria Vanderveer and Ginny Delamere were even members of the same species.

Valeria glanced at me and under her breath said, *"Jy krap met ń kort stokkie aan ń groot leeu se bal,"* and then turned and continued down the trail.

"That," I said, "is her special way of telling you you're being arrogant. And that it's a risk you don't want to take."

Even though Valeria's back was to us, I could just make out the side of her face and could see her expression softening into a smile. I had never known anyone whose flashpoint was so low and yet who could cool so quickly.

"So what does it mean?" Jon asked. "Exactly."

"It means," Valeria said without turning around as she walked on, *"Don't test the patience of the captain."*

But my laughter at her answer clearly told Jon there was more to it than that.

"And literally?" he asked me.

"It's an Afrikaner proverb warning you not to scratch the lion's testicles with a short stick."

Obviously shocked at Valeria's indelicacy, he turned and looked at her continuing along the trail ahead of him and seemed to have made up his mind — this woman was a species entirely to herself.

I had made the campfire especially large, so Jon would have something picturesque to describe in his chronicle and not disappoint his readers. The blaze also nicely knocked the edge off a cool night.

About thirty feet wide, the glade had been used as a campsite many times before, the massive charred area in the center of the clearing dating back probably decades.

"I don't see any human remains," I had said with a figurative elbow into Jon's ribs as I began clearing away some ancient debris. "So I guess we're safe for an hour or two."

"You two are merciless, I hope you realize that," he answered and then glanced at Valeria for a reaction.

However, the woman of the forest either failed to hear him or else ignored him as she circled the perimeter while her keen eyes scanned the jungle for any threats while I worked.

"I'll take the first watch," she said, and if one could not feel secure with such a sentry as she, all hope was lost.

An hour later we were stretched out on our bedrolls and sipping hot tea after our meal. Outside the circle of light from the fire, the enveloping forest, ominously opaque, draped around us like a shroud of black velvet.

Valeria was leaning back on her left elbow, a tin cup in her other hand, as she eyed Jon's expression like a tracker examining an interesting pug mark. Her rifle lay beside her.

Motionless, Jon was staring into the flames.

"Some squirrel hunt, don't you think?" I said.

He jumped with a start and looked over at me. "I'm sorry. . . what was that?"

"Sorry, I didn't mean to interrupt your ontological reflections."

"My . . . ?" He shook his head. "I don't even know that word."

"Some writer."

He tried not to smile but failed. "I was just thinking that any sane person should feel scared out here . . . ." He gestured at the surrounding darkness. "But I don't. And I'm not sure why."

"Valeria's Rigby."

He looked over at her. "Yes, but I'm talking about a different kind of safety. . . . Maybe that's not the right word anyway. . . ."

Valeria picked up the pot and went over and refilled Jon's cup.

He looked up as she smiled down at him.

He smiled back. "Just when I think you're all steel and no sheath, you startle me."

"I enjoy baffling people."

She returned the pot to the edge of the fire and lay back down on her blanket.

Jon turned again to me. "Not safety really . . . comfort, maybe. No, not that either. Completion, I think. And purity. Definitely that."

I smiled but said nothing.

"Out here in the bush everything is stripped away. Most of what I thought matters most doesn't matter in the least."

"And," I said, "things you never even stopped to think about matter most of all."

"Yes."

His voice was so low I barely heard it above the crackling of the fire.

"Out there," I said, "there's a man-eating cat. Brilliant and daring. And maybe watching us right now. And yet you feel at ease. Even though you know you're not completely safe."

"Yes," he answered with the serene and thankful look of a penitent in church who had just emerged from the confessional. "And I love that feeling more than I can describe."

"Welcome to the lowveld," Valeria said.

He smiled. "Thank you."

"You've learned something that few ever learn," I told him. "You've realized that there are only three things in life that truly matter. A good gun to see you through this day, the well-being of those you care for, and the integrity of your soul."

He hesitated and then said, "But deep down I wonder if I'm lying to myself."

"In what way?"

"Life can't really be that simple, can it? As simple as the jungle makes it seem?"

"Oh, yes it can. And is—for the fortunate few who come to comprehend it."

"But there are other important matters. . . ."

He turned to Valeria, as if for help, but she offered none.

"What kind of matters?" I asked.

He looked like he was about to speak and then burst out laughing. "I guess I'm not sure. I can't even think of them at the moment."

"You mean the hundreds of nothings that city people concern themselves with every minute of the day?"

"Yes, I suppose that's what I mean."

"Cobwebs destined to blow away on the wind."

"I just. . ." He looked away. "I don't understand how . . . how life honed down to the bone can seem so rich. Can *be* so rich."

"You do understand," I said, "but not with the logic of Aristotle."

"I'm not following you."

"You grasp it here." I hit my chest with my fist. "With a primordial wisdom born thousands of years ago. Before the bloodless rationality of wise old Greeks."

"Jon . . . ." Valeria said.

He turned toward her.

"You didn't know you had that understanding in you, but you did. It was always there. . . ." She paused, obviously searching for a word, and then she looked at me. "*Rus?*"

"Dormant."

"Dormant, Jon, inside you. But not anymore." She smiled at him with the affection of a wise older sister. "Because now . . . now you've come to Africa."

He seemed to consider that for a moment. "But don't you get lonely out here?"

"Sometimes," she said softly.

"And you, captain?"

"With Miriam and Joseph? How could I be lonely? They're worth ten legions of New Yorkers. And Buc is with me, too."

"I realize that and yet—."

"And besides," I said, sweeping my arm around at the thousands of creatures in the forest all around us, "was Noah lonely?"

"Well, you know I didn't mean that."

"Do I?"

"I meant lonely for other things."

"Like what? Noise and dirt? Pickpockets and streetwalkers? Or the squirrels in Central Park?"

"But you still come back to New York sometimes. You even have a home there."

"So?"

"Well, doesn't that mean something?"

"I return so I don't lose perspective."

"Meaning what?"

"Meaning I don't want to spend so much time in the jungle that I forget myself and start rubbing my face against tree trunks and urinating on bushes."

Valeria burst out laughing, and Jon turned away to hide his own laughter.

"I give up," he said, still facing away from me.

I nodded. "Wise choice."

After a minute or so of silence, he sounded suddenly serious. "I'm so grateful for this." He swept an arm toward the dark forest around us. "For all of this. Thank you."

"We haven't done anything," Valeria said.

"You're just like him. Never taking credit for what you do."

"Credit for what?" I asked.

"Don't you see? By bringing me here, you took a tiny pebble and tossed it into the water. And now the little waves are rippling outward forever."

"You make too much of too little," I said.

"Oh, no I don't. And I'll share this . . . how did you put it . . . this primordial wisdom. This deeper morality beyond the shallow values of unenlightened men."

Firelight plays tricks, but there might have been tears in his eyes.

"I'll share it with Ginny, and we'll share it with our children. And with our children's children. The waves will ripple on. To infinity."

He averted his eyes and looked toward the fire.

"And most of all I'm thankful for *Yingwe*. For the terrifying privilege of peering into the soul of the Lord of the Darkness." Jon turned back to me. "I'll be grateful to you for that forever."

We sat in silence for what seemed like a week, and then I stood up. "Let me bring you back out of the clouds." I walked across the clearing and picked up two small logs from our little pile and placed them beside each other near Jon about three feet from the edge of the fire. "Once when I was in India near Panar there were two orphan brothers. They were about fourteen and fifteen and survived by tending goats for others. Sometimes they slept in shacks. More often, though, out in the open. One night they were camping with a huge fire in a clearing. They'd just delivered some goats to their new owner." I pointed to the logs. "They were sleeping like that. In the middle of the night a tiger called in the distance and woke the younger one. When he opened his eyes, he saw a leopard carrying off his brother. They'd been sleeping about a yard apart, and yet the boy had heard nothing. No cry or struggle. Now the leopard was walking away with his kill about a foot from the edge of the fire and off into the jungle beyond." I went back to my bedroll. "So sleep lightly."

20

LEOPARDS . . . LEARN FROM THEIR MISTAKES (AND FROM YOURS), AND THEY LEARN MORE QUICKLY THAN ANY OTHER AFRICAN GAME ANIMAL EXCEPTING THE ELEPHANT.

----*SPORTSMAN BRUCE WOODS*

DEATH HAS A FACE, although few ever see it, at least without the delicate flatteries of the undertaker's hand. Soldiers see it. And doctors and policemen do as well. Yet most people who live in cities think of man's end, when they think of it at all, the way they read about it in storybooks or watch it portrayed on the stage. The gentle closing of the eyes and a soft loll of the head, and perhaps a not too severe drop of an arm to insure that those in the last row grasp the meaning of what they are seeing. Every nurse on earth wishes it were so. I know because one of my dearest friends is a nurse. Thinking of all I had witnessed on the American frontier and in the jungles of the world, I once casually asked her how often she saw people drift off and die with their eyes closed as in stories and plays. The question startled her—clearly she had never been asked that before—and also brought a look of sadness. She said it was probably less than one time in ten. The other ends were too bleak to contemplate.

I thought of her kind heart now as I knelt beside the body of a young white man slain by the most proficient feline predator I had ever known. Both of the corpse's eyes were open, hideously. Yet they did not gape in fear or horror, as some over-imaginative armchair adventurer might guess. Instead, the eyelids sagged like shrouds. Even more macabre, they did not do so equally. The right lid drooped halfway and the left about two thirds. No remnant here of a true human gaze but only a cold and gruesome simulacrum of it.

I tried to close the man's eyes, but *rigor mortis* sneered at me.

From what we were able to determine, he had been pulled from the tree in which he had been sitting over a tethered goat and had been quickly killed with little struggle. Then he had been carried about a hundred yards into the dense brush where we had found him thanks to the buzzing of the flies.

Compared to his unnerving stare, his wounds seemed almost incidental. His jacket and shirt had been sliced open and his chest had been stripped of meat, as had the right side of his face and neck. Evidently this had sated *Yingwe*, and so he had hidden the body here in the scrub in order to be able to feed later at his leisure. His pug marks were all around.

We had no idea who the man was. He looked about twenty-five and carried nothing by which we could identify him. My guess was that he was one of those naïve lads lusting for glory who had thought he could oh-so-easily bag The Man-Eating Leopard of Mpumalanga.

Valeria kept the little goat by her side with a piece of twine looped over its neck, and Jon held the dead man's rifle.

Valeria looked at me, and I knew what she was thinking.

"I believe he will," I said.

Jon turned to me. "Will what?"

"He stashed the body here, so he'll probably be coming back," I said.

"Could he be watching us now?" Jon asked, gazing off into the forest.

"Of course. But there's a stream not far from here, and he probably went there for a drink. He might be lying up near the water."

Jon glanced at the man's rifle. "This is clean, Hil. He never got off a shot."

"We'd have heard it if he had."

"Have you ever known of anybody being pulled from a tree like this?"

"Once. In India. But he wasn't eaten, just killed."

"Any idea how this happened?"

"I'd guess it never occurred to him that this leopard might have been shot at from a tree before. An ordinary leopard never looks up for enemies because there aren't any dangers to him from the trees. But this is an educated cat, as I told you a while back. He's learned."

"Why didn't he eat the goat?"

"Who can say? He didn't eat any in Lucy's village either."

"Is it possible he's developed a taste for people and prefers that now?"

"Anything is possible." I turned away and we headed toward the game trail. "We'll go back to camp and try to get some early sleep. We have a long night ahead of us." I pointed to the jackalberry trees all around. "There are plenty of good perches here, but I don't want you dozing and sliding out of one."

"Very kind of you."

"I do try."

"But, seriously, suppose I really did fall? What would—?"

"Oh, don't worry about that," Valeria said. "The leopard won't kill you."

Both of us turned toward her in surprise.

"Why not?" Jon asked.

"I'll shoot you before you hit the ground. Or at least on the first bounce."

I laughed, but Jon looked annoyingly grim.

"I don't understand the two of you," he said. "How you can joke after what we just saw."

"All we saw were the remains of a meal," Valeria said, walking toward the head of the line with the little goat. "Just accept it and move on."

"I'm trying."

She stopped and turned around. "I'm sorry. I know you are." She reached down and slid her hand along the goat's back.

"This happy fellow won't survive an hour out here alone. I'm going to take him back to Simon's village."

In my adventures with the volatile sex, I had learned that one could sometimes argue effectively even about cataclysmic upheavals, but prevailing in small matters was as likely as bagging a tiger with one of those little "Liquid Pistols" that mischievous boys were beginning to carry.

"Don't linger," I said. "Get back as soon as you can."

I was startled at the hint of anxiety in my voice. Evidently she was, too, because she spun around with a look of surprise.

"Don't worry," she said with a smile. "I won't end up as a cat's dinner. I know I have more than one little *bokkie* like this to look after."

21

LEOPARDS LURK IN DARK CORNERS.
----NIGERIAN PROVERB

JON AND I HEADED BACK to camp to rest, but our quest for Morpheus was only intermittently successful. So about an hour before sundown I brewed us some fresh coffee. As men often do, we nursed our coffee and our thoughts in silence.

"Hil," Jon finally said as he was finishing his third cup, "there's something I've been meaning to ask you about all those memoirs you had me read. Not many of those people seem to agree on when leopards hunt."

"When . . . ?"

"Time of day."

I smiled. "You've read well. They're all over the map."

"Why?"

"Because they're no different than the rest of the human race. They assume their experience is the only experience worth considering."

"And yours?"

"It varies. Some leopards rarely hunt when the moon is up. Unless they're starving and desperate, they'll hunt after dusk but before the moon rises or wait until it sets. Even if it's just a quarter moon."

"And the others?"

I smiled. "Some of them laugh at astronomy. And other leopards obviously don't care in the least about their reputation as lords of the darkness and will hunt on a beautiful sunny day at noon."

"And our friend out there?"

"That's a different situation. I've never known a man-eater to hunt in daylight. And at night rarely before the moon goes down. But *Yingwe* isn't hunting tonight. He's just finishing his own meal in a place he's hidden it, so I think he won't care as much about moonlight. At least that's what I'm hoping."

"This probably sounds crazy, but can you shoot by starlight?"

"No. But there's something called zodiacal light that can help in rare cases. But we can't rely on it here."

"I've never heard of that."

"At this time of year down here below the equator it's a soft light visible low in the sky in the morning. It's called false dawn. But it's useful for shooting only if you have open terrain. Only if you can see the horizon and can make out a silhouette. The forest is too dense here for that."

After a short silence, Jon said, "And what if we fail?"

"Then tomorrow we'll—."

"No, fail completely, I mean."

"Do you expect to?"

"What about the eight hunters you told me about who were eaten by the leopard in India? The one that's still alive and outwitting everyone. Or the tiger who killed the mail carrier and vanished. What if that happens here?"

"Then more helpless people will die. Is that what you're asking?"

"I guess what I really mean is how do we *know* if we've failed? When do we admit he's outsmarted us?"

Jon had no idea how much I admired him for the insight implicit in that question, an enigma that has tortured the hunter of man-eaters since the invention of gunpowder, and probably long before.

"There is no answer," I said, "except in each man's heart."

"And in yours?"

"My people are living in fear and mourning in darkness. I go on until the end."

"*Yingwe's?*"

"Or mine."

"I'll stay with you until the last act."

I smiled. "Or the final curtain."

"Yes," he said seriously. "Or that."

"But there's one exception. If he keeps moving north, others are going to have to deal with him."

"How far north?"

"Difficult to say. But if he roams back to Portuguese East Africa, then they're on their own. It might seem to you like we've come a long distance but we haven't. We're still not very far off my property. I'll protect my Shangaan family with my last breath, but I can't guard all of southern Africa."

Jon looked disappointed that the quest might have been for nothing. "Wouldn't that be ironic? For me to come all this way and never lay eyes on him."

"Don't worry," I said. "It won't come to that."

"How do you mean?"

"We're going to close with him. And it'll end, one way or another."

"How can you be sure?"

"Because it was meant to be."

He gave me that worldly and secular look that smelled of the alleys of Manhattan.

"Oh ye of little faith."

"All right," he said. "Explain."

"Too many strange happenstances. Do you think they were just random?"

"I guess I never actually considered it."

"Remember what I mentioned about my father? How he was a student of the Greeks and Romans? Well, so is his son."

"I must be really slow, because I'm not following you at all."

"The Fates."

"You believe this was foreordained?"

"Too many bizarre coincidences brought us here for this to have been an accident."

"What, the struggle between man and beast?"

"No, the battle between beast and beast. Written into the cosmos before the beginning of time."

"You mean Rixton of Africa and *Yingwe*? Why would — ?"

"A lowly *shikari* can never answer a 'why'. Only a 'what'."

I expected him to scoff, but he stared at me with the intensity of one of the scholars from Raphael's *School of Athens*. Then he poured himself more coffee but seemed to forget it was in his cup.

"Hil," he said finally, "if what you say is true, then I can't end up writing just a short series for *The Herald*."

It shocked me that he seemed to be relenting.

"I'm serious," he said as he saw my skeptical look.

"I agree that a few articles seem rather thin."

"I'll have to expand this later into a book. Something . . . maybe more philosophical."

I would have thought he would choke on the word, but he seemed to savor it.

"You have to realize it won't sell a hundred copies."

"I don't care. This is something that has to be brought home to people. I need to — ." Suddenly he burst out laughing. "Can you imagine a writer saying he doesn't care how many copies he sells?"

"Yes, I can," I answered in absolute seriousness. "If that writer is you."

He seemed touched but also baffled about what to say.

"Just remember to speak little of me in your book. Speak of *Yingwe*."

"But you're just as important."

"No. Don't ever think that."

"Then how can I — ?"

"Show your readers — even if there are only a hundred of them — that this isn't just a tale of a marauding cat with a brilliant intellect, a bad leg, and a will of iron. You have the talent and you have the courage."

He smiled but seemed unsure. "To do what?"

"To use your considerable powers to impress on your audience the truth of what you've learned."

He looked wary. "And that is?"

"That this cat isn't just a feline predator. That the leopard is—is above all—the living soul of the primeval."

Jon turned slowly away and stared off toward the forest.

"And," I went on, "that the half-mad Captain Rixton declares beyond doubt that the primeval is the beating heart of God."

Jon turned back and just stared at me for a minute, and then a slow smile began to spread across his face. "A hundred copies?" he said, laughing. "If I say that to the oh-so-clever Manhattan sophisticates, I won't sell ten."

"Well," I said, smiling, "you can always use the extra copies to soak up the cognoscenti's tears of godless laughter."

I noticed him look past my shoulder.

"The wild woman returns?" I asked.

"I've never seen a woman with a stride like that. A statement without words."

I stood up and turned around.

"Such a gentleman," Valeria said.

I removed my hat and bowed.

"See?" she said with a smile as she came into camp with all the delicacy of a thrown spear. "I wouldn't leave you poor little *welpies* defenseless out here."

"Thanks be to God," Jon said, trying to stifle his own smile.

"Did you think we were worried about your safety?" I asked.

"Desperately." She sat by the fire and laid down her rifle. "Aren't you going to offer a lady some coffee?"

"Lady?" Jon asked. "Do you know any?"

She sighed melodramatically.

He poured a cupful and handed it to her.

"*Dankie.*"

"All is well at the village?" I asked.

"Yes, but Simon told me he heard another white hunter was seen in the direction we're headed. But he didn't know who."

"Von Roon?" Jon asked, looking at me.

"Possibly. Maybe Kuskarohr." I shrugged. "Well, there's nothing we can do about it now." I turned to Valeria. "Have you eaten?"

"Yes. When do you want to start?"

"Finish your coffee," I said and began dousing the fire. "Then we can go."

She turned away and stared at the smoke rising from the hissing embers and slowly sipped her drink.

"Is something wrong?" I asked.

She looked up. "Why?"

"You look pensive."

She frowned slightly.

"*Peinsende*," I said.

She set down the cup. "I gave Sarah the little goat and she started crying. I can't stop thinking about it."

"I'm sure she doesn't get many gifts."

"That's what I thought, too, but that wasn't the reason. She saw I was startled and she said she wasn't crying about the goat. She was crying with happiness because she thought she'd never see me again. That I'd be devoured by the leopard."

"And did you tell her the truth?"

"What truth?"

I smiled. "That no leopard would dare."

"Oh, Hil," she said and reached up and took my right hand and just held it. "I really care for that girl."

"I know you do. Sarah and Philip will have a happy home at Hawthorne."

Valeria glanced at Jon and when she saw he was bent over and picking up his gear with his back to her, she quickly pressed her lips to my hand. "Thank you for saying that," she whispered.

"And I'll give them a place with me if you do get devoured."

She let my hand slide from her grasp and gave me a helpless smile. "You're aging me. Have I ever told you that?"

I reached for my rifle. "Jon, take the lantern. If we bag him late, I don't want to have to stumble back here in the dark."

We reached the small clearing with the leopard's kill about a half-hour before sunset. Shaped almost like a horseshoe, the clearing curled around about twenty feet at its widest. Before he had dined the previous night, *Yingwe* had dropped the corpse at the edge of the upper arc toward the base of a jackalberry. Dense forest stretched beyond that. I pointed to a tree to the right of the curve that I knew Jon would have no difficulty climbing, and he managed it easily. He settled into a fork and unslung his rifle and laid it across his lap. I had given him instructions not to shoot except in defense of his own life, and, if he did, to be certain neither Valeria nor I were behind the cat in the line of fire.

I pointed to a tree at the other end of the curve, and Valeria ascended it as though she had been born to it.

I had no idea from which direction *Yingwe* might approach. Yet in the chance that he would use as cover the tree near where the body lay, and so approach the kill from behind the trunk, I took my place in a large jackalberry at the open part of the horseshoe on the opposite side of the clearing to give me a clean view of the entire area.

If we were really lucky, he would come to feed at dusk when there was still plenty of light for me to see. Yet no such good fortune graced us here. In what seemed like only minutes, night enfolded us like Lazarus in his burial cloth.

It would be about an hour before moonrise, after which I expected that the chance of *Yingwe* appearing would be slight, unless, as I was hoping, he felt confident enough to return to his kill in moonlight. So we waited. In darkness, time does not "creep" or "crawl" or any of the other usual quaint expressions. Rather, it seems simply to lock in place. Even I, who had spent so much time peering from the forks of trees into blackness, was still helpless to gauge the pace of a night's passage.

At last the moon rose, and perhaps another half-hour had passed when the welcome sound of several vervet monkeys barking alarm calls alerted us. I pushed off the safety of my rifle, for these were not the alarms for a snake or a bird but of a predator on the ground. Given the area of origin of the calls, the animal seemed to be approaching from out of the jungle near the tree where the body lay. And, amazingly enough, doing so in moonlight. For once, the leopard had relaxed his caution.

I raised my rifle off my lap but did not shoulder it yet. It was foolish to risk getting arm weary before the animal even showed.

Then the last sound on earth I wanted to hear stabbed my ears like an icepick—the whooping of a hyena. And then more whoops and some gentle lowing as well.

The lead female, with the maddening arrogance unique to her kind, ignored the barking of the monkeys and emerged from the woodland behind the tree, and she was quickly followed by more of her clan than I could count even with the aid of moonlight. As eagerly as Ginny Delamere savoring the fragrance of lilacs on Long Island, their keen noses had picked up the scent of the putrefying corpse. In moments, the ripping of flesh and the crunching of bone melded into the uniquely primordial symphony of Africa.

I leaned my head back and took that deep breath of resignation that all too frequently signaled the hunter's failure, for I knew the keen ears of the leopard would have heard this killer choir from far off and he would never appear in my sights this night.

I slept poorly, and I suspected Valeria and Jon did no better. Valeria had taken the last watch, and all of us were now awake before dawn, and with little appetite. So we sat by the fire and just pumped coffee into ourselves to give our tired bodies some false reassurance.

Yingwe would have been on the move all night, of that I was certain. After having slept most of the day and then hearing the bestial chorus, he would have slipped silently away in the darkness in pursuit of other quarry. He was far ahead of us now.

"Hil . . ."

I looked over at Valeria.

"Yesterday I asked Simon if he might know anything about the young man pulled out of the tree by the leopard. I didn't mention it last night because I didn't want us to get distracted before the night ahead. . . ."

I smiled. "You're a wise Amazon."

"He said that late last year three young English soldiers had come through here searching for the man-eater. He thinks the dead man might be one of them."

"Did he give you a reason for believing that?" Jon asked.

"He said they told him they'd made an agreement. A kind of competition. Each one had put in twenty-five pounds, and whoever shot the man-eater would get the prize. If anyone quit, he'd forfeit his money. . . ."

She sipped her coffee.

"And?" I said, feeling my annoyance growing.

"After about a month, two of them wanted to go home. Too many people had been killed. It looked hopeless. One wanted to stay, though. The other two argued with him to go back with them—Simon overheard most of the conversation. The two told the other one he could have all the money, but they should leave the task to more skillful men. But the other soldier wouldn't relent. Simon thinks that's probably the dead man."

"Naturally," I said in disgust. "They're *Engelse*. Everything has to be a sporting contest to them. I know, I lived on that rainy rock. A cricket match or the Epsom Derby, it makes no difference. All the world is the playing fields of Eton, isn't it?" I tossed away the rest of my coffee. "For God's sake."

"It's brave, though," Jon said.

That was not even worth an answer.

"Well, isn't it?"

I noticed Valeria lay a hand on his arm for him to stop, but he seemed not to notice.

"No, it isn't," I said. "It's moronic. And it's obvious he wasn't doing it for the money. At least that might have made some sense. But this was for the glory. The man who slew the Mpumalanga Man-Eater! Maybe get his name in *The Times*. How grand. And for what?"

"Well, that's not nothing."

"And when he died in forty years, it might have earned a single line in his obituary. And four decades from now people reading it would've said, 'Mpumalanga? Where's that? Is it in Malaya? Was that a tiger?'"

Jon glanced at Valeria and then looked back at me. "You're harsh, captain."

"Am I? After all, I'm agreeing with you. You're absolutely right—it's not nothing. It's less than nothing. And now he's a meal for maggots."

Jon said no more but got up and began quietly pulling his gear together.

Valeria and I sat in silence for a while, and then she came and sat beside me. "Hil," she whispered, "trying to kill your own frustration by upsetting your friend or by cursing the foolishness of a dead man does you no credit." Her face was so close to mine I could count the soft strands in her ginger eyebrows.

"Thank you for the gentle slap," I said. "You're a far finer human being than I could ever hope to be."

"Oh, no," she answered with a hint of a smile. "Just prettier." She squeezed my wrist. "But one who's always had an incurable weakness for scarred men."

"Then I'm a very fortunate man."

She smiled again and pressed her lips to my forehead. "Yes, you certainly are."

22

THE LEOPARD STANDS OR DIES ALONE, AS A KING HAS TO.
----NATURALIST JEAN-PIERRE HALLET

I HAVE OFTEN THOUGHT the perfect time for a man to die is after the moon slips below the horizon on a cold December night. Not to imply a winter of discontent, not at all, but a poetically fitting dénouement to a fruitful life. And I have always believed that absolutely the cruelest time to be compelled to slough off this mortal coil is on a beautiful sunny morning with the birds caroling in the crisp air of a new day.

Such a day we savored now. We had heard a single gunshot somewhere north of us shortly before dawn when the birds had just begun, and we were now moving in that direction. The trees had thinned out to almost nothing, and we were advancing through thornscrub when we came to an open grassy area that spread out about a hundred yards in front of us.

Directly before us at the beginning of this open space sat one of the oddest constructions I had ever seen. A barrier about five feet high and perhaps twenty feet across and made completely of thornbush stretched in an arc and partly blocked our view of the rest of the area.

We went around this makeshift wall and discovered the body of a dead Shangaan boy about twelve years old. All his clothes had been peeled off, and about half of him had been eaten. I judged the kill to be about two days old. Whether the boy was from some distant village or perhaps a wandering orphan no one would probably ever be confident enough to say.

The man-eater's pug marks were visible everywhere.

The only explanation that seemed sensible to me for this curving thorn fence was that a canny hunter who was going to sit over the remains of the kill wanted to make sure the leopard had to approach and feed from a specific direction and thus present only one possible line of fire. Yet I was baffled because there were no trees anywhere nearby from which to shoot.

I looked at Valeria, but she just shook her head.

"Hil," Jon said and pointed across the clearing. "What's that?"

It looked like a mat lying on the grass about seventy-five yards away.

We approached it and saw that it was some sort of reed roof partly covering an opening in the ground. I grabbed an edge and pulled it completely aside. In a rectangular pit slightly larger than a grave sprawled the shredded body of Cyril Lloyd.

I handed Jon my rifle and jumped down inside.

What lay before me, barely recognizable as a primate let alone as a human, was not some half-eaten meal but a mutilated artifact of feline rage. Lloyd had not been consumed, not even a mouthful of him. Rather, marking him in his departure from life was the bottomless fury unique to the Lord of the Darkness.

It appeared from the pug marks that the leopard had pivoted and had sprung without warning into the pit of his enemy, and then Lloyd had reflexively thrust his rifle up in front of himself to block the animal. *Yingwe* had swiped at the weapon, apparently with his left paw, and knocked it out of Lloyd's hands. In the process, the leopard had raked his claws across Lloyd's face, completely stripping the flesh from his right cheek and tearing out both eyes. Then the infuriated leopard had delivered an equally brutal blow with his other paw that sliced along Lloyd's forehead and upward and across the top of his skull. Almost his entire scalp had been flipped backward like a cheap wig and was now hanging down the back of his head by a small bit of skin. The bare bloody skullcap was beginning to crust over, but some of the scarlet surface still glistened wetly in the sun.

Then the leopard had seized Lloyd by both shoulders and the cat's jaws had clamped on his throat and finished it.

Although more than enough blood to daunt the fainthearted soaked the clothes of the dead man, in fact there was relatively little when one considered the nature of his wounds. Lloyd's death had come too quickly for him to bleed out.

I extended my arm upward and Valeria gripped my hand and helped me out of the hole.

The shooting pit was just over six feet deep, about ten feet long, and about five feet across. The moveable roof was made of thickly woven reeds that Lloyd had even taken the considerable trouble of masking with dozens of fresh clumps of grass for better concealment.

"Have you ever seen anything like this?" Jon asked.

"No, but I've heard about pits like it. I think this is what Lloyd was talking about when he told me of a friend of his who'd shot a leopard in Bechuanaland in an area with no trees around."

"Did it work then?"

"He said it did, but the leopard was not a man-eater."

"Any idea what—?"

"Hil," Valeria said.

I turned and saw her ten feet away and down on one knee. I went over and she pointed to the ground at the most hopeful sight since Noah saw the rainbow.

"What is it?" Jon said as he hurried up beside me.

I squatted beside Valeria. "A fresh blood trail. The Fates are with us."

"It's only a nick," Valeria said. "It won't bleed forever."

"But we can follow it up?" Jon asked.

"If we move now," she answered.

"And that's what explains this," I said, gesturing back at Lloyd's grave.

Jon seemed surprised. "You know what happened?"

"I can make some good guesses."

"Can you describe it?"

"We have to go, Hil," Valeria said.

"Your move, tracker," I said to her with absolute confidence. "I'm sure you have better eyes than I and we need them now."

Without a word, Valeria took the lead.

"Remember the gunshot just before dawn?" I said to Jon as we moved out. "That was the hit on *Yingwe*. But Lloyd made a mistake that cost him his life. Did you notice how close the leopard was to the pit when Lloyd fired? Only about ten feet or so. My guess is the leopard had come up from somewhere behind the pit. Lloyd probably had the roof propped up a couple of inches and suddenly saw the silhouette of the leopard cross right in front of him. That was the end."

"I'm not sure I understand."

"If Lloyd had waited just thirty seconds, he could've bought his redemption. If the leopard had been three-quarters of the way across the clearing when Lloyd fired, the leopard would've bolted, whether he was hit or not. But Lloyd was too eager. He shot when *Yingwe* was still right in front of him. Since Lloyd didn't kill him, the man was doomed. No leopard—no big cat on earth—who's wounded from only a few feet away runs. Ever. He can't risk it. He turns and attacks his attacker."

As we moved into the forest, the morning birds sang cheerily. Valeria walked slightly ahead of me and to my right, and I positioned Jon off to my left as my left eye. I had been correct about Valeria. She was spotting traces of blood a honey badger would have missed. And she had been right as well, because it was rapidly thinning out. As the stands of acacias and jackalberrys grew denser, the blood drops became difficult even for her to see, and finally it no longer mattered because the wound had obviously clotted by now and could no longer help us.

After about a half-hour, Valeria raised a hand and signaled for a rest. We sat on the ground in silence and drank from our canteens. We now had no idea where the leopard might be. He could be nursing his little wound in some reed bank along a stream or ignoring that scratch entirely and sleeping on a branch somewhere up ahead. Or he could be on his way back to Portuguese East Africa.

After a ten-minute break, we moved on. Fortunately, we still had a game trail wide enough for the three of us and with considerable space between. Nonetheless, the quest was starting to look hopeless, at least for today. Yet I decided this was Valeria's decision to make. The knowledge of the jungle I had acquired, from years of experience and sometimes at great price, she somehow intuited from her very essence. I might be a sort of ramshackle prince in this world, but she was the uncrowned queen of this untamed realm. Wise was the man who deferred to that.

We entered a small clearing, but little sun penetrated the heavy forest canopy. As delicately as people walking on rice paper, we continued taking just four or five steps at a time and then stopping and listening. Our weapons were at our shoulders.

At the opposite edge of the clearing a small game trail pierced the jungle. If we went further, we would have to walk single file, an approach reeking with the smell of the grave. I looked toward Jon. To the left, a second path bored into the green tangle, but one barely wide enough for even a single man.

Like sacrificial lambs, we paused at the center of the clearing in front of the larger trail and I turned to Valeria. She gave me a knowing look.

"That's a death trap, Hil."

"Yes, we'll have to—."

Barks of vervet monkeys shattered the stillness, and the terrifying snarling grunts that melt elephants suddenly erupted to our left.

"Hil!" Jon screamed and spun around and fired down the narrow trail.

"Move!" I shouted, for Jon was completely blocking my shot and I could see nothing.

"Get out of the way!" Valeria yelled.

Lowering my rifle, I rushed to the edge of the clearing and grabbed him by the collar and jerked him away and he fell to the ground.

I shouldered my weapon, but it was far too late.

Yingwe broke cover and shot from the hole in the brush and hit me like a Spanish bull. Down I went beneath the furious cat, as my rifle flew from my grasp.

My left hand shot out and seized the muscled neck as the leopard's guttural grunting roar pounded my head and vibrated my breastbone.

The man-eater's sharp front talons thrust through my shoulder patches, and his warm and rancid slobber spattered across my face as those great yellow fangs strained to clamp my throat.

My right hand dived into my jacket pocket and closed on my pistol. I jammed it against the leopard and fired.

The stifled recoil against the cat's chest blew the gun backward out of my hand, but the leopard seemed unfazed by the shot as he furiously flailed at my thighs with his hind claws, and those front hooks sank further into my shoulders like steel through rotten meat.

"No!" I yelled as I saw Jon run up behind the cat with his rifle. "Don't shoot!"

But Jon had already tossed aside his weapon. He now jumped behind *Yingwe* and seized his tail to pull him off me.

"Let him go!" I shouted. "Get away!"

Suddenly the leopard slammed down harder onto me, and I stared in horror at the most extraordinary and terrifying sight I had ever seen in my life.

Completely atop the spine of *Yingwe* Valeria had leaped, just as the doomed clergyman had done so long ago. Her muscular right arm hooked around the cat's neck like a taut cord of braided steel and jerked his head back and away from me. Her powerful legs coiled around his narrow gut and the impala knife flashed. Straight into his side the long blade sank.

Yingwe exploded in rage and his roar seemed as if it would shatter my face.

Like a pagan deity hurling lightning, Valeria plunged the knife again and again deep into *Yingwe* behind the shoulder. He flew backward now to knock her off. Locked together, they crashed into the undergrowth, the leopard desperate to destroy the slashing predator astride his back and determined to strike him down.

I jumped up and snatched my pistol from the grass.

"Let him go!"

But she failed to hear me among the crashing and roaring.

They vanished into the thick brush, the weight of their tumbling bodies splintering and snapping branches all around them.

I bolted toward them across the clearing.

"Stay away!" Valeria shouted above the explosive roars of the leopard.

Suddenly they burst from the brush and rolled into view, Valeria's shirt now soaked with blood as she drove the knife home. Amazingly, the stricken leopard managed to spring to his feet with the blade still sinking over and over deep into his core.

"VAL! LET HIM GO!"

She instantly released her hold and was thrown across the clearing.

Yingwe whirled and bolted toward me.

With a calmness that surprised even me, *M'Dabula* fired the shot of his life. The gun flamed and *Yingwe* twisted and recoiled like a stricken snake and crumpled to the earth.

The bullet had shattered his spine. He lay on his right side breathing heavily as the knife wounds on his left side poured blood. He was paralyzed beyond hope. And possibly beyond pain as well. Nonetheless, to be safe I should have put another bullet into him and finished it, as any sensible hunter would have done, but I have always been a fool.

Across the clearing, Jon was aiming his rifle at the dying leopard, just in case.

Valeria, still breathless, rushed up to me and I grabbed her and pulled her close. The press of her heaving chest against me was the most glorious feeling in the history of the world.

I held her crushed against me for a century, and then I finally leaned back and just gazed at her face speckled with a dozen tiny cuts—not wounds by the leopard but thorn slashes from when she and *Yingwe* had tumbled through the underbrush in their battle for supremacy.

"Princess of the Amazons," I whispered.

She smiled and wiped the bloody blade of the knife on her trousers and slid it back into its sheath.

I went over to Jon and laid a hand on his left shoulder. "You, sir, are one of the bravest men I've ever known."

He seemed uncomfortable.

"And you tell your father that Rixton of Africa said so."

"Thank you."

"You can lower your weapon now."

I turned to *Yingwe*. He had lived his life alone, but I decided he would not die that way. I walked over and dropped to one knee beside him. I had no idea how much he could see, but I hoped he could make out my expression. He breathed what I thought was his last, but after a long pause another breath came. I watched as his light now flickered and died and his lungs emptied a final time.

I placed my pistol on the ground. Lifting his head, I rested it on my foot. I slid my hand across his face as a child might caress the petal a fallen flower. Old he was and marred, but his beautiful tawny coat felt mysteriously soft, like the first kitten I had ever held. His noble head was large, and heavy with the wisdom of his ancient race. Thin scars veined the bridge of his nose, each dark slash a witness to some forgotten victory from long ago. Both of his ears were nicked and notched with similar badges of valor. The only fresh injury was a graze on the left foreleg that had cost Cyril Lloyd his life. A thick keloid from an old bullet wound still showed on the right hind leg. Most striking of all, though, was the startling fact that he was sightless in his left eye. A strangely beautiful light blue cast shrouded the entire cornea. Injuries like that can have many causes but, oddly, the fur and flesh surrounding it were unmarked. I suspected he might have inadvertently flushed a spitting cobra, and even *Yingwe's* lightning reflexes would have been too slow for that excitable serpent. Most astounding of all was that it did not appear to be a recent injury. So for years this daring predator, robbed of the full perception of depth, had somehow managed to compensate during countless stalks and kills, as well as in life-or-death battles with invading leopards. In all my years in the bush I had never seen anything like it, and I doubted I ever would again. I reached down and gently closed his eyes.

As I continued gazing at the fallen king and stroking his magnificent fur, my surroundings seemed to blur and drift away. I no longer saw an old leopard beneath my fingers, but in my mind I had instead a vision of a happy little cub rolling around with a littermate and then leaping at the tip of his indulgent mother's flicking tail as she taught her two young how to spring and snatch at moving prey. I saw a big two-year-old going off now from his mother forever to claim his own place in the emerald Eden. I saw ever more skillful stalking and taking, brief but torrid romances, and healthy cubs he would never see, as he had long since moved on. I saw him frighten off rash invading leopards who soon thought better of their folly, and I saw him age and pass his peak, and finally lose the realm he had ruled so long. I saw him patrol the borders of alien domains and daringly snatch the prey of the resident princes, for though now he was weaker than they he was so much wiser — wiser, perhaps, than any cat had ever been. I saw him stumble and fall and rise again in triumph over the errant bullet that had failed its task but that had slowed him now forever. I saw him settle at last, perhaps without relish, on the sluggish and stringy two-footed ape as the prey he could now reliably catch. And I saw him wander year after year slowly south toward the predators who would finally slay him, the half-crippled cat and the half-blind man and the half-feral woman advancing inexorably to the fated destiny of their final embrace.

And now he lay here to be devoured. What were the words of the poet? *"The knell, the shroud, the mattock, and the grave; The deep damp vault, the darkness, and the worm . . . "*

But there could be none of this for *Yingwe*. He would not become a portion for foxes. I would gather him up and send him to my friend in Pretoria and then take him home. He would come to my house on the Sabi, not to be shown off but to be with me alone while we waited for the end time. For the New Heaven and the New Earth, when the leopard would lie down not with the lamb but with the man. And we would be together again at last, for eternity.

"Hil," Valeria whispered as she laid a gentle hand on mine.

I looked over at her.

"We have to treat your wounds."

I laid *Yingwe's* head on the ground as delicately as if he still breathed.

The heavy leather patches over my thighs had protected me from *Yingwe's* hind claws, but those sharper front talons had thrust through my shoulder patches as though they had been made of paper. I pulled off my jacket and handed it to Jon and then peeled off my shirt.

Valeria seemed surprised there was so little bleeding, but that was not uncommon with cat punctures.

I removed the leather thong with the tiger claw and looped it around Valeria's neck. "Please take care of this for me."

She touched it tenderly and tucked it inside her shirt and then pulled the carbolic and gauze from the first-aid kit.

Before she could minister to me, I took the wet gauze and dabbed it against the little cuts on her face. Then I let her continue.

Had the injuries been broad slashes rather than stabs, they would have been much easier to sanitize, but Valeria performed the task as thoroughly and delicately as possible and with the cool dispassion of a surgeon.

"Like Florence Nightingale," I said with a smile, but she ignored me.

The pain from the wounds was not as intense as the inexperienced might think, but the carbolic might as well have been molten lava searing my flesh. Finally I reached my limit and waved Valeria off. Then she used rubber adhesive plaster to fasten fresh gauze over the wounds.

I put on my shirt and jacket and slipped my pistol into a pocket.

"Hil," Jon said, "why did he attack instead of letting us pass by?"

"Were you looking in his direction? At that moment?"

"I think I was."

"He thought you'd made eye contact with him. So he attacked."

"That's right. You'd told me about that before."

"Now I need a favor."

"Anything." He handed me my rifle.

"Stay here and guard *Yingwe* to keep the scavengers from desecrating him. Will you do that?"

"Of course."

"I'll send Joseph back here immediately to takes some pictures and skin him and get him into the salt as fast as possible before the hair slips."

"I'll guard him with my life."

I smiled. "I know you will."

I turned to Valeria. "Let's go find Dusk."

"Oh, Hil, we have to get you home. We can come back later to —."

"All right, let's compromise."

She seemed wary. "How?"

"We'll skirt The Dragon's Tail and listen for any alarm calls. If we hear nothing from the birds on the way, we'll go straight home and come back when I'm feeling better."

She gave me that fake-fierce squint. "I think you were already working that out when I was caring for your wounds with the tenderness of a saint."

"Saint Valeria . . . now that *would* be a miracle!"

She tried not to smile and turned away and packed up the first-aid kit.

I got to my feet and felt surprisingly steady.

"I'll be here," Jon said.

"I know," I answered with a smile.

At that instant a resolute ray of golden sun pierced the trees and graced the leopard with dappled light. Nothing more than a coincidence, perhaps. Yet San Juan de la Cruz would surely have held a different view.

I reached down and stroked *Yingwe* one more time. "When the stars threw down their spears, and water'd heaven with their tears, did he smile his work to see? Did he who made the Lamb make thee?" I slid my hand across his sleeping face. "Good night, sweet prince."

The view from The Dragon's Tail could have made even a cynic weep. From the high ridge where we stood, a long green incline, curving gracefully downward like a child's slide, swept away before us and softened into the curiously bluish tint that thick foliage always seems to assume as it fades off into a hazy infinity.

On the flatter slopes, with their mixture of trees and grassland, we had seen wildebeest and reedbuck and eland and had heard the chattering of chacma baboons as well. It was ideal leopard country, especially with the dense tree cover that did not always make its way up to the higher reaches of the escarpment.

Valeria and I turned away from the edge of the gorge, and went to rest on a couple of rotted logs in the shade at the edge of a clump of trees.

I was beginning to feel a bit off, as the toxins from *Yingwe's* claws had begun accomplishing their dark magic within me. Valeria had noticed this, as she seemed to notice everything, but I brushed it aside and told her we would be home soon. What I had not mentioned, because I had no evidence other than hunter's intuition, was the disquieting feeling of something following us on our backtrail for the last mile or so.

After a short rest and a drink, we continued along the line of trees about fifty yards from the edge of the escarpment. We had gone perhaps a quarter of a mile when several screeching shrikes shot upward out of a thick stand of trees about a hundred yards ahead of us, and the hideous squawks of guinea fowl were unmistakable.

Valeria turned toward me.

"Would Dusk come if you called him?"

"Yes," she said, barely above a whisper.

"Try it."

We stood up, and she slung her rifle over a shoulder and cupped her hands around her mouth.

The sound she let loose stunned me. Though only a single word, the leopard's name, she drew it out so it seemed to be a mile long, and she voiced it with all the feeling of a contralto at Albert Hall. Here was a half-wild creature of the forest, still stained with the man-eater's blood, giving voice like Maddelena in *Rigoletto* in order to call to her side a remorseless predator spawned in the mists of prehistory. For the first time in my life I was witnessing something entirely beyond my comprehension.

Before that one word had died away, a magnificent black panther burst from the brush and bounded toward Valeria.

"Oh, dear God," she whispered in thanksgiving.

Dusk had come only about twenty-five yards when a rifle boomed to our rear and the slug hit the ground in front of him and launched dirt straight at him. He rubbed his right foreleg against his face to get the grit out of his eye.

I spun around.

Von Roon had emerged from the trees fifty yards behind us and now had braced his rifle on a boulder near the edge of the escarpment.

"NO!" Valeria shouted.

Dusk saw him, and, to the great cat, to see was to think and to think was to act. He swerved and, grunting in rage, bore down instantly on Baron Erich Von Roon.

In no more than two seconds, the leopard was running full out, his powerful spine a miracle of flexion and extension as he closed on his enemy at the edge of the abyss.

"They're going to kill each other!" Valeria yelled.

I shouldered my rifle, dropped to my right knee and braced my elbow on my left and the Mannlicher roared.

"NO!" Valeria screamed and spun toward me in horror.

She looked back and Dusk was gone.

"No! No! No! You blew him over the cliff?! Why?!"

She turned and bolted toward the rim of the escarpment.

I ejected the spent shell and picked it up and slipped it into a pocket. Then I stood up and followed her and kept the action of my rifle open.

I walked slowly and by the time I got to Valeria she was on her knees peering over the edge. Then she looked up at me in disbelief.

I gazed down. Two hundred feet away at the bottom of the chasm lay the remains of a decadent aristocracy in the form of the twisted wreckage of Erich Von Roon.

"How?" Valeria whispered.

I pointed to an area of smeared soil near the edge. "Here's where he slipped."

She examined the spot. "*Ja*," she said, and then her glance fell to my rifle.

"No one believed me about the boy who was beaten to death."

"And the power of the *Sangoma*?"

"Do you remember what I told you? That at the proper time he would adjudicate the law of the veld?"

"I remember. Someday he would throw out his leg . . . and send Von Roon to damnation."

I rested the stock of my rifle on my right foot. "The Law of the Primeval is greater than the laws of man."

She stood slowly. "Yes."

I looked back at the corpse. "I'll notify the authorities. If someone wants to fish him out, they can try. But by tomorrow there won't be anything left. So no one will see what finally became of him. Except Captain Hilton Rixton and God." I chambered another round and flicked on the safety. "And *that* I can live with."

A sudden whoosh by my side startled me, and in an instant a great black phantom swept by me and reared and draped his forepaws over Valeria's shoulders. He rubbed the sides of his face back and forth against one of her cheeks and then the other as he marked her as his own. She braced herself against his weight and wrapped her arms around him and just held.

After scent marking her, Dusk dropped to all fours and sinuously slid serpentine style around the outside of her legs again and again as he rubbed his flanks against her.

I stepped away and sat on a log and let them enjoy their special moment.

Carefully, and with an animal sense rarely seen in woman or man, Valeria slowly walked toward me and sat beside me. She neither touched me nor paid any attention to me, in order that her actions would tell Dusk I was simply a natural and unthreatening part of the landscape.

Dusk approached us with his eyes on me. He took my measure not with dilated pupils of fear or with pinpoints of rage but with what I might call a gaze of relaxed caution. But was that not always the way with leopards?

Dusk appeared to weigh, at most, about a hundred and twenty pounds. More gracefully proportioned than lions, and a thousand miles more remote than even the tigers I had known, he seemed to impart flowing form to the mysterious essence of the feline soul. His color, a pooling of pigments, was a silent symbol of his own remoteness. Black as onyx, he was unsoftened by the tawny warmth of the lion, so appropriate to that cat and his social set. His spots, just barely visible, were hopelessly lost within his own blackness, as almost every ray of light that hit him was snatched and consumed — except for the light in his eyes. That was returned to anyone with the will to look. Unlike the lion's warm and sepia-eyed invitations to friendship, the great panther's gaze was the stare of the isolate. Dusk confronted the world with eyes of the coolest crystalline green, like Coleridge's emerald ice from The Land of Mist and Snow. His mouth was partly open, the smooth tips of his ivory lower canines just visible. A bright trace of pink tongue lay at ease between them, and a string of saliva, like a silken filament sprinkled with dew, stretched from a hidden upper canine to a lower fang and vibrated with his breath. The three contrasting colors, so different from the enveloping black and yet so fundamentally one with it, created the most breathtaking vision I had ever seen in my life.

Dusk turned away from me and lay down and relaxed in front of Valeria. With that preternatural awareness unique to the soul of the leopard, Dusk knew that now, now at last, all was right within the heart of the world.

23

IF EVER I WERE TO BE FOUND WORTHY ENOUGH OF
BEING ACCEPTED BEYOND THE PEARLY GATES INTO
THE GREAT HUNTING GROUNDS IN THE SKY, I
IMAGINE THE LEOPARD WILL BE THE SHINING LIGHT
ILLUMINATING PARADISE.
--HUNTER RONNIE ROWLAND

EVERY ONE OF THE PUNCTURE WOUNDS in my shoulders festered
despite the carbolic. I remember little of the next few days except
lying in a shaded room and being scorched by fever. I have a
faint memory of Joseph changing my dressings, and I recall once
waking in the middle of the night with a single lamp lit and
Valeria leaning over me and sponging my burning body with
alcohol to help douse the fire that seemed to be consuming me.
Then one morning I woke up feeling cool as marble. Sunlight
that seemed like rays from Heaven was streaming in.

I felt pressure across my lower body. I tilted my head
forward and saw Buc lying against my feet. As soon as he
noticed my change in breathing, he jumped up and began licking
my face until I finally had to stop him before I drowned. I leaned
my head to the right and saw Miriam sitting in a chair beside the
bed and smiling at me. She put a finger to her lips and gestured.

Valeria was kneeling on the floor next to the other side of the bed with her body slumped forward and her head resting on my thigh. She was sound asleep on her knees.

Miriam stood up to leave, but I reached out for her. She extended her arm, and I kissed the back of her hand. I had never seen her tremble like that before, and she blinked hard several times and hurried away.

"Thank you," I whispered before I let her escape.

Then I turned to Valeria, and I suddenly realized that my treasured tiger claw had been placed back around my neck.

"Ginger."

She woke up sleepy-faced and disheveled and turned toward me.

"That's hardly dignified," I said.

She pushed herself up and smiled that half-wild smile that was hers alone.

"Feel my forehead," I said.

She touched the cool skin and her lower lip quivered.

"Will I ever understand redheads? I doubt it. How many days has it been?"

"Just two," she said in a near-whisper.

"Is Jon all right?"

"Oh, yes. Joseph took him to Pretoria with him. He said Jon needed a holiday."

Buc finally settled in next to me and I wrapped my arm around him. As always, he knew when to be gentle and quiet.

"The crisis is over."

"Never lie to the Princess of the Amazons," she said. "But you do seem much better."

"I'm sure I looked like an unembalmed corpse."

"Only if a corpse can talk. You were delirious for a while."

"I hope I didn't say anything embarrassing."

"You called out for Buc, but he was already here beside you praying his dog prayers."

"Did I say anything else?"

She stood up and began adjusting the covers around me.

"Val . . ."

She looked over at me.

"Anything else?"

"A woman's name," she said, acting as nonchalant as someone juggling cobras. "Many times. But it wasn't very clear."

"Probably my first love. It happened once before when I had blackwater fever."

"Harriet, I think," she said, fidgeting with the sheet. "The woman who fancies Quakers, isn't it? You must still care for her very much. I understand."

It appeared, though, that the understanding was not coming easily.

"Would you get me my pocket watch?"

She seemed confused.

"There's a picture of her inside, and I think you deserve to see it."

Valeria went to the dresser and got the watch but seemed as reluctant to open it as if she knew a scorpion lurked there.

"Please, Val."

She popped it open and stared at the ivory miniature and tears filled her eyes.

"Her name is Hirannmaya," I said. "That's 'Golden' in Sanskrit. She lives in a palace in India. Perhaps someday we can visit her together."

Valeria moistened her lips but still did not speak.

"*She* was my first love."

Valeria came back to the side of the bed and slowly dropped to her knees. Then she lowered her face to the covers and wept. Not about my golden leopard or about Dusk or about any single thing, but with the accumulated relief from everything.

I had never seen anyone cry silently before. I had not even known such a thing was possible. But the feral creature of the jungle primeval had no doubt mastered many things I dared not even imagine.

Buc immediately wormed around me and began licking the side of her face.

I leaned forward and pressed my lips to the top of her head and just held them there against her hair, and then Buc eased off.

Finally, when she had cried herself out, I leaned back.

She looked up through joyously red eyes and whispered, *"Ek is lief vir jou meer as my lewe."*

"Should I understand that strange tongue?"

"It means 'I love you more than my life.'"

"Soos ek is lief vir jou, Prinses van die Amazons."

"A strange tongue?" she said, grinning. "You're a terrible person. Has anyone ever told you that?"

I smiled back and knew I would be perfectly happy simply lying there and counting her freckles until the stars paled out.

We went to New York for the wedding of Ginny and Jon. Marjorie and Ginny met us at the dock, and Ginny greeted Valeria Vanderveer as if she were a long-lost older sister.

A woman of the African bush like Valeria was dazzled by New York, but no more so than were the gentlemen who fell under her spell. This was especially true after Ginny graced her with gowns from the finest dress shops in Manhattan.

It amused me immensely to see her confused by so much male attention. Marjorie Delamere provided entrée to the homes of many society notables. At these soirées, I was pleased to vanish into the background like a dappled moth and be charmed by Valeria's bewilderment. I learned later from Marjorie that Jon had added to the piquancy of these gentlemen's captivation by quietly telling them that they were being enchanted not simply by a flame-haired beauty with an exotic accent but by a fearless woman of the forest who was one of the finest rifle shots south of the Limpopo.

"Few real men can withstand that sort of intoxicant," Marjorie had whispered to me with a smile.

Most overwhelming of all, though, was when Ginny and Marjorie invited us to dinner and Ginny reached out and took my hand and asked me if I would give away the bride. I believe she actually enjoyed my astonishment, but there was no jest in her request or in my humble acceptance. Without doubt, many whispers were traded among the guests as this delicate Manhattan flower walked down the aisle of St. Mary's on Long

Island on the arm of a bronzed and scarred man of the veld. Several society columns even speculated, although without success, on the identity of this one-eyed stranger who obviously had swept in from some antediluvian outland beyond the imaginings of civilized man.

Other than the wedding itself, the most touching moment of the visit for me was when Ginny presented me with my portrait by Lord Hardwicke. She had originally intended it as my gift to her, but she now insisted it belonged in my home. In the painting, entitled *Late Afternoon in the Transvaal*, I am leaning casually against a desk near an open window in a small bungalow. No firearms or skins or dusty trophies clutter the field. Yet there is one delicate touch that means more to me than this flattering portrait of an aging *shikari*. If one looks carefully through the window, one sees, resting along a limb of a giant jackalberry in the distance, a tawny, spotted phantom just at the outer reaches of ocular resolution. The hint of an image could be simply a trick of the light or of the artist's brush, but to the wisest and most perceptive it is far more haunting than that.

Jon has begun the final polishing of his chronicle for the *Herald*, but he told me he would not submit it until the publication of an account by the one person he insists is most qualified to record a memoir of these events. Hence, my taking up the pen to compose this narrative.

As I write these final words, I am seated against the trunk of an acacia and facing a sky flushed with crimson by the setting sun. Comfortable again in her plaid shirt and khaki trousers, Valeria is leaning against me and resting her head on my shoulder. Buc is sleeping beside me on my right with his chin across my thigh.

An eight-foot tall termite mound rises about twenty feet in front of us to our right. Atop it reclines a great black cat staring off to the west. A study in ebony, he might be a carving were it not for the twitching end of his tail, as he grows ever more active and alert as darkness falls. What thoughts animate those tics only the Almighty can know, but he is God's own sentinel, of that I am sure. With absolute mastery and with a hint of that mysterious squint, he watches over his humble and grateful charges, the Rixtons of Africa.

AFTERWORD

FOR THOSE who would like to learn more about big cat conservation, Captain Rixton recommends these organizations, and he sincerely thanks you for your interest.

http://www.altaconservation.org/

https://www.panthera.org/cat/leopard

http://www.21stcenturytiger.org/

www.ingramcontent.com/pod-product-compliance
Lightning Source LLC
Chambersburg PA
CBHW070050260626
47160CB00004B/1162